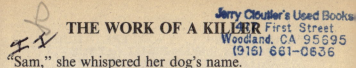

"Sam," she whispered her dog's name.

There was no response.

"Sam!" This time a little louder, more commanding. Nothing moved outside in the darkness.

And then Sam was there, cowering close against the glass, trying to touch her, to be comforted by her nearness. He whimpered. The hackles were up on the back of his neck but his attitude was one of terror.

"Sam," Elizabeth said again, letting the curtain trail and drop from her fingers. She stood and moved reluctantly toward the kitchen.

There was nothing there. She pushed open the utility room door.

Something rattled across the floor, striking the opposite wall and rebounding, spinning with the momentum. A knife, the blade and handle smeared with blood . . .

DEADLY FRIENDS

Mary Monroe Brown

ZEBRA BOOKS
KENSINGTON PUBLISHING CORP.

ZEBRA BOOKS are published by

Kensington Publishing Corp.
475 Park Avenue South
New York, NY 10016

First Printing: January 1994

Printed in the United States of America

Chapter One

Elizabeth knew she was dreaming. She was lucky this time.

The snow was falling, falling, drifting gently into the open grave. There was no coffin. The woman's face was turned up to the pewter sky. She might have been sleeping but for the gash that opened her throat, the black flow of blood that had dried upon her blouse.

The raw, damp earth began to fall upon the body. Methodically, emotionlessly, one shovelful at a time, the man flung in the suffocating black soil.

Elizabeth staggered to him. She clutched his arm and cried for him to stop, but he didn't respond. He looked through her. He couldn't feel the desperate pressure of her hands. He filled the grave while the snow fell as serenely as a Currier & Ives Christmas card, and that was ironic, because it was Christmas.

He turned then. Elizabeth could see the whiteness of his shirt, immaculate beneath the perfect cut of his dark car coat, see the enigma that was Stephen Kenwood. She could see the blood on his hands.

She struggled awake, gasping and crying, wet with

perspiration. The phone was ringing, echoing the screams inside her head.

She let the machine take it. There was nobody there. There never was.

Elizabeth sat up, smoothing back her damp dark hair and breathing shallowly over the pounding of her heart. The digital face of her alarm clock read 4:02 A.M.

It was already hot. Or still hot. September in Phoenix. She got shakily to her feet, turned down the air conditioner until the unit switched on, and then stood beneath the ceiling vent, letting the cool air flow over the dampness of her bare throat and arms.

It would be autumn already in Portland, the leaves turning. In another month the vines in the canyons would be as red as fire.

The telephone began to ring again.

She waited tautly for the prolonged silence after the tone, but a man's voice said, "Elizabeth? Pick up, hon. It's Keith."

Keith Vanfossen. Elizabeth sat down on the bed and slowly picked up the receiver.

"It's an odd time to be calling, isn't it, Keith?"

"Yeah, sorry about that. I figured you'd be up already, working on your sketches. Don't tell me I was wrong."

"I was awake," she admitted. "Where are you? Are you at Sky Harbor?"

"Don't I wish. I'm at LAX, on my way to Vancouver. Miss me?"

"Listen, Keith . . ."

"No, Elizabeth," he broke in sharply. "Don't say it. Give us a little more time to work this out. We've got to talk."

"We do? Or I do? That's what it's all about, isn't it, Keith? Me talking? Talking too much?"

There was a long moment of utter stillness on the line, and then Keith's quick, persuasive voice.

"Elizabeth, listen to me. It's not like you think. I can explain everything. Give me a chance to . . ."

"I'm moving out, Keith."

"No, damn it! You can't!"

"I'm going today."

"Listen to me! Don't do anything till I get home. That'll be on Friday. You can put everything on hold until then, can't you?"

"I'm sorry, Keith. I can't."

"You mean you won't! Damn it, Elizabeth, what am I supposed to do? What's going to happen to . . . ?"

"To you? Is that what you were about to say? I don't know, Keith. What *is* going to happen to you? Maybe you won't get paid."

"That's low."

"The truth hurts," Elizabeth said sharply. And then, "I'll leave the keys on the counter. You shouldn't have any trouble with the lease. I've spoken to the landlord."

"I'd like to know where you'll be living. I want to see you."

"Why?"

"Damn it, Elizabeth! This is the way you do it, isn't it? You just disappear."

"Do I?" Elizabeth's voice was flat, without inflection. "How would you know that, Keith?"

There was a pause.

"I . . . hell, that's what you're doing, isn't it? Disappearing? Leaving no forwarding address?"

7

"I'm staying with an old college friend. I'll leave the address, if that's what you want. But I don't want to see you. Not now, anyway."

"Okay." She could hear him breathe out, she could imagine him running a hand over his craggy face in that way he had when he was exasperated or angry. "Okay, Elizabeth, we'll play it your way. When can I see you?"

"I don't know. Later. You can forward my mail to Constance's when you're through with it."

"Elizabeth, for God's sake!"

"Or I could come by your office and pick it up. You do have an office, don't you, Keith? It's hardly something a man would lie about."

The incredible stillness of the night and the room and the moment picked up the hard exhalation of his breath.

"Okay. Maybe I don't look so good in this. Maybe I haven't been entirely square with you. But you know I love you, Elizabeth."

"I've got to go."

"Sure. You've got to pack, right? That shouldn't take five minutes. You travel light. Fast and light."

"Goodbye, Keith."

She broke the connection and with a leaden arm dropped the receiver back into the cradle. Her head was beginning to ache in time to the heavy, dull thuds of her heart.

Keith was right about the packing, except that she was already finished. Everything she owned was arranged in a few meticulously labeled packing boxes: coffeemaker and cups, linen and towels, clothing, shoes. It needed only the cotton camisole she wore, her mother-of-pearl hair brush, a few cosmetics, and her toothbrush, and she was gone. Again.

Elizabeth walked to the bedroom door.

"Here, Sam," she called.

The dog wasn't on the landing, and she knew what that meant: he was watching something, someone, through the downstairs window. Despite the heat of the early morning, a shiver ran down her spine.

"Sam!"

He raced around the corner and up the carpeted stairs, an oversized golden retriever by anyone's standards, but certainly so within the confines of a condominium. He sat when he reached her, his tail sweeping the landing and his mouth lolling in a grin.

"There you are, Sam Gamgee. Keeping out burglars, are you?"

His tail thumped. Elizabeth dropped a hand to his head and scratched his ears.

No one would be frightened of Sam. He was too good-natured, too friendly. But his canine senses were keen, and he knew when someone was outside. Perhaps he even knew who it was.

Elizabeth shivered again. She turned abruptly and went back into the bedroom, crossing to the bureau where her handbag lay. The half-light of the room was picked up in the mirror, reflecting back shadowed gray eyes in a finely boned, almost colorless face and a mass of dark hair that spilled over shoulders that were too thin.

Elizabeth wasn't looking at her reflected image. She retrieved a key from the lining of her handbag and walked across and picked up the telephone.

God, she was growing to hate the sound of the telephone ringing. The silence that followed her own voice on the answering machine. The elusive whisper of someone breathing before the machine cut off the caller.

Maybe she wouldn't get a phone when she moved. Maybe she would sever that last chance of contact . . . Maybe.

Elizabeth unscrewed the earpiece and took out the tiny microphone that nestled inside. She flipped it into the wastebasket. She knelt and unlocked the cabinet by her bed.

Elizabeth eased up the false bottom of the night table and took out the tape recorder. It looked innocent, harmless in her hands. She sank back on her heels and activated the rewind button and it began to whir.

Sam wasn't listening to it. There was something else he heard, too faint for human ears. He charged back down the stairs to take up his post at the living room window. Elizabeth's flesh stirred.

Keith's voice came over the recorder as if he were in the room: "Keith Vanfossen here."

He must have been alone in the condo during the day while she was at work at Everhold. When he had told her he was in Sacramento.

"What do you have?"

"I appreciate you returning my call so quickly. I thought you'd want to know I was back in Phoenix."

"I already knew. Who do you think you're dealing with, Vanfossen?"

Elizabeth leaned forward tautly. A whisper of familiarity, of memory, stirred just beyond her reach. She rewound the tape and listened again.

"What do you have?"

"I appreciate you returning my call so quickly. I

thought you'd want to know I was back in Phoenix."

This time she could hear the tension in Keith's voice.

"I already knew. Who do you think you're dealing with, Vanfossen?"

She didn't know the voice, did she? There was something, the clipped enunciation, something . . . She could almost put her finger on it.

"I need more time."

"I thought you were supposed to be good at this sort of thing, Vanfossen."

"What sort of thing, for Chrissake? Seducing children?"

"Don't lose your head," the man advised coldly. "When you start thinking she's not a player in this, take a good, hard look at what she's done. You'll live longer if you do."

"What's.that supposed to mean?"

"Just what you think it means. You wouldn't be the first person Elizabeth Purdin has killed."

"I'm shaking," Keith sneered.

"Please yourself. I wouldn't turn my back on her."

"Maybe you have reason not to."

"And you don't, Vanfossen? You're the Judas here. She's probably well on her way to figuring that out. No one ever said she was careless. Or stupid."

"That's just it. That's why I need more time. And she's not suspicious. She's beginning to trust me."

"How nice. That only took four months. You're everything they said you were, aren't you, Vanfossen?"

Keith cleared his throat.

"You knew it wasn't going to be easy. Especially since half the time I'm on the road running down

11

leads. But I'm making progress. She's pretty close to talking."

"How close?"

"I don't know. Hey, pressuring me isn't going to get us anywhere. I'm pushing as hard as I dare."

"You think she might bolt?"

"No! No. I just . . . give me a little slack, will you?"

"I'll give you a little slack, Vanfossen, along with a warning. You're the only person I've been able to maneuver into a position close enough to her to be of value. Don't think for one instant that I'll stand by while you let her walk without handing me the information I need. If you fail me, I'll kill you myself. Is that enough slack for you?" The line went dead.

Elizabeth closed her eyes and leaned back against the bed.

"Who are you?" she whispered.

Chapter Two

Elizabeth moistened her dry lips as she watched the taxi drive away. Then she turned and ran her eyes over the posh condominium complex. She could imagine Constance LeMirre against the distinctly Mediterranean flavor of arched doorways, plastered walls, and red tile roofs. The lush entry courtyard with its palms and scarlet bougainvillea would appeal to her flair for the dramatic.

The door opened abruptly as she reached for the bell.

"Elizabeth! Lord, it's good to see you! I've been watching out the window for the last hour, in case you had second thoughts about staying with me. I know how stubbornly independent you can be. I was going to tackle you if I had to." Constance laughed as she drew Elizabeth into the cool, tiled foyer. "Admit it, love. You almost backed out, didn't you? Remember, I knew you very well in our college days."

Constance had always been beautiful. Now she was stunning. Tall and golden-blond in an elegant green silk pants suit that emphasized her long legs and glowing tan skin, she seemed to crackle with the energy Elizabeth remembered. Looking at her, the years rolled away. Elizabeth blinked before the powerful flood of memories and somehow managed to smile.

"I'm here, aren't I?" She put down her suitcase and gave Constance a quick, hard embrace. "Thanks for letting me stay, Con. My house should be ready in under a week."

"That's too soon. We can't begin to catch up on each other's lives in anything less than a month. Oh, Elizabeth, how long has it been now? Five years? Six?"

"Closer to seven," Elizabeth said. She should know. She had lived each of those years one agonizing second at a time. She had strung them like beads upon a string, and she wore every one of them in her heart.

"That long? Lord, the years fly, don't they? And we swore we would keep in touch. So much for idealistic promises."

"Idealism is for children."

"You sound like Stephen. That edge of cynicism that was always as natural to him as breathing." Constance shook her head and her smile was suddenly strained. "But then, we're probably all hard. The Royce Pharmaceutical survivors."

Elizabeth hoped Constance couldn't hear the deafening thud of her heart. After a long, still moment, she managed, "Is that where we're heading, Con? Straight back?"

"No! I'm sorry, hon. I told myself I wouldn't do this, dredge up the past and cut myself to ribbons on it. It's so damned self-destructive.

"But it's hard not to, looking at you. You haven't changed, Elizabeth. The same arresting gray eyes and somber mouth, the same fine-boned air of fragility. No one would guess you're the strong one. The one who pulled us through that nightmare." Constance made a wry face. "Sorry. I'm doing it again. There have to be other things we can talk about after all these years."

There had to be. Elizabeth found her voice.

"Such as what you're doing so far from the New York fashion houses. I couldn't believe it when I saw your picture in the *Republic* advertising the new Miche's here in Phoenix."

"That was a stroke of luck, that ad. If you hadn't seen it, we could have lived in Phoenix for years and not known each other was here. We might never have known. It doesn't bear thinking about, how close it was."

"So how did it all happen? You said something on the phone about owning your own design company. Tell me more. And what happened to the lure of the Big Apple?"

Constance chuckled.

"The lure of the Big Apple? I'd have to say that it still whispers my name from time to time. I love the place. But you know me, always restless.

"When we all split up after college, I went to the job I had waiting in New York as a designer for a major house. I was there a couple of years. I liked what I was doing at Marston's, but it was so limiting. No artistic control, someone forever breathing down my neck and taking credit for my designs. I had to get out.

"So I bought a small, struggling design company

and ran it myself. When my father died, I was able to invest serious capital into the company. It took off, and some of the bigger chains began making offers to buy me out. Miche's Southwest Exclusive was the highest bidder and a company I respect, so I sold. I came out a major stockholder in Miche's, as well as publicity and promotion head for the new stores they're opening in the Southwest." She shrugged in the self-mocking way Elizabeth remembered. "Your basic little-rich-girl-makes-good theme."

"I'm impressed. But I still can't get over the fact that you ended up in Phoenix. It's such a coincidence."

"I suppose it is, really. Moving west with Miche's as I was, I could still have chosen Pasadena or Albuquerque. I liked both cities. But the Valley of the Sun had a special appeal. I couldn't resist it. Thank goodness.

"And just look at this weather, love. Back in New York, it's already on the icy edge of winter." She laughed. "I couldn't believe my ears when I heard your voice on the phone. I never dreamt you'd leave Portland."

Elizabeth cleared her throat.

"Everyone is a transplant in Phoenix."

"Isn't that the truth? How long have you been here?"

"Two years."

"I can't imagine you alone, Elizabeth. In college it was always you and Stephen. I really thought . . ."

"It was a long time ago."

"You're right. I'm sorry. And you're probably wondering when I'm going to remember my manners. Well, I have. Let me show you your room. Then

16

I'll mix us a cool drink." She picked up Elizabeth's suitcase. "Is this all you have, love? You travel light. I couldn't fit my makeup in this."

Elizabeth let out the breath she had been holding. She followed Constance across the exquisitely decorated living room.

"This place is beautiful, Con. I recognize your genius. It's uniquely Constance LeMirre."

"You bet." Constance laughed merrily. "I've just finished the dining room. Come see what you think."

It was very formal, with hand-painted Chinese wallpaper on frosted leaf setting a subtle tone. Ivory Chippendale dining room chairs were upholstered in coral suede. Carved ivory Chinese figurines reinforced the coral accent.

"You are so good at this." Elizabeth shook her head. "I mean it, Con. Interior design lost a major talent when you chose fashion. If you hadn't proven yourself such a success, I'd be tempted to say you made a big mistake."

"Are you kidding? Do you know what I pull down each year thanks to the clothing industry?" Constance tossed her golden head and laughed. "Let's just say Mr. and Mrs. LeMirre's little girl Constance can continue to live in the luxury she's accustomed to. Remember how you and Ellen and Mary used to taunt me about my decadent life-style'?"

"We were jealous. Entrenched in that cold old barracks of a dorm while you ran around in your little sports car and wore designer labels."

"And I flaunted it, of course. I always was a brat."

"No," Elizabeth demurred. "You saved my life."

"Elizabeth, no." A spasm of remembered pain flashed across Constance's face. "No. If we start talking about debts, than it's I who owe you. And you know where that kind of talk will lead us. Back to Portland."

Everything led back to Portland. Everything always would.

Elizabeth walked across the deep pile of the carpet to stare out at the street. Heat waves emanated from the black asphalt. There was no one there.

"And Royce Pharmaceuticals," she murmured.

"Sure," Constance agreed, and her beautiful voice was hard. "Good old Royce Pharmaceuticals."

"Have you been back?"

"Been back where, for God's sake? The building was razed years ago."

"To see Mary Prill and Damon. To see Ellen."

Constance stared.

"Ellen Glover? Sweet Christ, no! I never heard that she *was* back, but I wouldn't cross the street to see Ellen Glover. As for Mary Prill, she was a nothing. I imagine she's still a nothing. If Damon Baille isn't dead of an overdose of his favorite arm candy then he's probably died of cirrhosis. Why in God's name would I put myself through that?"

"Because we were all friends once?"

"Huh-uh. No way. Why, you lived in the same city as they did until two years ago, right? Did you look them up? Get together for old times' sake?"

"No."

"Okay. Neither would I. Listen, hon, the only thing I've bothered to remember about Ellen Glover was how she complained about you walking the dorm halls all night when you were roommates. I've taken that to heart and put you in the downstairs

18

bedroom. You can pace the floor at all hours and never disturb my sleep. All right?"

Elizabeth turned back from the window.

"If you're having second thoughts about me staying, Constance, I hope you'll say so. No one in their right mind would welcome an insomniac as a house-guest."

"I have nothing against insomniacs. Sleepwalkers? Maybe. I think I'd have a heart attack if I came upon you drifting around Ophelia-like with your long hair undone and your eyes glazed. If you walk in your sleep, tell me now, and I'll put knockout drops in your evening wine."

Elizabeth smiled faintly.

"Your imagination is running away with you. The only reason Ellen knew I was up was her repeatedly tiptoeing in after curfew. As roommates we had little contact. I saw more of her at Royce Pharm."

"I remember. She was always throwing herself at Stephen." Constance gave Elizabeth a quick, searching glance, and then looked away. "Let me just put this case in your room and then show you the rest of the place."

It was a large, two-level unit with an open, airy floor plan. Constance's signature design flair was apparent throughout the bed and sitting rooms, as well as in the Eurostyle kitchen. An upstairs balcony looked out over the entry courtyard and a high security wall to the towering dark shape of Camelback Mountain.

"It's beautiful, Constance. You make me feel like a transient with my rental lifestyle. I'm jealous."

"Oh, good," Constance chuckled. "If you're not locked into a lease already on that old-neighborhood house of yours, I'd like to offer this to you. Easy terms. The light is great up here with the balcony and all the windows. It would be perfect for a studio."

"You've got to be joking. You haven't been here six months, have you? You just finished the dining room."

"Maybe I'm restless again," Constance smiled. "Maybe I have other plans."

Elizabeth was surprised at her sense of disappointment, of loss. She hadn't allowed herself to count on anyone for a long time.

"You're leaving Phoenix?"

"Oh, lord, no! I have my hands full with Miche's. But there's a lot more to life than work, you know, old friend."

"Is there?"

"Always. I love having a man in my life. And I'm very serious about this one."

"You're planning to move in with him?"

"Of course."

Of course. Constance had always been able to have any man she wanted.

"Poor Constance. The complicated life of a property owner."

"It doesn't sound like you're going to be much help."

"Sorry, I'm committed. One year lease."

"A *year?* On a dead-end street in a quiet neighborhood whose idea of excitement is signing up for irrigation? Hon, break the lease. You can use my lawyer. I'll have you in here in no time. Think of the *light,* Elizabeth."

"I like the light, Con. I love it. But Sam Gamgee

wouldn't. He's been shut up in a condo too long. I promised him a yard."

"We're talking about a dog here, right? He's going to choose your life-style?"

"He *is* my life-style. Sorry."

"Okay, okay. Can I help you decorate your house?"

"I'd like that. It's going to be stark when the painters finish with it. Navajo white throughout, if I know anything about landlords."

"I can see you as pure twenties, love. Georgia O'-Keefe. Vases of fresh cut flowers. One of your seascapes against a background of warm dusty rose. And, of course, a basket of dog biscuits on the hearth."

"It sounds like you've seen my last batch of greeting cards."

"I do my homework, love. As soon as I heard what you were doing with your talent, I had to see. I can only imagine the power of the original oils when the prints are so good." Constance shook her head. "When are you going to get serious about your painting, Elizabeth? Greeting cards may pay the bills, but they can't leave much for caviar and champagne. And believe you me, life without caviar and champagne is a poor substitute for the real thing."

"I like Everhold. They've been great to me. I have my own line of greeting cards, and my calendar will be out soon. That's enough."

"Enough is never enough. Let me talk to some people. You could have a show this winter in Scottsdale. Dazzle the snowbirds."

"No! Please, Constance."

"Oh, all right, if you feel that strongly about it.

21

You were always as independent as hell. I have to savor that you're leaning on me just that little bit while you get over this breakup. It looks like it's all you'll let me do." She smiled wryly and laced an arm through Elizabeth's. "Come on, love. I promised to mix us a drink."

"I really do appreciate you letting me stay, Constance. Now, when do I get to meet this 'very serious' new man of yours?"

Constance seemed to hesitate.

"I'm not sure you want to, love."

A terrible sense of disaster exploded full-blown in Elizabeth's breast. She could feel her color drain away.

"Do I know him?" she managed to ask at last, but it was a rhetorical question. She had already read the answer in Constance's eyes.

"You used to. It's Stephen, of course."

Of course.

Chapter Three

Elizabeth's hands trembled. In slow motion she picked up the pale blue envelope from where it lay with the rest of her mail on her desk. It was addressed to Libby Purdin.

The office complex was deserted at this hour, but she deliberately swiveled her chair so that she faced the room. She turned the envelope over.

It was from a dead man.

No, no, no! She was being hysterical. David Royce was dead. His company had folded years ago. This was no more than an envelope from those old days, bearing the Royce Pharmaceutical logo. The company that had died with David Royce.

Someone, one of the old circle, had run across an envelope and decided to send it. It was as simple as that. They had all worked for David Royce during their college days: Constance, Mary Prill, Damon Baille, and herself. Stephen Kenwood. Even Ellen.

Dear God, this brought it back! The familiar Chritton Street address, Portland, Oregon.

Constance would be amused. Elizabeth told herself that if she hurried, she could catch Constance at home and they could open the letter together. Share a laugh. It was probably Damon, with his bizarre tilt at life, saying something like "Ha! I'll bet I scared you!" and God, he had no idea!

Elizabeth ran her fingers blindly over the envelope. It had been so long. In April it would be seven years. Damon wouldn't have a clue as to how to find her, even if he wished to. And they had never had anything in common but Ellen.

And the postmark. It had been mailed here in Phoenix only yesterday.

Damn! She was scaring herself. Elizabeth tore the end off the envelope with quick, trembling fingers. Three newspaper clippings fluttered onto the blotter of her desk.

She would never show Constance, after all.

The body of a woman was discovered late Tuesday by a city maintenance crew clearing a ditch along the Washington Street on-ramp. There was no identification. The woman is described as 45 to 55 years old, 62 inches tall, and weighing about 125 pounds. She was wearing a blue t-shirt and windbreaker, gray jogging pants, and white tennis shoes.

The police refuse to comment, but the men who found the body say the victim's throat had been cut.

Elizabeth pressed a shaking hand to her lips. She read again the sentence that had been underlined in bold red ink: ". . . the victim's throat had been cut."

The other two clippings were similar.

Police have confirmed the identity of a young woman fatally injured in a knife attack on the lower East side late Saturday. Mariel Hinckley, 25, of Baton Rouge, died at the scene after sustaining a severed artery when a knife-wielding man slashed her throat before fleeing on foot.

No motive for the slaying has been revealed.

A Fresno, California man is in custody tonight after fatally stabbing his estranged wife in her parents' home. Ronald Calvin Hale, 46, will face charges of first-degree murder in the death of Marie Todd Hale, 36, in the Orange County slaying.

Hale, a retired cannery foreman, allegedly broke into the home of his father-in-law, where his estranged wife was sleeping, and cut her throat. Hale then called police and turned himself in.

"Slashed her throat" and *"cut her throat"* were sharply scored in the same red ink.

Elizabeth pressed the tips of her fingers into the sockets of her aching eyes. She must have read without blinking. She must have thought she could close her eyes when the harsh words quit dancing before her and the clippings would be gone. A bad dream, a nightmare; God knew she had enough of them to recognize one from reality.

Only this *was* reality. Elizabeth exhaled on one long sigh and let her eyes refocus on the articles. Her heart was pounding in her ears, but it didn't matter.

She was going to have to think. Think hard, and, please God, emotionlessly.

None of the clippings bore either the date or the name of the newspaper in which it had appeared. That made them virtually unidentifiable as to city and state, except in the third, where the slaying had obviously occurred in California. The first referred only to "Washington Street," a name that must appear on thousands of city maps across the country. The second mentioned the "lower East side," an equally vague description.

In the first and second articles, the murders were unsolved and without known motive, but the third gave little doubt as to the identity of the killer.

All three victims were women. All three had their throats cut. There seemed to be no other connection in the articles.

Each clipping had been precisely ruled with a pencil and then a black marker and carefully trimmed. The damning red line was as straight as a die.

All right. She could stare at the clippings until the night gave way to morning and it would change nothing. It didn't matter where the women had been killed, why, or even who had done it. It was the "how" she was being taunted with. *The victim's throat had been cut.* Threatening her. Reminding her . . .

It was starting all over again.

She picked up the telephone.

There was a slight vibrational hum as the elevator rose to Elizabeth's floor. She put down the phone and in one sharp movement swept the clippings and envelope into her desk drawer and slid it shut.

"Burning the midnight oil again, eh, Miss Purdin?" the elderly security guard observed, as he went down the corridor, checking doors. Then, checking the other side, he retraced his steps, the same ones he made every night on the half hour.

"I'm almost done, Arthur. Another twenty minutes."

He always said the same thing. "Take your time. If Mr. Eliot doesn't have a guilty conscience about the long hours you work then I surely don't." He chuckled and sketched a salute. "I'll check everything when you're gone. See you tomorrow, Miss Purdin."

He pushed the elevator button, but then turned back.

"You know, miss, if you're ever nervous about leaving the building late, give me a ring downstairs. I'll walk you out. Crime never sleeps, you know."

Elizabeth ran an unsteady hand across her mouth. "It's only 9:30."

"All the same, miss." The elevator opened. "Give me a shout. No use taking chances." He stepped inside and the doors slid shut.

No—no use taking chances. Elizabeth let out her breath and, opening the drawer, took out the clippings and envelope. She shredded the newsprint and then the envelope, and gathering up the confetti-sized scraps, she took them down the hall to the waste disposal unit.

Her fingers were smeared with ink; she must have been sweating. She went into the washroom and the harsh glare of the overhead fluorescent light revealed ink smudges on her face as well, where she had pressed her fingers to her lips. She scrubbed at them with unnecessary force, removing the stains from the

27

shocking pallor of her skin. She went back to her desk at last and picked up the telephone.

It rang three times before the answering machine in Constance's home clicked on. Elizabeth waited through the recorded reply, and when the beep sounded, she said sharply, "Are you there, Constance? Pick up the phone, Con."

"Hi. Don't you sound intense. All work and no play makes Jill et cetera et cetera."

"I thought you might have gone out."

"I'm about to. Some of us *do* have social lives, you know."

"Constance, how long has Stephen been in Phoenix?"

"A couple of months. Why?"

"Why did he move here?"

"Lord, I don't know. Because of me? What do you want me to say?"

"Then he knew you were here?"

"Elizabeth, what is this, the third degree? I don't know how it happened that he moved to Phoenix. You're the one who's so fascinated with coincidence. All that matters to me is that he's here."

"But he left Portland a few months ago?"

"I didn't say that, love. He's been in Denver for the past two years."

"So what brought him here?"

"Good God, I don't know. Didn't I say I didn't? All I know is that he worked for a lab in Denver until a couple of months ago. Maybe he got tired of the cold. Maybe he was transferred."

"So he's still with the same company?"

"No-o. He's with Execucon Labs in Tempe now. Is that significant?"

"Constance, did he know I was here?"

Constance sighed.

"No. All right? I told him. Your name came up. Sorry, I don't remember how. I said you were here . . ." She paused sharply, and after a long moment went on. "He may have known already. He didn't say so, but he may have. I don't see what difference it makes. Elizabeth, are you all right? You sound odd."

She must, she was sure she did. She was walking too near the edge. She took a deep breath.

"Con, I'm sorry. Really sorry. But there's something you should know about Stephen."

"Oh, for God's sake, Elizabeth! Don't you think you've made your point with your cold little silences when his name comes up? I'm not dense. I know you don't approve. Okay? I'd really like to leave it at that, if you don't mind."

"Constance . . ."

"No. No, love. Listen, Elizabeth, I know you mean it for the best, and I appreciate that. But I just don't want to get into the bad old days, okay?" Constance's sigh came distinctly over the line. "You know, hon, for a woman who is as tough as Ollie North, you've got a wide streak of protectiveness for your friends. But this is one who doesn't need it. I'm a big girl. I've been a big girl for a long time. All right?"

"All right."

"Good. And Elizabeth?"

"Yes?"

"Don't you think that you and Stephen could be friends again if you were willing to try?"

"We were never friends," Elizabeth said harshly.

Constance sighed again.

"No, I suppose not. I really don't mean to be an ass about your concern, love. I'm not likely to forget what you did for me in college. It was your talent that landed me that first design job. I wouldn't be where I am if you hadn't pulled me through that dark patch. I'll always owe you."

"It's I who owe you, Con," Elizabeth managed. "I'd have lost everything if you hadn't covered for me. Everything that mattered."

"Forget it. It was a long time ago." There was a pause, and then Constance said in a low voice thick with tears, "Those were bad times, Elizabeth. Anyone could be forgiven for making a mistake."

Yes, they *were* bad times. But some mistakes were never forgiven.

"I'd better let you go, Constance."

"Right. Before I ruin my makeup. But, Elizabeth?"

"Yes?"

"We can thank God it's over."

Chapter Four

Elizabeth got out of her car and locked the doors. It was still early morning and the parking lot was empty. She started toward the big building that was Everhold Greeting Card Company.

A man was waiting for her.

The sun was in her eyes, and for a moment she felt a shock of alarm. And then she recognized the security uniform and Chuck Lester, one of the young men from Everhold's security division.

"Morning, Miss Purdin. I think I startled you. Sorry."

"I didn't expect to run into anyone this early. You do work all hours, don't you? Didn't I see you on duty yesterday afternoon?"

"Hey, you're observant! I like that. Most people can't describe what a co-worker was wearing five minutes ago, do you know that? Of course, you're an artist. You probably notice such things. You would be what my prof describes as the perfect witness."

Elizabeth's scalp tingled.

"Witness for what?"

"Oh, gosh . . . I don't know. Some kind of crime.

Or a car accident . . . Who was at fault, that sort of thing. Do you know that statistics show that . . . I forget the percentage . . . a high percentage of people get the color and the make wrong when describing a 'high emotion' scene. That's like something where they're scared or freaked, that sort of thing. Can you imagine?"

Elizabeth could imagine. Unless it was a scene replayed in nightmares so many times one could close one's eyes and describe every detail.

"I remember now. You're studying to be a police officer."

"Hey, not bad. Who'd think upstairs would know something like that?"

"I wouldn't think you could fit your classes into the hours you work, Chuck."

"I couldn't, most places. But Mr. Eliot has been really decent. I can pretty much determine my own hours, and the other guys trade off with me sometimes. You never know when I might show up around here."

Elizabeth smiled faintly. She was beginning to believe he hadn't been waiting for her, that it was a chance encounter and he was passing the time.

"I hope that isn't meant to be sinister," she offered, but she was joking. She couldn't imagine anyone less menacing than Chuck Lester. Standing close enough to him for conversation in the morning light, she was struck by how young he was. Or perhaps it was herself, feeling older than time.

He shook his head.

"Nope. But that's a good word—sinister. I was waiting to talk to you about something that may just be a little sinister."

Elizabeth looked at him and her eyes were clear. He would not have guessed that she was struggling with the desire to stop him, to walk away, to cover her ears with her hands.

"What is it?"

"Somebody is watching you."

The parking lot was quiet. For a handful of seconds Elizabeth said nothing. Then she put her hand on Chuck Lester's arm and drew him into the shadow of the building, surprising him with how suddenly she moved, and the strength of her fingers.

"Did you see who it was?"

"It wasn't quite that simple, Miss Purdin. First of all, see, I noticed the guy you date. Vanfossen? I didn't think much about it until I saw that he never went into the building. Into Everhold. He hung around, quiet, glancing at people as they came and went. And then, when you came out at lunch, I looked for him and he was gone. So I knew he wasn't waiting for you. That happened a couple of times."

Elizabeth let out the breath she had been holding. Better a known, she thought bitterly. Better a friend or its facsimile, than God-knew-what.

"But then, a couple of days later, just after my days off, I see this guy. Not Vanfossen. He's sitting in an older model car, over there." Chuck motioned toward the far corner of the lot. "He's reading a newspaper and that was okay, it wasn't as if it was a hot day and sweat was running off the guy. I wouldn't even have noticed him if I hadn't just had a class about surveillance and been thinking about it, watching cars with particular interest, you know, practicing my observation skills.

"So anyway, when you come out at lunchtime, this

33

guy throws down the paper and starts the car. He pulls out and sits idling on the street. As soon as you've driven away, he falls in behind, several cars back." Chuck took a piece of paper from his pants pocket. "I ran the number through DMV. I got a guy by the name of Royce. David Royce."

No. No, no, no!

"David Royce is dead."

The security guard frowned at the paper in his hand.

"No kidding? I always heard the IRS would follow a guy to the grave. I didn't know DMV would."

"There was no grave." Elizabeth didn't recognize the black "cop" humor. She hardly heard him. "David Royce went out into the ocean one cold April day. And he never came back."

"He killed himself?"

"Yes."

"Well, gosh, I don't know what to tell you. Somebody is paying the registration fees on a dead man's car, and they're paying it in his name. The plates were current."

"Did you see what the man looked like? Could you describe him?"

"Nope. Sorry. Like I said, he was just a man reading the newspaper until he started to follow you. Then it was all I could do to get the glasses on his plates and take down the number. But it wasn't Vanfossen. I'd have recognized him."

"Was that the only time you saw the man?"

"Just the once. I put the other guards on the alert, too, giving them the car make and number, but nobody has seen him. There is one other thing, though."

"What?"

"This may have nothing to do with the guy in the parking lot, but I figured you'd want to know. It's probably harmless."

"Tell me."

"Well, you know I rotate shifts. So I know everybody that works in security. And we talk and pass on stories that might not get told otherwise, if you know what I mean. And sometimes at night the guys get a little bored and they kick back maybe a bit more than the people upstairs, like yourself, might think is professional."

"Go on."

"So they tell me this morning that they were goofing around last night, listening in to conversations coming through the switchboard. Hoping to catch Harv talking to his girlfriend, you know the sort of thing. So they heard a call come in for you."

"For me? At night?"

"Yeah. About midnight, one o'clock. I don't know if you know, Miss Purdin, but Everhold uses an operator rather than shutting down the switchboard or using an answering machine. It's supposed to be Mr. Eliot's idea. Heaven knows why."

Elizabeth knew why. Mr. Eliot's daughter was a runaway. He wanted someone to be on the phone if she ever called, whatever the hour.

"Yes?"

"And this call comes in, like I said, around midnight. It was a woman, and they said she sounded really upset. Like it didn't occur to her that you wouldn't be at your desk at that hour. And I guess she didn't say much or leave a message. That's why

35

I thought you might not even hear about the call if I didn't tell you."

It was an Indian summer day in early October. The leaves were just beginning to turn gold and orange on the fruit trees, the chinaberry and ash. But a chill ran down Elizabeth's neck as if a cold wind were blowing.

She looked across the empty parking lot, the empty years. There was a knot in her throat, and it may have been tears or it may have been hatred, but it was interminable. She could scarcely remember the beginning, and she doubted she would live to see the end.

"Miss Purdin?"

She would call again. And again. Until her cold, nervous fingers were hopelessly tangled again in the skein of Elizabeth's life. In Constance's. In Stephen's.

"Miss Purdin?"

"I beg your pardon?"

"Myself, I figure any calls I miss in the middle of the night are all to the good and I'm not going to give my home number to a kook that thinks he can call me at all hours. But I thought you might want to know, especially on top of this business with the guy in the car."

"I appreciate it. I'm sure it's nothing, but thank you for your concern."

"Right. Well, I've got to check in, or Howard will think I ran into trouble. But don't you worry, now. I'll keep a close eye on the parking lot."

"Thank you, Chuck."

"No problem," he assured her, but Elizabeth was already gone, even before she walked away. She was waiting for the ringing of the telephone. Her nerves were tensed for the sound.

And it came. Exactly two minutes after the lines opened for the day.

"Elizabeth? Thank God! I've got to see you."

"Mary?"

"Yes, of course."

Of course. After six and a half years of silence. Mary Prill.

"Where are you?" Elizabeth asked, but she didn't want to know. Or worse, she already knew.

"I'm here in Phoenix. I have to see you, Elizabeth. *Now*. It's vital."

Elizabeth leaned back in her chair and ran a hand across her eyes. Not "It's important," but "It's vital." The difference seemed to carry a whisper of threat or of hysteria. Or perhaps, Mary being Mary, it was both.

"It's been a long time," Elizabeth said.

There was a pause. And then Mary clipped, "You sound just the same. I didn't expect it."

"Didn't you?" Elizabeth asked bitterly. "I recognized you. You sounded exactly as I expected."

"And how is that?" Mary snapped. "Shallow?"

"Self-serving."

"Isn't everyone?"

Elizabeth put her elbows on the desk and leaned into her hands. Her brief flare of anger was gone. It was wasted effort, as wasted as the tears.

"Perhaps. Where are you? I can come now."

"Don't sound so thrilled," Mary said sarcastically. "It's only been seven years. Are you sure you can fit it into your schedule?"

37

"I can fit it in," Elizabeth responded. "But I don't want to. I'm asking myself why I should."

"Then by all means let me give you the answer, Elizabeth. It's because you always honor duty. You always do what's right, by your lights, no matter who gets hurt. Don't tell me you've forgotten your role: Elizabeth the Perfect."

"And yours," Elizabeth clipped. "Mary the Traitor."

There was a long silence.

"You haven't changed," Mary said bleakly.

"You've no idea. I'd like to keep it that way."

"Of course. You never had any use for the rest of us, just Constance LeMirre with all her money. And Stephen Kenwood. Which lasted the longer, Elizabeth? Your friendship with Constance, or your passion for Stephen?"

"Shut up, Mary."

"My, my. Struck a nerve? Well, let me tell you what I heard. I heard you and Stephen are history. Constance, I hope, is in hell, where she belongs."

"You don't think she'd go without you, do you?"

Again the silence spun out. When Mary spoke at last there was a cautious edge, a retreating, perhaps even a whisper of fear.

"Where *is* Constance?"

"You didn't come all the way from Portland just to see her? I'm surprised."

"She's here?"

It *was* fear. Elizabeth couldn't miss it.

"She's been here for six months."

"Christ!" Mary gritted between her teeth. And then, "I'm slow, aren't I? You're probably laughing at me for taking so long to catch on. Everybody's here, right? Even me. And I almost believed it was my idea to come, despite the circumstances."

"What *are* the circumstances, Mary?"

"As if you didn't know. You almost convince me." The brittle edge was still there in her voice, but it was thinner; it shook. "Elizabeth and Constance and me. And Stephen? Is he here?"

"Yes."

"Of course. Not David. David is dead. What about Ellen? Is Ellen Glover here?"

"No."

"She wouldn't be! Not when her disappearance can drag us all through hell! Damn that woman! Damn her to hell!"

Elizabeth pressed her fingers to her temples. She had to suppress the hatred in Mary. "You've forgotten someone—if you're making a roll call of everyone who worked at Royce Pharmaceuticals at the same time as you and I did."

"You mean Damon Baille?"

"That's right."

"Oh, Damon will be here," Mary gritted. "He's coming."

That was it, then. The vultures were gathering. They scented weakness, vulnerability. They wanted to be in on the kill.

Elizabeth shivered.

"Where do you want to meet?" she asked grimly.

Chapter Five

It was a quiet morning at Encanto Park. It was still too early for picnickers but it would to be a good day for them, and they would come. Now there was only Elizabeth and Mary Prill, sitting at a table near the lagoon, and a host of noisy ducks paddling about in the warm amber water.

Elizabeth doubted she'd have recognized Mary had they passed on the street. At nearly thirty, Elizabeth's own age, Mary looked middle-aged. The fleshy roundness of cheek and chin that Elizabeth recalled had thinned to angular lines, emphasizing the large jaw and pale blue eyes. Her skin was sallow and her sandy hair thin and limp. The habitual expression of discontent that she had often worn was now indelibly etched into the long lines of her face.

So many years apart should have given them a dozen things to talk about. It gave them none. It had been too long, too grim, and the only thing they had ever shared was grief.

Even their silence was bitter.

Mary kept turning the plain gold band on the third finger of her left hand. Elizabeth supposed she was expected to notice, to comment. It seemed ridiculous to play games. Mary had wanted to see her, she had traveled some twelve hundred miles to see her, and now she sat moodily twisting her wedding ring.

"Why are we here?" Mary demanded abruptly.

That was a good question. It was Elizabeth's question. For a second it crossed her mind that Mary was confused or ill, and then she recognized the expression in the pale eyes. She tested it.

"Am I supposed to know?"

"God, why do you do this? What sick, sadistic kick can you possibly get from it? You sent for me. You demanded I come. And now you play some deep game with me that is so absolutely characteristic. I'm risking everything and you're laughing at me."

Elizabeth turned and looked out across the water of the lagoon. It was restful, despite the cola cans and paper cups. It was quiet after the tumult in Mary's flushed, angry face.

"I didn't send for you."

Mary came off the bench with all her nervous, ragged energy. She caught Elizabeth by the shoulders and her hands were trembling.

"You did, Elizabeth! You did! Admit it! Don't taunt me!"

Elizabeth looked steadily up at her. She pushed at the clutching hands and they fell away.

"I didn't. You may prefer to believe it was me, but it wasn't. If someone sent for you, you'll have to look a little further. It may surprise you to know that I don't even know where you live. That I have no interest in knowing."

The stiffening went out of Mary. Her color

blanched away and she sat down slowly, awkwardly, on the stone bench beside Elizabeth.

"Oh, lord, Elizabeth. What am I going to do?"

"I don't know, Mary. Maybe you should ask Mark Russell."

"Mark Russell? Was that his name? Lord, I couldn't have recalled it."

"Perhaps," Elizabeth said bitterly, "that's because someone you considered a friend didn't betray you over him."

Mary leaned back against the cold, hard ridge of the concrete table as if she didn't feel it. She closed her eyes.

"You can't begin to know how sick I was about that. And do you know what the irony was? He dumped me. He got me to betray my friends. He said they weren't good enough for me. And then *I* wasn't good enough for him." She laughed harshly. "I suppose he decided he wanted a girl who was loyal to her friends."

Elizabeth felt an unwilling stir of compassion. Mary had always been weak, malleable. She was a person looking for someone to melt into, to give her form and decision.

"You got over him. You married."

Mary jerked, closing her fingers around her wedding ring as if Elizabeth had threatened it. Her face closed up and it was tight and ugly, like a child on the verge of a tantrum.

"Yes! I married! I have children. Little babies, tender babies. Now do you see what you're doing?"

"No," Elizabeth said grimly. "What *am* I doing?"

"You're destroying us."

For a few seconds Elizabeth thought of getting up and walking away.

"It's getting to be a stale theme with you, Mary. Is it because you believe it or simply want to believe it?"

"I want to believe it!" Mary said vehemently. "I want you to tell me it's true!"

"Then you're out of luck."

"Oh, I am that, all right! There's not a day goes by that I don't remind myself of that! When I got your letter, I thought . . . God, I must have been crazy . . . that you had decided to quit playing cat-and-mouse games with us. That you were going to let us go."

"What kind of letter?" Elizabeth clipped.

"Now, that was the good part. The straightforward part. I should have been suspicious right off, shouldn't I? Not some thief in the night. A straightforward letter, like a real human being would send."

"Did it say it was from me?"

"Of course it did. It was every word your handwriting. Your signature, too. I especially liked the touch where you used an old Royce Pharm envelope. You've no idea of the impact. You would have been pleased."

Elizabeth ran a hand across the pressure in her temple. She let out her breath on a long sigh.

"I didn't write you. You can believe it or not."

Something stirred in Mary's eyes. Terror.

"You did, Elizabeth. Of course you did."

"Listen, Mary. Someone wrote to you using my name, signing my name. They wanted you here so badly they coerced you into coming while they hid

43

behind someone else. Now deal with that. Face that. Because it's reality.

"There's nobody here to lean on, Mary, not even me. You want to believe I'm evil but you would rather cling to me than stand on your own. You're out of luck. You're on your own, and God knows the danger."

Mary had paled as Elizabeth had spoken. She wrapped her arms across her body defensively, and there was no more pretense. She said tautly, "It's been hell. Sheer, living hell."

"You're being watched?"

Mary twitched, a tremor. She wanted to accuse Elizabeth all over again. But Elizabeth's eyes were as clear as the gray stone slab that lay over David Royce's grave, the one where his body would never lie.

"Yes."

"How long?"

"Lord, I don't know. Forever. No, for the last year, maybe. And it's not only that. The house has been broken into a number of times and nothing has been taken. The phone rings. It rings and rings and no one is there. The people at work tell me someone comes by asking about me, but never when I'm in the office. I never see them." Mary's voice was ragged. "I'm scared, Elizabeth. I can't go to a park in the daylight over a thousand miles from home without wondering if I'm being followed."

"Tell me about the letter."

Mary shook her head helplessly.

"It was . . . threatening. Quietly menacing. And then the Royce Pharm envelope . . . I didn't dare *not* come."

44

"Did you save it?"

"No. I burned it in the sink five minutes after I got it. It wasn't the sort of thing I wanted James to run across, I can tell you. He doesn't know about any of this. He doesn't know about . . . you know. Royce Pharmaceuticals, Ellen's disappearance. I've made sure he didn't know."

"You're talking about your husband?"

"Yes. James Rhinehardt. He's a dermatologist. I run the office for him and two other physicians. And trust me, Elizabeth, I can't afford him knowing it's because of me that our home is being violated." Mary closed her eyes tightly. "He thinks I'm in New Mexico. My folks are in Clovis, and my mother has been ill. I told him I needed to spend some time with her."

"If you want my advice," Elizabeth said darkly, "and I doubt you do, go to Clovis. Go to your hotel and pack your bags and take the next flight out. Or go home."

"I can't. I've got to see this finished." Mary's chin quivered, but her voice was surprisingly resolute. "I'm not going back till it's over. I refuse to go on as I have, terrified every minute of every day."

"I don't think you know what's happening here. I'm not sure you want to know."

"I don't know," Mary admitted bitterly. "Do you? Does Damon?"

Damon. Damon Baille. Elizabeth looked back into the past. There were so many shadows. Damon was one of them.

"What about Damon? You say he's coming."

Mary shuddered.

"He'll be here. Maybe he's already here. I don't

know. He's horrible, Elizabeth. I live in fear of James discovering that I ever knew such a man."

"He's still using drugs?"

"Oh lord, yes. And the cheapest liquor he can buy. He looks like a caricature of his old self. I doubt he's ever sober. He calls me at the office and even at home and I have to lie to James. It's awful."

"What does he want?"

"It's always the same. He says we all have to get together and talk about Ellen. He's obsessed with it. He called me the day I was leaving Portland. I was scared to death he wanted to travel with me. But he was just checking up on me. He was planning to hitchhike. Can you imagine? Hitchhike from Oregon to Arizona! Why anyone would pick him up is beyond me, and I swear, he probably got here before I did. What are we going to do, Elizabeth?"

It seemed to Elizabeth that the sun was gone. She was cold though the air around her was in the low nineties.

She had schooled herself in passivity, in waiting. Years spent like that, braced for the next blow. And here was Mary, an expert at dissolving into the strongest person near her, suggesting action. And brilliant, beautiful Damon Baille, ravaged by drugs and his own private hell, trying to force a confrontation among them all. It was some kind of distorted alter-reality.

Elizabeth tested its perimeters.

"What do you think we should do?"

"I think Damon's right: we have to meet. All of us. Everyone who worked at Royce Pharmaceuticals that last year. We've got to talk."

"What will that accomplish?"

Mary's eyes narrowed.

"Don't toy with me, Elizabeth. I'm not simple, whatever you may think. You know as well as I that we all have . . . let's call it information. Dangerous information. But one of us, one of us, Elizabeth, is being eaten alive by it. He is preying on the others, and there is no estimating how far he will go. And I don't mean the 'he' literally. It's just as likely to be you or Constance as it is to be Stephen or Damon."

"Or you."

"Or me," Mary said tightly. "Or Ellen. You notice she's not here. Not that we know of, anyway."

Elizabeth could feel her scalp prickle.

"David Royce is dead," she reminded Mary.

"I hate that about you, Elizabeth. The way you come up with something a person is thinking. But you're right. David is dead. It would be a lot simpler if he weren't. We know he was crazy."

"And Damon isn't?"

"Yes, well, there's that, of course. He's marginal at best. And he's dead set on bringing us all back together."

"I got a Royce Pharm envelope too," Elizabeth said. She watched Mary carefully, every flicker of light and shadow in her face. "There were newspaper clippings inside. About murdered women."

Mary's breath went in on a hiss.

"Good God! And you mention it like it was no more than an afterthought. You're as cold as ice, Elizabeth. Colder. There's no melting in you."

"Do you want hysterics?"

"It might be refreshing," Mary snapped. "But I won't hold my breath."

"Which of us would have kept old supplies from Royce Pharmaceuticals?"

"I would have. Isn't that what you want me to say? I'm the one with the scrapbooks, the mementos, the fetish about order. But I didn't. There was nothing about Royce Pharmaceuticals that I wanted to remember. Absolutely nothing."

"The company was liquidated years ago. It may interest you to know that I went to the auction. But it was just office equipment and the like. The actual paper goods, stationery, had been sent to the incinerator or for recycling. They were already gone."

"I can imagine you there," Mary said bitterly. "You *would* watch it all be torn apart."

"It was torn apart when David killed himself." Elizabeth hesitated, she took a chance, "When Ellen disappeared."

"Ellen! Christ! She *would* run through the whole fabric of this thing! Never one to be left out, that's Ellen. Even when she's gone, she's here."

That was close. It was uncannily close.

"Is she here?" Elizabeth dared.

"You tell me! Is she? She walked out when the company was still alive and well, if you'll excuse the expression. Why not take an armload of stationery with the company logo? What's a little pilfering to Ellen Glover? So she could write to us. So she could scare the hell out of us."

"Why?"

Mary made an exasperated sound in her throat.

"Don't be naive, Elizabeth. There's more to this than the obvious. And it doesn't have to be Ellen. As I said before, it could be any one of us."

"But there's still got to be an object to it," Elizabeth insisted. She was pressing so close to the truth that her flesh felt clammy, cold. She had to take Mary past it, offer it to her, and let her dismiss it. If she would. "The object of one of us deliberately scaring the others?"

"You're suggesting it has to be for financial gain, I suppose?" Mary snapped. "You've been around Constance LeMirre too long. There could be a dozen reasons, and none of them material."

"What, then?"

"Oh, for Lord's sake! Don't you watch television, go to the movies? Does terrorizing innocent people usually have a motive? Does Freddy Krueger expect to get paid for slashing some teenager to ribbons? To be able to frighten someone is to have power over them. That's enough for some people. Even you will have to agree, Elizabeth, that whoever is doing this isn't normal."

Elizabeth felt the relief slide through her veins. She said quietly, "Do you remember what was in the letter?"

"Every word. It said that I couldn't hide the truth any longer. That I had been lucky so far, and that I didn't want to watch it fall apart now. I was to come to Phoenix immediately, to call you at Everhold.

"And I did. I dared not ignore a letter like that. But I didn't expect it to be like this. I thought, I hoped, I could appeal to you to understand, to leave us alone." Mary's voice wobbled. "I didn't want to find that it was more complicated than some . . . I don't know. Sick reunion or something. Oh, God, Elizabeth, I'm scared! I wish it were you. I wish it were no more frightening than a slender woman with ice water in her veins. I could live with that."

49

"Go home, Mary," Elizabeth advised bluntly. She stood up and the breeze caught her dark hair. She smoothed it back and looked down at Mary on the bench. "Go home while you can."

"Are you threatening me, Elizabeth?" Mary asked, and her voice was odd, fluttering. Perhaps with hope, perhaps she was grasping again at the possibility that it was only Elizabeth, that there was nothing more sinister here than what she could see before her.

Elizabeth shook her head in exasperation.

"Goodbye, Mary," she said resolutely, and turned and started walking away.

"Wait, Elizabeth! What about a meeting among the five of us? We've got to talk."

"Count me out."

"We were your friends once, Elizabeth."

Elizabeth shook her head and kept walking.

Chapter Six

The headlights swung across the high oleander hedges and the signs on either side of the road proclaiming it a dead end.

Elizabeth parked the car on the street and got out slowly, looking across the darkened expanse of lawn to the lightless house beyond. Her skin crawled.

She had been living here for over a week, long enough to know that something was different tonight, that something was terribly wrong. And yet she could see nothing.

Sam was silent. The houses on either side were mutely lit, welcoming in their way, although Elizabeth had met neither family.

Usually she parked in the garage, but tonight the thought of driving into that dark maw seemed menacing. She got out of the car and moved slowly, deliberately, up the drive, until she stood in the shadows the palm trees cast across the front door.

Somewhere in the neighborhood, not close, a dog barked. It sounded primitive, primordial on the dark, quiet street.

Elizabeth reached out a hand and pressed it

against the hardwood panel of the door. She could feel it: something terrible within. It trembled in every nerve of her hand, up her arm. With frozen fingers she tried to turn the knob.

It was locked. She knew it would be. She had locked it herself.

Elizabeth fumbled with the key. She inserted it into the lock, and when it gave, she slowly pressed the door open.

She could see nothing amiss. The living room sprang to life at the touch of a button, bathing the room in normalcy.

Elizabeth moved along the wall to the picture windows. She slid back the draperies and reassured herself one by one that the locks were fast.

The bedrooms were next. She moved deliberately, stiffly, searching out every corner and closet, checking the lock on each door and window.

There was nothing she could see. No chair, no magazine moved even a quarter of an inch, no door left ajar that she had closed. But still she moved carefully, as certain of the intrusion as she was that the security was unbroken.

She reached the arcadia doors. She drew back the drapes and the darkness rushed in, but nothing more. None of the locks had been touched. She knelt and placed an open hand against the glass.

"Sam," she whispered.

There was no response.

"Sam!" A little louder, more commanding. Nothing moved in the darkness.

And then Sam was there, cowering close against the glass, trying to touch her, to be comforted by her nearness. He whimpered. The hackles were up on the back of his neck, but his attitude was one of terror.

"Sam," Elizabeth said again, letting the curtain trail and drop from her fingers. She stood and moved reluctantly toward the kitchen.

There was nothing there. She pushed open the utility room door.

Something rattled across the floor, striking the opposite wall and rebounding, spinning with the momentum. A knife, the blade and handle smeared with blood.

Oh God, the blood! So much blood! Across the wall, the ceramic tile backboard, the laundry sink, the floor. An ocean of blood, more than the whole of a body might contain, Elizabeth thought hysterically. More than in the most grisly horror film she had ever been unwillingly compelled to see. And the smell: cloying, filling her nostrils with death.

There was nothing else.

Through the outer utility room door lay the closed garage. Elizabeth moved toward the door mindlessly, reaching out a hand as if to fend off the waiting horror that might at any second hurl itself upon her. Her fingers trembled above the doorknob. The lock was intact.

But she had to try the knob. Even seeing the metal hardware that rendered the door immobile, she needed to feel that the door did not give beneath her hand. That it did not begin to turn from the outside when she touched it.

And then she remembered the reality of fingerprints, their importance here. She shook herself and took a paper towel, a handful of paper towels, and forced herself to grasp the knob.

It was secure. She let out her breath on a long, ragged exhalation.

Elizabeth's mind refused to function. She felt ill, shocked, frozen. She was totally at a loss. And then she remembered the knife.

She sank down onto her heels, her arms wrapped about her body. She could see the knife where it had been flung by the opening door.

Elizabeth knew that knife. But God, it had been years ago, lifetimes ago. Lives ago.

She knew what to do now—what she had to do. She wrapped the paper towels about her hand and reached out for the knife.

It felt cold and hard beneath her fingers through the padding of coarse, protective paper. She dropped it into the sink and it clattered noisily, spattering blood.

Elizabeth winced. She turned on the water quickly, washing her hands, letting the flow rush over the knife. Taking away the blood. Taking away the truth.

She fought to breathe. Short, quick gasps through her mouth. She didn't wish to smell the blood, to see it.

Elizabeth washed the knife until the water flowed clear and then she scrubbed it dry with more paper towels. She folded the blade away inside the distinctive handle, and clutching it tightly in her hands, she stood looking at all the blood. Staring.

Finally, she called the police.

Elizabeth could hear the sirens as she sat on the floor in the spare bedroom with Sam Gamgee. It was impossible to know which of them was trembling more. When the loud knock came at the front door, she got up shakily, ordered Sam to wait, and went

54

out, closing the door behind her. There was no furniture in the extra bedroom, but it seemed kinder than leaving Sam alone in the dangerous, darkened back yard.

"Miss Purdin? Elizabeth Purdin?"

"Yes. Come in."

Elizabeth stood aside and the officers moved past her, filling the room, overflowing the house. A police van was just pulling up in front of the driveway. The flashing lights on the white police cars ran the length of the street, the housefronts. They disappeared and started all over again. There was the crackle of distorted radio voices. Elizabeth closed the door on it.

"Miss Purdin, I'm Detective Roy Sibben. You reported a murder?"

He was a big man, well over six feet tall, with the build of a football player who has let himself go. The press of officers separated and Elizabeth was surprised to see that there were only four of them.

"This way," she said tautly, and led them through the kitchen. When she would have opened the utility door, Detective Sibben stopped her.

"If I may?"

The door was off the latch. He took a felt-tip marker from his breast pocket and pushed the door wide.

Elizabeth didn't watch. She leaned against the kitchen cabinets and waited for the police to complete their inspection. She could hear the scuff of shoes, the jingle of keys as they knelt, moved about, studied the room and its grisly contents.

"The body's in the garage?" Sibben wanted to know.

55

"No . . . I don't know. I haven't been out there. I thought . . ."

Elizabeth heard Detective Sibben turn the dead-bolt on the door, the familiar scrape of the metal molding across the threshold as the door was opened.

She had to look, to know. She came into the utility room and stared past the officers to the garage beyond.

There was nothing there.

Sibben motioned to one of the officers to open the garage doors. When the flashing lights wheeled through the empty garage interior, Sibben waved in the men waiting by the van. Over the din of the radios, Elizabeth could hear people's voices shouting questions. The neighbors had to be in shock.

Sibben drew back into the house, leaving the door wide for the men and equipment. He gave Elizabeth a hard stare.

"Where's the body?" he wanted to know. "Or are we supposed to look for it?"

"You can look," Elizabeth said stonily. "But you're not going to find it. I've shown you all there is."

"Nichols," Sibben addressed the female officer. "Check out the rest of the house."

"My dog is in the room on the left," Elizabeth said to the retreating back. "He's friendly." She was glad it was a woman. Sam was used to women.

"Have you touched anything?" Sibben wanted to know.

"Everything."

Elizabeth described her progress from door to windows, checking locks. She watched him take notes. He was listening carefully, he was absorbing it, but she had the feeling that he was bored. As if he had seen all this so many times it had lost the power to horrify, to shock.

His thick black brows ran together in a single bar above his eyes. He was a machine with a thousand questions to ask and then he would go. He would write it all up and forget it. This was simply another night, routine perhaps.

Elizabeth shivered. She felt ill.

There was the tramp of feet and the sound of men's voices in the garage and utility room. Powerful floodlights moved across the drapes of the arcadia doors in the back.

"What time did you get home, Miss Purdin?"

"9:15."

"But you didn't call the police right away. Why was that?"

"I searched the house. It took some time. When I found the blood I called the police."

"Why did you search the house? Find an unlocked door?"

"No. I was nervous coming home alone. I've only been living here for a week. I was frightened."

"Now, Miss Purdin." Sibben shifted his weight and smiled slightly, skeptically. "You don't mean to tell me that you go through this routine every time you come home in the dark? It's not a high-crime area . . . I'd have to say it's a no-crime area. Do you know how rarely we get calls to neighborhoods like this? Maybe once a month."

"I told you I was scared," Elizabeth said coldly. "You'll have to take my word for it."

"So scared, in fact, that you parked on the street and walked up to the house, right? Do you want to

57

know what I think, Miss Purdin?" Sibben leaned forward in his chair so that he could read her face, and he didn't look bored anymore—he looked hard and calculating. "I think you don't scare so easily. I think you'd skip right up here in pitch darkness ninety-nine times out of a hundred without even looking behind you. But this was the one-hundredth. This time you knew something."

"Then let me tell you what I think, Detective," Elizabeth gritted. "I don't believe I was under any obligation to call you. There's no body. I think I could have taken the garden hose and sprayed down the room and shaken my head over the mess the cat made of the place while I was out. But you know, Detective, I don't have a cat. And I *did* call the police."

Detective Sibben said sarcastically, "You're too broken up about this, Miss Purdin. Perhaps I should get the police surgeon down here to order you a Valium."

Elizabeth *was* broken up. She was shattered. But perhaps not like he was used to seeing, helpless with shock. She said quietly, "You want me to say that I knew a murder had been committed in my house. I can't. I didn't know it. Not until I saw the blood."

"You saw nothing suspicious on the street when you approached the house?"

"Nothing."

"There's been no talk in the neighborhood of prowlers or burglars?"

"None that I know of."

"Do you own a gun, Miss Purdin?"

"No."

Officer Nichols had come back from her inspection

58

of the house. Elizabeth looked from her to the other officers. They all had guns. The rubber grips were thrust up high in the holsters, close at hand, in deadly menace. Whenever Sibben leaned forward Elizabeth could see the straps of the shoulder holster he wore beneath his plainclothes jacket.

"Carry mace? Tear gas?"

"No, I don't."

"Correct me if I'm wrong, Miss Purdin, but we have, by her own admission, a nervous young woman who lives alone. She spends half an hour creeping along the walls and windows every time she comes home and it's dark, looking for something threatening. Wouldn't you think she'd arm herself in some way?"

"Not necessarily."

"Why not?"

He was insulting, making a mockery, a lie, of her every word. Her response was too quick, reflexive, to temper with cooler judgment.

"Because I'm not in danger!"

The silence was deafening.

"I see," Sibben said at last, and his voice was smooth. "Don't I ever wish I was a clairvoyant like you. I'd know when to wear my vest and when to leave it home. And if I chose to do something . . . criminal, I'd know to have a solid alibi. Do *you* have an alibi, Miss Purdin?"

"Do I need one?"

"Now, you tell me. You're the one who knows what's going on here. Do you?"

An officer came in through the kitchen and motioned to Sibben, who got up and joined him there. They spoke together in low voices. Officer Nichols, a small, middle-aged blonde with dark roots, gave Elizabeth a glance that was somewhere between impersonal and compassionate.

"You've got a nice dog," she offered. "Dobermans and rottweilers aren't as pleased to see strangers as yours is. I can appreciate it."

Elizabeth pressed cold fingers against her closed eyes. She was trying to hear what the men were saying. She was afraid to hear.

Sibben came back. He stood towering over her, trying to intimidate her, perhaps, before sitting down. He looked at the papers on the clipboard in his hand for a long time.

"Well, Miss Purdin? Guess what? The rental supervisor says nobody has a key to this house but you. You *did* say the house was locked when you let yourself in?"

"That's right."

"So let's hear about the key."

"I'm sure you already know. I insisted on having all new locks installed before I moved in. Isn't that consistent with the behavior of a nervous young woman?"

He ignored her sarcasm.

"You paid for the work. You even insisted on hiring locksmiths of your choice and on being here to oversee their work. Is that right?"

"You know it is. You probably know that when he asked for copies of the keys to the new locks, I gave him ones that didn't fit."

"Yes, how about that? May I see your keys, Miss Purdin?"

Elizabeth took her key ring from her purse and handed it to him.

"We'll check these for wax residue, clay, see if copies have been made. But, Miss Purdin?"

"Yes, Detective?"

"You might want to be thinking about getting yourself a lawyer."

Elizabeth didn't need a lawyer. She needed a good strong headache tablet. She wondered if they would let her get an Excedrin from her medicine cabinet or if she had already passed the boundaries of moving freely in her own house.

The men propped open the door between the kitchen and utility room. Elizabeth could see them drawing circles around the spatters of blood and a photographer was taking pictures from every angle. Two men went down the hall with a briefcase—lab technicians, Elizabeth supposed, and if they were looking for fingerprints, they would find them, but they would be hers.

"Detective Sibben?" Elizabeth managed. "I heard one of the officers say something about blood tests. Is it possible you already know the blood type?"

"Tentatively. Fresh blood doesn't take more than ten minutes to run a prelim on. Of course, if you'd taken a few more passes around the house we'd have been out of luck. It's three, maybe four hours on dried blood."

Elizabeth didn't want to hear it. She could feel her heart beating in the pulse at her throat.

"May I know the blood type?"

Sibben consulted the sheet in his hands. He took his time, reading her tension perhaps, and playing on it. He didn't even need to look at the paper. It wasn't something he ran into every day.

"It's human blood. AB negative."

Elizabeth felt her color recede. She said faintly, "Excuse me," and walked down the hall to the bathroom.

Officer Nichols went with her.

Whether they considered her a suspect or were only protecting the scene from unwitting interference in their investigation, it didn't matter. Elizabeth placed her hands flat on the cold tile on either side of the basin. She leaned over, doubled over, the violence of her sickness taking her strength and her will. Her head pounded mercilessly.

When the spasms passed, Elizabeth turned on the water. She let it run, washing her face repeatedly in the icy water. But that brought to mind the bloody knife, and she closed her eyes tightly against the image. She pressed cold, wet fingers to her burning eyes.

"You know who the victim is, don't you?" Nichols suggested gently from just behind her.

Elizabeth nodded. She took the towel that Nichols offered and pressed it to her face. She felt hollow, used up.

"Keith," she said. "Keith Vanfossen." She hung up the towel carefully, deliberately, as if it mattered. The face reflected in the mirror was as white as death.

Elizabeth turned away, opening the door, and they went out into the hall.

Furious voices met them.

Elizabeth went still. For a handful of seconds she was frozen, mindless. And then she stepped forward, she said tonelessly,

"Hello, Stephen."

Chapter Seven

"Good God, Elizabeth!"

She might have planned this, this macabre gathering, as furious as Stephen was. He stood in the doorway, across the room from her, but Elizabeth could see that two years had made no difference in him. His lean, hard features, perhaps a little pale in the garish light, were as unreadable beneath the anger as the last time she'd seen him.

Detective Sibben raised a staying hand to the officers. Policy demanded that the two be separated immediately. They were both suspects at this point in what was a particularly grisly murder. But Sibben waved aside procedure. He could sense the tension, feel it. Something was happening here, something unexpected. He trusted his instincts.

He was wasting his time. As if she possessed the clairvoyance he had derided, Elizabeth turned and met Sibben's glance. She didn't look weak and shaken now. Her steady regard mocked him.

"I'll have to apologize, Detective Sibben. I should have told you that I called Stephen Kenwood and asked him to come."

"Is that a fact?" Sibben taunted. "And when was that, Miss Purdin?"

"Just after I called the police. I believe that's the proper sequence for this sort of thing, isn't it?"

She hadn't called Kenwood, Sibben had seen the shock in her face. But the damage was done. She'd had the opportunity to cover him with a lie and she'd taken it, and any pretense at breaking down the story was only that, a pretense. Which didn't help her, but it gave Kenwood an excuse for being in the neighborhood, and probably spared him a night being grilled at the police station, if not a hell of a lot worse.

Elizabeth looked at Stephen. Immaculately dressed as always, he wore a light gray suit with a blue silk tie over a crisp white shirt. His dark hair was slightly ruffled, as if he had just run a lean, agitated hand over it, but there was no other suggestion of turmoil in him. Even the anger was gone. He returned Elizabeth's glance without expression.

Elizabeth's heart was beating in her throat, and that was appropriate. In the throat, where Stephen's knife had plunged, and Keith's blood had flowed away with his life.

"I think you'd better sit down," Officer Nichols advised. She stepped close to Elizabeth, taking her elbow and urging her to the sofa.

"I'm all right," Elizabeth managed weakly. Her mouth was dry. She had never come so close to fainting and this was not the time to begin. "Could I have a couple aspirins? My head is splitting."

"Sorry," Sibben said coolly. "We haven't finished our investigation of the premises."

"I'm not asking for cyanide capsules, you know. How sinister is aspirin?"

"You don't stay down long, do you?" Sibben observed distastefully. He looked at Nichols. "Get her a couple aspirin. I don't want to hear about police brutality or some such rot." And to Stephen, "Stick around, Kenwood. I want to hear more about Miss Purdin calling you. And why, if it was so urgent, you came on foot. That's right, isn't it? There's no other car out front."

"Am I a suspect?"

"Maybe not . . . yet. We'll see what we can do." Someone was calling him from the utility room, and he gave Kenwood a steady look and went to see what the yelling was about.

Elizabeth didn't look up. Stephen came and stood in front of her and she closed her eyes so she wouldn't have to see him, see the hardness in the glance he bent upon her.

"Are you all right, Elizabeth?" he clipped.

That was too much.

"Of course," she gritted. "Perfect. And you?"

There was a sudden moaning cry, rising on a crescendo and falling away. Nichols, coming across the room with the aspirin and a glass of water, stopped in midstride. It was an unearthly sound.

"It's Sam," Elizabeth said. "My dog. He hears Stephen."

She looked at Stephen then and she had been wrong. He had aged. This close she could see a dusting of gray in the dark hair at his temples, the tiny fine lines at the corners of his eyes. The price, she thought grimly, of being one of the top chemical engineers at the Royce Chemical conglomerate.

The wailing cry came again. It might be a dog, but it sounded like a soul in torment.

Sibben came through the kitchen, a pained expression of his face.

"That's a dog? My kid's cat sounds better when its tail gets stepped on. Okay, Miss Purdin, if the dog wants to see Kenwood, I'm all for it. Anything to stop that racket. If you don't object, I don't."

Elizabeth shrugged, swallowing the tablets.

"First door on the left."

Not that Stephen could miss it with Sam's excited crying coming through the door. No more than he could miss how lost Sam had been without him.

"We're done in there, right, Nichols? The lab boys been over it?"

"Yes, they're working on the second bedroom."

"Okay, Kenwood, if you want to see the dog, we'd all appreciate it."

Stephen did. He must have. He turned without a word and went down the hall and opened the door. Elizabeth looked away.

"Dog knows him pretty well," Sibben observed.

"He used to," Elizabeth clipped. She lifted her chin and challenged the sardonic expression Sibben wore.

"Incurious sort, isn't he?"

"I beg your pardon?"

"Guy walks in off the street, police everywhere, somebody's been murdered in the other room. He doesn't even comment on it."

"Perhaps you're forgetting," Elizabeth said evenly. "I called him."

"Oh, that's right. You called him. You told him somebody was dead. Have I got that straight?"

"Straight as a string."

"That *is* what you said? It slipped your mind to mention that you'd called him?"

"I believe that's what I said," Elizabeth retorted coldly. "Check your notes."

"You know, maybe I'll do that. While you're checking the Yellow Pages for an attorney."

"Am I under arrest?"

"Officer Nichols tells me you know who the victim is. A guy named Vanfossen."

"That's right. He had a rare blood type. He was proud of it. He told everyone."

"I see. You're saying you didn't know him especially well?"

"That's not what I'm saying, Detective. We lived together for a couple of months. When we split up I moved in here. I suppose he stayed in the condo. I don't know. I haven't seen or heard from him since."

"He didn't have a key to this place?"

"That's right. He didn't."

"Now's the time to change your story, Miss Purdin. Before it gets too complicated. Vanfossen didn't have a key?"

"Thanks," Elizabeth said dryly. "But it's not necessary to change my story. Keith didn't have a key to my house. He's never been here."

"Never before tonight, I guess you mean," Sibben taunted. He inclined his head almost imperceptibly toward the utility room and its grisly contents. "The ME will be giving us a time of death. While we're waiting on that, maybe you'd like to tell me where you were all evening?"

For long, long minutes Elizabeth didn't reply. In the garage the van door slammed. Sam was quiet.

"I was at the South Command police station."

"No." Sibben denied. "No no no. I don't even want to hear this. The whole thing is starting to stink." He threw down his clipboard and called to an officer in the kitchen. "Carlton, check this out. Miss Purdin claims she was at the South station all evening. Let's get some times and a positive ID."

He said sarcastically to Elizabeth, "I suppose you're going to tell me some perfectly plausible reason why you just happened to be in a police station while your ex-lover was being murdered in your house?"

"I had a flat tire when I got to my car after work. It was dark and the parking lot was deserted."

"And the police, having nothing to do, took you down to the station for coffee and sandwiches while they changed it for you. Makes sense to me."

"I was nervous about the neighborhood I was in at that hour. I didn't know what I should do. And then I saw that the other tires were flat, too. They'd been slashed."

"Slashed? You mean deliberately punctured?"

"Yes."

Sibben dropped into the chair and gave Elizabeth a hard stare. He began to drum his fingers on the clipboard on his knee.

"All right. Let's hear it. Run it by me. I'm sure you've got it letter perfect."

Elizabeth hoped so.

"I was scared. I didn't know if it was random vandalism or something more sinister. Maybe someone was trying to set me afoot so I could be mugged."

"So you went back to your office and called a garage while you waited safely inside. Or no, I got it—you got security to take a look around, call a garage for you."

"No." Elizabeth moistened dry lips. "I couldn't

get back into the office once it was locked. There aren't guards. The security is completely electronic. And I didn't know where there was a public phone. I walked to the police station."

"You decided to take your chances with the mugger?"

"I didn't see that I had a choice. It was either that, or lock myself in my car all night."

"Okay. So you get to the South station. You call the garage. Why didn't you get a cab and go on home? Why didn't you call Kenwood?" Sibben tossed his head in the direction of Stephen, who was coming down the hall. "You knew it could be a couple hours. Why waste the time? Why not get your car in the morning? Go on home?"

"I wish I had," Elizabeth said sharply. "I wish to God I had."

"Why? So your blood would be all over the floor in there with your boyfriend Vanfossen?"

Elizabeth winced. Her eyes touched Stephen's and flinched away.

"I think you're forgetting, Detective Sibben—I told you I'm in no danger."

"That's right, you did. And what was the basis for that deduction? Maybe you'll fill me in."

Stephen cut in sharply.

"You don't have to answer any questions, Elizabeth. Not without an attorney." And to Sibben, *"Does* Elizabeth need an attorney, Detective?"

"We're checking on that, Kenwood. In the interim, maybe you'd like to answer a few questions? Or do you feel a need to call in counsel on *your* behalf?"

"I'll let you know," Stephen retorted. "It depends on the questions."

"I'm sure it does," Sibben said dryly. He consulted the sheets in his hand. "You were in the neighborhood because Miss Purdin called you. Isn't that the story? Not much we can do with that, is there?"

"I doubt it."

"On foot."

"That's right."

"Why?"

"I was near."

"I see. A young lady calls you. I won't say she's hysterical . . ." he gave Elizabeth an ironic glance, " . . . but she's upset. Somebody has just been killed in her house. And what do you do? Walk over. You must live pretty close."

"I don't," Stephen said shortly. "I was out walking. I left my car at Execucon Labs."

"In Tempe? That's a hell of a walk. Five miles, six. And I guess you were going by an AM/PM when you heard the phone. You picked it up and it was Miss Purdin, all full of a murder at her house. You don't even call a cab. You just continue your walk till you get here. And you almost beat us. Although Miss Purdin insists she called the police first and then you. And we were here in five."

"I was already in the neighborhood. You've heard of cellular phones, haven't you, Detective?"

"Sure. Wouldn't want to show it to me, would you?"

Stephen took the phone from his coat pocket and slid it across the coffee table to Sibben.

"Okay. So you were already in the area when Miss Purdin called you. You came right over and here you are. Any idea whose blood is all over the laundry room in there?"

"You said it was Vanfossen's, didn't you?"

"Something like that. Did you know Vanfossen?"

"No."

"But you knew that he and Miss Purdin were, shall we say, more than friends?"

"I knew."

"But you hadn't met? You never met him here, say?"

"No. I've never been here before."

"Is that right? So the lab isn't going to find any of your fingerprints in what they're lifting off around here?"

Elizabeth felt the slightest hesitation in Stephen. Her skin crawled.

"That's right."

"Have you seen where the guy was murdered?"

"You know I haven't."

"Maybe you'd like to take a look. You too, Miss Purdin. I want your opinion on something." He grinned wolfishly at Elizabeth. "No? All right, Kenwood, then. Miss Purdin feels she's seen enough. And I'll just bet she has."

Stephen came to his feet.

"How do you know it's Vanfossen?"

"We don't know, as a matter of fact. Miss Purdin says it is." Sibben mocked Elizabeth's lowered head. "Our methods are a little slower than hers. We have to wait until after something has happened to know about it."

"What do you want me to see?"

"In here." Sibben led the way to the utility room. He stood aside for Stephen to get the full view of the blood-spattered room. He said cheerfully to the lab technicians, "Let me know when it's a wrap. I guess there's nothing like having enough blood for your specimens, eh?"

Stephen stood for a long moment.

"I think I've seen everything," he drawled.

"Good. Let's go out and discuss it with Miss Purdin." They passed Carlton, still on the phone with the police station.

Elizabeth didn't look up as they resumed their seats.

"Did you notice anything written in the blood on the wall when you were in there, Miss Purdin?"

"No."

"What? I don't believe I heard you."

"I said 'no,' " Elizabeth gritted.

"Kenwood?"

"It says 'baby,' " Stephen said without expression.

"That's right. That's just what *I* thought. What do you make of that, Miss Purdin?"

Elizabeth was silent.

"Come now, Miss Purdin," Sibben mocked. "I want your opinion on this. After all, you wrote it."

Chapter Eight

Elizabeth raised her head.

"I've changed my mind. I'd like to call my lawyer."

"Now, why doesn't that surprise me?" Sibben grated. He looked impatiently at Carlton, who'd just put down the phone. "Okay, Carlton. Let's hear it."

"Her story checks out. She didn't leave the station until just on nine P.M. And there's no question it was Miss Purdin. I talked with a Lieutenant Forbes. She showed him her ID and auto registration."

"Why?" Sibben demanded. He turned from Carlton to Elizabeth. He repeated grimly, "Why?"

Elizabeth sank back, her hands, palms up, lay open on the cushions at her sides. She looked tired, pinched, but there was no missing the resolve.

"May I use the telephone?"

Sibben swore under his breath.

"Okay now. Let's run over a few things one more time. No one, and I mean no one, has a key to this house. Is that right?"

"Someone has," Elizabeth demurred. "But I don't know who and I don't know how. They're new locks and I didn't give a key to anyone."

"Not Vanfossen?"

"No."

"How about Kenwood? Give him a key?"

"He told you he'd never been here."

"Just answer the question, if you don't mind."

Elizabeth sighed and closed her eyes. She had never felt so tired.

"I did not give Stephen a key."

"I think you're way out of line here, Sibben," Stephen interjected sharply. "She asked to call her lawyer. I doubt if you're prepared to deny her that right. And if it hasn't escaped you, she's proved she wasn't here when Vanfossen was killed. What more do you want?"

"What more do I want? Well, let's see. How about the truth? How about how somebody killed a man in a locked house and removed his body from the premises without ever having had the means to enter it in the first place? And why? And how Miss Purdin knew it was going to happen. How she knew she needed an alibi and had time to plan one that couldn't be broken. And why she didn't stop it. She says she wishes she'd come right home so that it wouldn't have happened. And with blood all over the room in there, she insists she's in no danger. I'd like to know the answers to *all* of that." Sibben tossed the handful of papers and the clipboard onto the floor at his feet. "But I'm not going to find out, am I? Not from Miss Purdin. Who may, by the way, call all the lawyers in the phone book if she wants to. Like you say, her alibi is as solid as a good mind and a little time can make it, so I'm not holding her. She can go."

"*I* can go?" Elizabeth gritted. "This is my house, if you've forgotten."

74

"Wrong. It's not your house. It's a crime scene. It'll be sealed off until everybody's done checking fibers and prints, the works. Maybe a couple of days."

"A couple of *days?*"

Sibben shook his head.

"You seem to be missing something here, lady. Some guy got himself murdered in there in your laundry room. And whoever did it has a key. Think about that. You may be as hard as you pretend to be, but you still wouldn't weigh in at a hundred pounds, soaking wet. How would you plan to defend yourself if it turned out this killer and you had different ideas about the danger you're in?"

"It's a 'no-crime' area," Elizabeth taunted.

"Sure," Sibben said disgustedly. And then, "Why did you write in the blood?"

"I didn't."

"Sure you did. But you didn't waste him. You probably had the time between arriving home and calling us, but you couldn't have disposed of the body. Your car's clean. Nice new tires, too. A classy touch. But I just don't get the blood." He turned away and started toward the kitchen.

"Can I get some things out of my room?"

"Yeah. Officer Nichols will help you pack."

Stephen watched him go and then looked down at Elizabeth.

"He's wasting his time," he said coldly. "He's yet to learn that no one can lie like you when you try."

She winced.

"Is it all right if I take my car?" she asked Nichols.

"I'll drive you," Stephen clipped. "Constance will expect you."

No.

"I'll go to a hotel."

"What about Sam?"

"I'll board him."

Elizabeth didn't want to look at Stephen. He was a traitor. God, no, he was everything worse than a traitor.

Nichols was speaking with Carlton. For a moment there was just the two of them, walled off from the room's activity by the bitterness that bound them together.

"Sam can stay with me," Stephen said shortly. "You both can."

Elizabeth straightened. She said between her teeth, "You *bastard!*"

He didn't retort. He looked at her without expression, his eyes as flat and unreadable as the surface of a lake.

"You stab me in the back . . . !" Oh, God, that was awful, that was a terrible choice of words. Her fury and her horror took her breath away. She pressed her hands to her mouth and waited for the paralyzing ache in her throat to ease. She was going to cry.

"Stop it!" Stephen wrenched. He took her arm in hard, biting fingers and walked her smartly to her bedroom. He let her go, taking the case from the closet and beginning to pack it. He slammed in hairbrush, lingerie, and sleeping gear as efficiently as she could have done herself. "Pick out the clothing you want to take," he said evenly. He went into the bathroom and began to gather her things, a toothbrush, makeup bag, a comb.

Elizabeth followed him.

"Get out!" she hissed.

Her eyes fell on the violation that had been done. The walls and countertop, the light switch, the doorknob where powder had been sprinkled to lift off fingerprints that weren't there. The fingerprints of a killer.

The anger went out of her, the fire. She was beaten, after all.

Stephen gave her a sharp look. He put down the articles that he held.

"This is no time to cave in," he advised.

"I know," she said tiredly. "Sam can go with you. His leash is under the sink in the kitchen, if they'll let you get it."

"Good," he said, but he didn't move. Her eyes were too bright. She was about to shatter.

Nichols knocked on the bedroom door and came in.

"Sorry. The dog is howling again." She looked from one to the other. "Anything you want me to do? I'm not half bad at helping pack overnight bags."

"Good," Stephen said. "We've got a start." But still he didn't move. He studied Elizabeth.

"Thank you," she said to Nichols. She broke Stephen's glance. She went to the closet and slid back the doors. She could hear him walk away.

Elizabeth looked at the dresses and it didn't matter. She wanted to lie down on the bed and weep until all the pain and horror were gone. Until this nightmare was over, until she knew it for what it was, an illusion of hell.

Her hands began to shake.

Nichols came up beside her. She must have done this a hundred times, a thousand. Helped people to

77

pretend that it was an ordinary day when it was never going to be that again.

"What do you think? Will you be going to work? This dress is nice."

Elizabeth drew a deep breath and willed her brain to function. She took down several dresses, some slacks, a blouse and sweater.

"I can't understand why it will take so long to finish with the house," she managed.

"I know. It's unbelievably disruptive. But I'm afraid it can't be helped."

Disruptive. Elizabeth tested the incredible limitations of the word.

"Yes, well . . . someone being killed in your home *is* disruptive, isn't it?" her voice was thin, tremulous. She had promised herself she wouldn't cry. "I'm sorry. I . . . I don't know if I'll be able to come back here."

"Many people can't."

Many people. As if this were something that happened every day. Elizabeth shivered.

"I suppose I'm ready," she said. She snapped the case shut and then opened it again. She couldn't remember if she'd put in the things Stephen had gathered from the bathroom.

He was waiting when they came out of the bedroom. He had Sam's leash on him, but it wasn't necessary. Sam was going nowhere. He stuck as closely to Stephen as a shadow.

Elizabeth looked away.

"I should have brushed him," she said tonelessly. "He'll shed all over you."

Stephen took her case.

"I've called a cab."

Sibben stood in the doorway, blocking their path.

"We'll be in touch. Miss Purdin," he taunted. "You get to feeling like talking, you give me a call. We could write a book on what you know."

"Excuse me," Elizabeth said tautly. She moved around him and kept walking. The cold night air hit her in the face.

Chapter Nine

The street was in chaos. Small knots of people stood in their shirtsleeves, trying to talk above the crackle of police radios. The flashing lights from the patrol cars made eerie, avid patterns on their faces. They all stared at the man and woman and dog that came out of the storm's center.

"Jeez!" the cab driver exclaimed. "What's going on here? Who died?"

Stephen gave the address of Execucon's parking garage. A television news van came down the street as they pulled away from the curb.

"You can see about it on television tomorrow," Stephen said shortly. He looked at Elizabeth's set face. He patted Sam. "Thanks for letting Sam stay with me."

"I forgot to get his food. I give him HiPro, but he'll eat anything. Except Crave. He won't touch it."

"Crave is cat food."

"He doesn't know that."

"Of course he does. It smells like fish."

"It does not. There's half a dozen varieties. I wouldn't give him fish-flavor."

"I don't know why you'd give him cat food at all."

Elizabeth gave Stephen an exasperated look.

"Let me give you the scenario," she said tartly. "It's late, I'm just getting home from work. I realize that I forgot to get dog food. The pet stores are closed, the grocery store is a hassle. So I run into Circle K. I don't want a whole bag of dog food at those prices. So I pick up a box of something that's designed for carnivorous housepets. Okay? No problem, right? Ha! Sam hates it."

"He's a lot of trouble," Stephen observed blandly. "Maybe I don't want him after all."

"Try to tell Sam that."

Stephen patted the dog.

"He's glad to see me because he knows I won't feed him cat food."

"I don't usually let animals in my cab," the driver informed them. "I got regulations. But, hey, I got a heart. Somebody die back there?"

"Yes," Stephen clipped.

They drew into the entrance of the Execucon Laboratories parking garage.

"This is it," the driver observed. "Too bad about the stiff. Some people are ghouls about things like that, but me, I just want to know what's happening out there. A guy like me, he's up close to a lot of types. It pays to know what kind of weirdo is operating the streets. Murder, was it?"

Stephen took Elizabeth's elbow as she climbed from the cab. She hoped he couldn't feel her trembling.

"Thanks," he said noncommittally to the driver. He paid him and slammed the door.

Sam pressed close. The auto exhaust and noise of traffic on University Avenue unnerved him.

Within the garage the outside sounds fell away. It was almost deserted on the second floor as their footsteps resounded on the silence. They found Stephen's white Buick Regal and he unlocked the door.

Elizabeth was suddenly aware of the isolation. The recessed fluorescent lighting cast eerie shadows, as distorted as reality was beginning to be.

She should have kept the cab. She should have found her own way to a hotel. She wouldn't be standing here now, alone with a . . . what? A killer? A violent shiver ran down Elizabeth's spine.

"Get in," Stephen said sharply.

She must be insane. It was past midnight. They were alone here in this vast, echoing tunnel. It was the end of the earth.

"I'm sorry," she managed. "I'm putting you to a lot of trouble. I can get a cab. You take Sam and get him settled. I'll find my own way." He wouldn't hurt Sam. He would never hurt Sam.

His face hardened.

"Get in," he repeated, his face now dark with controlled anger. It was as menacing as the nightmare she had walked away from.

Elizabeth got into the car.

He slammed the door and walked around to his side and got in. He put the key into the ignition, but he didn't turn it.

He was too close. She could feel the cold of the night coming off his jacket, his skin. He turned his head and looked at her.

"I didn't kill him," he gritted.

She could almost believe it. Almost.

"You had no reason to," she managed.

Stephen didn't reply for a moment. He looked through the windshield at the vast concrete banks beyond the circles of light.

"You're wrong," he said. "I had every reason."

He turned the key in the ignition. They swung out of the garage and down onto the street. Elizabeth hunched her shoulders against something that wasn't the cold.

"The police would have liked to know you had no business in the neighborhood. They would have demanded to know where you were when Keith was . . ." Elizabeth faltered ". . . in trouble."

Stephen studied her in silence. Perhaps she had forgotten that about him, the way he had of considering each word before he said it.

"You don't believe I could have provided an alibi?"

He was probably referring to Constance, and maybe she hadn't been totally demented to cover for him. It kept Constance out of it, at least. It occurred to Elizabeth that the only thing left to salvage from all this was her friendship with Constance. And even that might not be possible.

"I don't understand why you're here," Elizabeth said abruptly, sharply. "Is this some horrible, distorted coincidence that you wind up here? After two years, why all of a sudden can't I turn around without tripping over you or hearing your name? It's making me ill."

"Is it?" he wondered mildly. His eyes were on the road. "You're asking me what I was doing on your street tonight?"

"Yes. No. Why *were* you on my street? Why are you in Phoenix? Why *here,* for God's sake?"

"I was on my way to see you. I left my car and walked because it was a nice night and I wanted to think."

It might be a nice night to someone just out of the middle of a Colorado winter. It could be. But the five or six miles between her house and the parking garage was a great deal of thinking. She didn't believe it.

"Have you come by before?"

"Why?"

"Sam acts like there's someone outside at night. I can't see anyone."

He gave her a sharp glance.

"You can't stay there."

It sent chills down her spine. She wished he'd said it was he, whatever madness it implied. Heaven knew what stirred out there in the darkness.

"You were telling me what you're doing in Phoenix," Elizabeth prompted hastily.

"No," he clipped. "I wasn't. I was telling you to move back in with Constance. Give yourself a chance of surviving this damned mess we're all embroiled in! Call Constance. I'll stop at the next Circle K."

"Why Constance?" Elizabeth gritted. "Why not Mary Prill? Why not Damon Baille? God, I've got all kinds of old friends I can call, haven't I?"

His mouth tightened in the glow from the dash, but he didn't reply. He didn't even try to deny he knew they were all here.

"And Ellen Glover. We mustn't forget Ellen! Whoever went to the trouble of assembling all of us was really rude not to invite Ellen!"

84

"Stop it!" Stephen ground out. He pulled the car to the curb. He looked angry enough to shake her, but after a frozen moment he let out his breath. "You've been through hell tonight, Elizabeth. Let's just leave it at that."

She'd been through hell, but not just tonight. She said bitterly, "That's right. Ellen's dead, isn't she?"

He went on looking at her, his eyes glittering in the half-light of the car. And then he pulled the car back out into the infrequent stream of traffic. His movements were controlled, smooth, and each word fell like ice.

"You'd better watch who you say that to."

God, yes, she had better. She had better close her mouth and keep it closed until the danger of breaking down, of shattering, was past. She had been careful for too long to risk everything now.

"I will," she said grimly. She drew her coat more tightly about her although the heater was running. "Where are we going?"

"I don't know," he admitted. "Where do you want to go? If not to Constance's, a hotel. Or you can come by my place and see Sam settled, if you're worried about him."

Sam didn't need her. He had Stephen. She turned her head and looked at the dog stretched out asleep. For a moment she almost wished he were clinging to her. She was alone.

"A hotel will be fine."

"Which one?"

"I don't care. I've never stayed in one in Phoenix." She couldn't help it, she couldn't stop her tongue. "You can advise me. You're probably familiar with any number of them."

He understood. He said coldly, "I never cheated on you, Elizabeth."

Of course not. Not once. Not even with Ellen.

Elizabeth hunched her shoulders and stared out the window. She could feel the weight of his eyes on her, but it didn't matter. After a moment she managed, "So you were coming by tonight. Why?"

"I wanted to talk about your sister."

It was the last thing she had expected.

"No!"

"Yes," he said harshly. "She's lost without you."

Elizabeth shook her head in mute protest, but he went on.

"She can't understand it. Why you won't answer her letters or return her calls. Why you wouldn't come to see her when you were in Portland. But I can." He spoke between his teeth. "I can. I know it's because you don't care a damn about anyone. She can't seem to catch on to the fact."

Elizabeth put her hands over her ears, but it didn't shut him out. It shut him in.

"No," she repeated.

"She's got a baby, Elizabeth." He took one hand off the wheel and caught her wrist, forcing her to listen. "You've got a nephew that you've never seen. Christ, he's half grown now! And you won't go see him. You won't stop hurting your sister."

"Don't you think I *want* to see Sara and her boy? Don't you think I . . ." No, no, she was talking too much. "Please, Stephen. Please don't do this."

He flung her arm away.

"Of course," he said bitterly. "Of course." He drove fast, the street signs blurred past the windows. "Is the Royale all right?"

"It's fine." God, she had to get away. She had to think. No, no, she didn't dare think.

"I wonder about Vanfossen," he said flatly. "Did you just disappear one day while he was at work?"

There was no misunderstanding what he meant.

"Perhaps I thought," she countered wearily, "you were drinking too much to notice I was gone."

"It makes a good story."

The bright lights of the Royale lit up the night as they pulled into the forecourt and cut the engine.

"Make your goodnights to Sam. I'll get your case."

Elizabeth looked over her shoulder at Sam in the back. The dog lifted his head and his tail thumped, but he had no intention of leaving Stephen.

"Thanks a lot, old friend," Elizabeth said wryly. "For being so broken up over me."

Stephen had gotten out of the car, but now he paused. He looked at her and he could hear the tears behind the roughness in her voice, her hurt over Sam's defection.

"You little fool," he ground out. She seemed so slight a breeze might carry her away. It was hard to remember that she was steel.

Her chin came up.

"You know something, Stephen?" she began mockingly. She wasn't folding up and she wasn't dissolving, however much he expected it. "You came very close to blowing it back there. Sibben couldn't miss that you showed no interest in what had happened. He thought you'd have wanted to know who had died, at least."

"I didn't care who died," he clipped. "As long as it wasn't you."

Chapter Ten

Elizabeth was the last to arrive. She followed the maître d' across the large garden room of the Monte Cristo. Windows bathed the restaurant in light, but the view below looked gray and unappealing. Winter had trapped a blanket of smog in the Valley of the Sun.

They were all there, and someone—Constance, probably—had chosen a secluded table. Despite the hurried pace of the lunch hour they would be undisturbed.

They were seated in an irregular circle around the table with Constance and Damon across from Mary and the empty chair for Elizabeth. Stephen was at the end, as much apart from the others physically as he had always been in spirit.

Constance came to her feet as Elizabeth approached.

"Here you are," she said warmly, giving Elizabeth a quick, hard hug. She breathed close to Elizabeth's ear, "Are you all right, love?"

"Yes. Thanks, Con. I'm fine."

"I wish you'd come to me. You know you're always welcome."

Elizabeth squeezed her hand.

"I know. Anyway, I'm moving back into my place tomorrow or the next day." She smiled faintly. "You *are* looking gorgeous. Are you trying to impress us?"

Constance smoothed a hand down the arm of the short mink jacket and smiled silkily at Mary.

"I thought Mary would like this little touch."

"Of course," Mary snapped. "There's nothing quite like seeing someone draped in the skin of a dead animal." She tossed off her drink and motioned peremptorily for another.

"Unless, of course, it's watching them eat one," Constance said sweetly, giving Mary's roast beef sandwich a pointed glance.

Just like old times.

"Hello, Damon." Elizabeth offered her hand across the table. "It's been a while."

He had been attractive once, with the clear eyes and clean jaw of an ascetic. Now he was an aging junky and he looked the part. His hazel eyes were bloodshot and his dark blond hair rough. The flesh clung skeletally to the angular bones of his face.

He took his time responding to Elizabeth's greeting, putting down his cigarette and exhaling through his nose. But when his fingers closed over hers, they were surprisingly firm.

"Hello, Lizzy. You look like hell."

She hadn't been sleeping well and she looked it, but she couldn't describe how ravaged Damon was. Eaten up from the inside.

"So do you," Elizabeth countered. And then,

"Hello, Mary." Her glance touched Stephen briefly, slid away. "Stephen."

"I knew you'd come," Mary taunted.

Of course she'd come. That was what it was about, wasn't it? Forcing everyone out into the open?

"Why wouldn't I?"

"You've changed, Lizzy," Damon observed. He hadn't taken his eyes off her face.

"We've all changed," Stephen said sharply.

"You haven't, Stephen," Damon drawled. He took a long drag on his cigarette. "Not you. You're still defending Elizabeth."

"Elizabeth doesn't need defending. She hasn't done anything wrong." That from Constance. "We're all friends here, remember, Damon?"

He laughed mockingly.

"Sure, I remember. The best of friends." He tossed his pack of cigarettes across to Elizabeth as the waiter approached the table. "What are you drinking, Lizzy?"

She ordered the house wine. Damon was drinking Scotch on the rocks, Mary a White Russian. Stephen was having coffee. Constance raised her eyebrows at Elizabeth and waved off a second rum-and-coke.

"What brings *you* to Phoenix, Damon?" Elizabeth asked, when the waiter had gone.

"You do, love. All the troubles you have on your pretty head."

"Right." Mary mocked. "Add that to a cheaper street price for smack and we'll believe it."

"What did *I* say?" he feigned surprise at her animosity. "Don't you believe I'm here for our good friend Elizabeth?"

"Cut the crap, Damon," Constance advised. "We

knew you were on your way before the ugly business at Elizabeth's house. What we'd like to know is why."

"What's Mary's story?"

"You know damned well what 'my story' is, Damon. Elizabeth wrote and told me to come."

"And of course, you couldn't do enough to help out Elizabeth. You've always been right there behind her. Ready to knife her in the back, as I remember."

Mary flushed.

"That's a nasty metaphor, Damon, and probably not coincidental, knowing you. Are you suggesting I had a hand in murdering that poor man at Elizabeth's?"

"What poor man, Mary, my love? He hasn't been identified, has he? No body? Isn't that the story?"

"Go to hell. We all know it was her boyfriend. The police know it. You're trying to distract us from the real issue: what you're doing in Phoenix."

Damon ground out his cigarette, squinting into the smoke.

"I'll tell you why I'm here. I got a letter from David Royce."

A current ran through them. No one spoke for long, long seconds. And then Constance broke it with a hard little laugh.

"And was it difficult to read, dripping with seaweed and saltwater?"

"Maybe he's not dead," Damon said.

"Oh, he's dead, all right," Constance said flatly.

The tension evaporated.

"Yes. We know he's dead. Despite . . ." Mary paused.

"Despite what, Mary?" Damon wanted to know.

"Despite you getting mail from him? Despite you seeing him?"

Mary stared into her glass.

"I haven't seen him. There was one time that I thought . . . I thought it was him until I got a better look. I was mistaken. Obviously."

"Obviously." Damon's eyes, red-rimmed but surprisingly clear, came back to Elizabeth. "What are *you* doing in Phoenix, Lizzy, my dear? Did you put in for a transfer with your company and then just wait for an opening to come up?"

He must know it hadn't been like that. That she hadn't planned it. That she had just disappeared into the darkness.

"What difference does it make?" she challenged. *"You followed me."*

"That's a good point, love. Just think of the trouble you'd have given us if you'd decided to settle in, say . . . Baghdad. Or Moscow, for God's sake. It's a half-decent time of year in Phoenix. Only a couple of days out of Portland."

Constance shook her head.

"Damon, you're full of shit. You and Mary both. Elizabeth didn't tell you to come to Phoenix and David Royce sure as hell didn't. Did you ever think about getting a life? Preferably one that doesn't include hard drugs and hard liquor?"

"Oho! Another country heard from. Getting a little too close to a nerve, Con? What are you doing in Phoenix, my pretty?"

"I beg your pardon? Who chose you as our interrogator? I think I must have missed the election."

Damon cackled.

"Shit, we've got it all right here, don't we? Judge,

jury, the works. Constance, of course, is the judge. Always the center of attention, the control. And Mary has got to be vice. Turning over rocks to confirm her faith that slime really exists. And always ready to adapt to whatever plays to her advantage."

"And the dope addict," Mary sneered. "Stoned out of his mind on his best day."

"Right," Damon agreed. "And Elizabeth is the murderess. Advised to remain silent by her counsel, our own Stephen Kenwood." He put back his head and laughed. "We're God-damned self-contained."

"I suppose you see yourself as the prosecutor?" Constance mocked.

"It's a dirty job, Connie. You know the rest. Which brings us back to what you're doing in Phoenix. Get kicked out of that cushy job in New York?"

"Something tells me Mary turned over one stone too many. But what the hell? Miche's was opening a new outlet in Phoenix. They sent me to get it going."

"As simple as that."

"Not quite, but close enough."

Damon reached for his cigarettes.

"Don't tell me you've kicked the habit, Lizzy. You used to smoke like a chimney."

"We all grow up," Elizabeth said evenly.

"Excepting you, Damon," Mary gritted. "You'll never grow up."

"My turn," Stephen said abruptly. He was as detached as if he were no part of them, had never shared their dark secrets. "After David's death brought an end to Royce Pharmaceuticals, I worked for Royce Chemical Conglomerate, the mother company. After that, I went to Colorado and signed on with Selbe Drugs in Denver for a couple of years.

"In June I heard that Execucon Pharmaceuticals in Tempe was looking for chemical engineers. And here I am."

"In Phoenix, of all places. Are you suggesting it's a coincidence?" That from Damon.

"I'm not suggesting anything," Stephen clipped.

There was a long moment of silence. Damon drained his glass and waved it at the waiter.

Constance shook her head.

"He's a romantic soul, our Damon," she mocked. "He wants to hear that you came to Phoenix, Stephen, because you knew I was here."

"Then he's out of luck. I didn't know."

"Ouch, Con. Same old same old. He came for Elizabeth."

"Who wouldn't?" Mary snapped. "If he got a letter anything nearly as threatening as the one I got."

"He didn't say that. Did you, Stephen?"

"No," Stephen drawled. "I didn't."

Damon took his drink from the waiter's hands and sketched a salute before drinking. He leaned toward Elizabeth.

"So now we're all up to date, right? Maybe you'll explain to us who this guy was you killed, Lizzy. And why."

"Don't call me Lizzy."

"You don't like it? That's what Stephen always called you, isn't it? No, maybe you're right. It wasn't quite Lizzy. Help me out, someone."

"Shove it, Damon," Constance snapped.

"Always the lady, right, Connie?"

"Always."

"This is cute," Mary gritted. "But hardly productive. Unless we're here to remember how we always hated each other."

"Hate, Mary? That's a dirty word. You don't mix that word with murder unless you want to find yourself in a very hot chair."

"Shut up, Damon. Your sense of humor is as revolting as ever."

"Yeah, how about that? I've heard it said before." Damon lit another cigarette from the butt in his hand. He must have felt the weight of Elizabeth's eyes. His glance came up sharply to meet hers.

"*I* know why you're here, Damon," she said. "You want to know where Ellen is."

No one moved. And then Damon leaned forward, a jerky, taut action that almost upset his Scotch. His eyes were red, but they were as lucid as Elizabeth had ever seen them.

"That's right," he bit out. "I want to know where Ellen is."

"And we're supposed to know?" Mary demanded. "What's it been, seven years? And she walked out on us, if you'll remember."

"She disappeared."

"Yeah, right. Ellen's a slut. She always was a slut."

Elizabeth hadn't taken her eyes from Damon. She said tightly, "Ellen is dead."

It crackled through them, electricity and horror.

"For God's sake, Libby!" Stephen ground out.

She didn't look at him, she couldn't. She watched Damon.

"Libby," Damon said with satisfaction. "I knew it was something like that. Libby. I'll remember that."

"She's dead, Damon."

He leaned back, sprawled, as if the tense energy that had kept him going was suddenly spent.

"I know," he said.

Constance stirred uneasily.

"What are you two talking about?"

Mary was reeling too. She said, she demanded, "Wait a minute! You're saying that Ellen has been dead all this time? Since the last time we saw her?"

"Yes."

"There's no way," Mary denied flatly. "Absolutely no way. Ellen was always her own biggest fan. She certainly wouldn't consider self-destruction."

"You're talking about suicide," Constance interjected. "Is that what you're saying, Damon? Elizabeth? Ellen killed herself?"

"You tell me," Damon drawled.

"Well, Christ! That's cute!" Constance gave Elizabeth an exasperated look. "I can't believe you're in on this, Elizabeth."

"She's not," Damon denied. "Are you, love?" He looked at Elizabeth, but his words were addressed to Constance. "Ellen was pregnant. And no, it wasn't suicide."

All eyes were on Damon. Elizabeth could feel a fine line of perspiration break out on her upper lip.

"You're kidding. Ellen was pregnant? With whose baby? Christ, how do you know this, anyway?" Constance demanded.

"Ellen told me."

"Was it was your baby?"

Damon laughed.

"Who knows? My guess is it was David Royce's."

"Oh, now wait a minute! You're not saying that David killed her! I don't believe it!" Mary looked

96

disgustedly from one face to another. "You can't believe it any more than I do."

"Why not?" Damon mocked. "Because it wasn't David's style to bump off someone he knew?"

They all froze, wordless. And then Constance tossed off the last of her drink and said evenly, "Shut up, Damon. You never did know when to close your mouth."

"You're drunk," Mary snapped at Damon. "You don't know what you're talking about."

"I think he does," Elizabeth said quietly.

Constance stirred. She patted Elizabeth's clenched hand.

"Listen, hon. We all know Damon is as crazy as hell. He'll say anything. And you've been through a terrible ordeal and you're vulnerable. Remember who it is that's talking this garbage."

"Thank you, Connie," Damon mocked. "I didn't say David Royce killed Ellen. I don't think he did. I do know for a fact that Ellen was pregnant when she disappeared. So what does that mean? Maybe nothing. Unless you put it together with what was written in a murdered man's blood. A man killed in Elizabeth's house."

"It said 'baby,' " Mary said thinly. "So what? That's reaching, even for you, Damon. You would have to believe that Ellen *is* dead and that this Vanfossen's death somehow ties to her. *And* an infant you say she was carrying at the time. I don't believe it. It's classic Damon Baille. Ellen's alive and laughing at us, and if she ever *had* a baby, out of wedlock or not, she'd probably strangle it with her bare hands and dance off to a party."

Elizabeth winced. She could feel her color drain away.

"Elizabeth, hon, you're white," Constance said in alarm. "Don't you feel well?"

That was an understatement. She was sick.

Damon's head came up sharply. He looked beyond Elizabeth with chilling focus.

"What?" Constance followed his glance.

"A cop."

"You would know," Mary said sarcastically. "I'm sure you've had enough experience sniffing them out."

"I have."

Elizabeth didn't turn. She ran a steadying hand over her eyes, the dampness of her forehead. Stephen murmured close to her ear.

"It's Sibben. He's coming over."

Of course. She had made the mistake of leaving word at Everhold that she would be here.

She let out her breath on a sigh.

"How is Sam?"

"He misses you."

"Can he come home?"

"Whenever you're ready."

"Tomorrow. I . . ."

"Well, well, well. If it isn't Miss Purdin and all her friends. Having a party, are we?"

He towered over them. His voice suggested something obscene, as if she'd killed Keith and was dancing on his grave.

"Detective Sibben. This is a little out of your jurisdiction, isn't it?"

"Good of you to be concerned, Miss Purdin," he

said smoothly. "But murder kind of blurs the lines. My jurisdiction might just lead anywhere."

"Meaning?"

Sibben looked from one face to another around the table.

"Kenwood, I suspected I might find you here. Maybe I've gotten a touch of Miss Purdin's clairvoyance. In fact, I'll bet I have. I'll bet I could tell you the name of every person at this table." He took out a notebook and leafed through it. "Damon Baille. That'll be you, of course. One of Portland's finer citizens, from all I hear."

Damon didn't blink.

"And Stephen Kenwood, of course, and Miss Purdin. That leaves one Mary Prill Rhinehardt and one Constance LeMirre. That'll be . . . ?" He looked inquiringly from Constance to Mary.

"I'm Constance LeMirre," Constance said flatly. "What in the hell is this?"

"This is trouble, Miss LeMirre. All five of you are being sought for questioning by the Portland Police Department."

Chapter Eleven

"Why?"

That from Stephen, matter-of-factly. The rest of them might be frozen with the possibilities that loomed before them, but he seemed unaffected.

"That's a good question, Kenwood. I asked myself that on the way over here. Why a perfectly nice little reunion of old college friends would have anything to do with a murder."

Elizabeth asked thinly:

"You've found Keith's body?"

Sibben snorted.

"That's interesting, Miss Purdin. I'd swear you just the same as said you think your friends are tied to Vanfossen's death."

She did think so, God help her.

"You're the one who brought up the subject of murder, Detective."

"I was talking about a bunch of Portland pals being questioned about a murder. You drew the conclusion that it was here in Phoenix." He looked expectantly at the circle of faces. "Isn't anybody going to ask?"

"It isn't necessary," Damon clipped. "We know who they found."

"I thought you might." Sibben's glance lingered on Elizabeth. She had gathered her composure. She met his eyes without a flicker of weakness.

"Yeah," Damon mocked. "Jimmy Hoffa."

"Shut up, Damon!" Mary shrilled. "For God's sake, just shut up!"

Constance looked tautly at Sibben.

"Tell us," she demanded.

"It seems that there's been some construction going on, oh, maybe a mile from where you five all used to work back in '85, '86. They were doing some digging back then too, incidentally, building a little shopping center. Looked like it would be there for years. But that's progress. It was bought by some big company that felt the property'd be more valuable as a parking lot for its new chain grocery store.

"So here they are, heavy machinery ripping up concrete and earth, and they find something they hadn't bargained for. A woman's body."

"Ellen," Mary said faintly.

"Now, look at that. You've got Miss Purdin's gift, too." Sibben swiveled around and looked at Elizabeth. She was glad he couldn't see how tightly her hands were clenched beneath the table.

He looked at each of the others.

Kenwood's attention was caught, held, but he showed no expression. Baille was hunched forward. His eyes were bright, almost wild. He didn't look quite sane.

The two women were pale. He had seen witnesses to violence look like that just before they folded up

101

on the floor. Or before they came up with a weapon and smoked the place.

"Ellen Glover," he agreed. "Very, very dead."

"She disappeared," Constance managed. "Years ago. We thought she'd run away. You're not saying she . . . that she died then? That she's been dead all this time?"

Constance's eyes flicked to Damon, no more than a twitch. He had said it. He had seemed to know.

"That's about it. She never went anywhere. Just a one-way walk down the street."

"How did she die?" Mary choked out.

"Her throat was cut."

Stephen leaned forward sharply. He didn't seem to feel the shock and horror that electrified the others.

"What's going on here, Sibben?"

Sibben feigned surprise.

"You tell me, Kenwood. It's *your* little class reunion."

"That's right, it is. So suppose you explain just what you're up to. We're obviously not under arrest. And if you're planning to question us, why are you feeding us information? It looks damned strange."

"What are you suggesting, Kenwood? That I'm setting you up?"

"I'm not a lawyer. But if we were suspects in Ellen's death, you'd have us each in separately for questioning. You wouldn't feed us information unless you're deliberately trying to confuse the investigation."

Sibben had drawn up a chair and now he leaned back in it. He looked pleased.

"Portland's got an old murder," he said. "I got a new one. I think it's kind of interesting, having all of you around right now. I'd hate to see you dragged back to Oregon just when I might be needing you here."

"What does that mean?" Constance demanded. "The equivalent of 'don't leave town'?"

"Something like that."

"Oh, God!" Mary put her face into her hands.

"I'll expect each of you to come by the station in the next day or two. We'll need statements. Portland is putting it together at their end. But I'd advise you each to be thinking about an alibi for the time that Ellen Glover disappeared." He looked mockingly at Elizabeth. "That should be no problem for you, eh, Miss Purdin?"

Elizabeth didn't have an alibi. Neither did Constance. Their eyes met.

Sibben got to his feet.

"Oh, and Miss Purdin? If you're thinking about lying, I wouldn't recommend it. These things have a way of unraveling on a person."

Elizabeth could feel her face stiffen. She looked up at him in silence.

"Like your name, for instance. You've been lying about that, haven't you?"

She surprised herself. She replied evenly,

"Yes."

"Right. And what *is* your name? Your legal name?"

Elizabeth didn't look at Stephen. She turned her eyes to Constance and she was sorry. She wished it didn't have to be like this.

"Kenwood," she said. "Elizabeth Kenwood."

"Is this supposed to be a revelation, Sibben?" Stephen clipped. "It isn't. It's no one's business but Elizabeth's and mine."

"Sure," Mary agreed. "Big deal. If anybody cares it's Constance."

Elizabeth couldn't bear it. This was the last thing she had wanted, Constance hurt. And it was a sham, anyway. As if a past could make a future. They had proved it could not.

Constance's eyes were very blue, very bright.

"Detective Sibben?" she managed. "May I go to Portland? I believe Ellen has family there. They must be sick with grief."

"Yeah, well, I don't suppose I can stop you. But see that you check in at the station when you get back. And I'll want your statement before you leave."

Mary shivered. She was on the shrill edge of hysteria.

"She was *your* roommate, Elizabeth! If it weren't for you, we wouldn't have met her. She wouldn't have gone to work for Royce Pharmaceuticals. She'd probably still be alive!"

Damon snickered.

"Déjà vu, Mary, my dear. You've got to keep that knife sharp to stab in Elizabeth's back, don't you?"

"You bastard! Stop saying that!" Mary slapped the table with the flat of her hand, sloshing water glasses. And then, hissing, "I mean it, Damon! Shut your filthy mouth!"

"Ouch! I'm crushed."

Sibben stood up.

"I could listen to you people all day, but darned if I don't have things to do in the office. I'll be waiting to hear from you."

"Wait a minute," Damon interjected. "You wanted us to know all the grisly details about Ellen, right? Aren't you forgetting a big one?"

"What's that, Baille?"

"The baby Ellen was carrying."

"You're saying she was pregnant?"

"Yeah, that's what I'm saying. Surely the lab ghouls wouldn't miss it."

"I don't know. I'll check it out. Seven years is a long time in that damp climate, but . . ." he shrugged, perhaps relishing the imagery he presented. "They're pretty good. Who would think they could figure the cause of death this long after the fact? Knife scored the bone, they say. Almost cut off her head." He nodded pleasantly. "Have a nice day."

They sat in frozen silence after he had gone. It was Damon who broke it.

"Maybe she'd already had the baby."

A long time ago, before the liquor and the drugs, he had been a mathematics whiz kid. He could never stop looking for the logic in insanity.

Elizabeth held herself rigid with a conscious effort that made the blood pound in her temples, in her breast. She waited for the next sentence, the next words, the cry that would damn her. She could feel Stephen's eyes, the weight of his glance as heavily as a hand on her shoulder. She dragged her glance to his.

He was not a man to show emotion no matter what went on behind the shutters of his eyes. So she would not have believed it possible, the shock registered now in the dark pupils as he looked at her. The shock and the horror.

Chapter Twelve

Elizabeth walked the length of the hotel room and back again. Her steps left footprints in the deep carpet as if she'd walked in snow. On the fourteenth passing she stopped abruptly and picked up the telephone. She dialed.

The answering machine wasn't on. The phone seemed to ring forever.

"Hello?"

"Hello, Constance."

"Elizabeth." There was the slightest hesitation, and then Constance said coolly, "I can't talk now."

"Please, Con . . ."

Elizabeth could hear her take a deep breath.

"What is it?" Coldly. As cold as those remembered prints in the snow.

"I'm sick about what happened. That you found out the way you did that Stephen and I were married."

"*Are* married, don't you mean?"

"Yes, well, legally. Until a few days ago, we hadn't seen each other for over two years."

"Because you ran out. Because he didn't know

where you were to start divorce proceedings against you."

Elizabeth sat down on the bed. She said finally, "That's right," but it wasn't necessary. It was obvious that Constance knew all about it now, about them. That Stephen had told her.

"You know, Elizabeth, I'm not a child, and I'm hardly naive. I've certainly no compunctions about sleeping with a married man. That's not the issue. It's really us, you and me, our friendship. I should have been told about you and Stephen. Even without my telling you I was interested in him. That's the ultimate sellout, isn't it? Worse than what Mary did to you."

"I wanted to tell you. I tried to." Elizabeth hated how that sounded to her own ears. One didn't *try* to do something, they did it. She drew a deep breath, but Constance spoke first.

"I know you did. I remember. I wouldn't listen. I thought you were trying to tell me about Stephen and Ellen." She gave a little laugh that was nearly a sob. "As if any of that matters now, with all that has happened. God, Elizabeth, who killed her? I can't get it out of my head."

Elizabeth shivered.

"I don't know," she admitted. She didn't mean to say more, but the words were suddenly there, too late to be recalled. "One of us."

"Christ, that's what it comes down to, doesn't it? I've looked at it until I can't see straight, and I still can't come up with anything else. It has to be one of us."

"Constance, David *is* dead, isn't he? That sounds absurd, I know. Of course he's dead. But the things he was doing . . . If he was alive, we'd know he was behind this."

"Listen, Elizabeth . . ." Constance was silent for a long moment. "I'm not proud of this. I've wished a thousand times . . . Elizabeth, I saw David drown. I was there."

"Are you serious?" Elizabeth was staggered. "You never said . . . Con, the police, the witnesses . . . they never mentioned you."

"I know. They didn't see me. God, this seems to be the time for dredging up old secrets. I hate it.

"It was a Sunday and I'd run by the lab to pick up something. I can't even remember now what it was. David was there, of course. He was always there. Even after he'd been banned from the pharmaceuticals section.

"Anyway, he was writing letters in the office and he seemed really low. He said he was about to drive out by the Chutes and would I come along.

"Elizabeth, looking back, I should have been suspicious. He always said he hated the ocean. He rarely left the office. Writing letters? Christ, I don't doubt he was working on a suicide note and then gave it up! Remember how the police found where he'd burned something in the sink?

"Well, a lot of help he got from good old Con. I didn't want to spend the day with him. I sure as hell wouldn't get in the car with him behind the wheel. Oh, no, I drove. It was the least I could do."

"Constance, you couldn't have known. No one could."

"Sure. I told myself that a few thousand times. You can't imagine how little comfort there is in it."

Elizabeth could. Hadn't she done the same with Ellen?

"So we went for a drive. With me cursing my luck at having to spend the day with him, of course. You know how he got after Ellen disappeared? Depressed doesn't come close to describing it."

Elizabeth could hear her own breath resounding off the mouthpiece of the telephone. God, she didn't want to take this last ride down to the ocean with David Royce. She didn't want to know.

"He left me at the car. He said he needed a little time alone to walk on the beach. I didn't question it, even though nothing but a duck would be out in weather like that. The wind off the ocean was like ice."

"That's why no one saw you. The area was deserted."

"Oh, there were a couple of hardy souls. But they were down on the spits. I was up at the car. Anyway, I didn't see David for a while, but when he did come into view, he was walking along the point, right at the edge of the water, and God, the sea was rough. I think one of the men yelled to him. It was too far away to hear, or to be sure the man was warning him back, but that's what the papers said later, and that's what it looked like. I suddenly got scared. The enormity of what I was seeing just came crashing . . ." Constance drew a shaken breath. "I wish the men who'd tried to save him had said he'd slipped. I think I could have found some peace in that. I think I could have quit seeing him plunge deliberately off the rocks into the crashing waves if they'd said it."

"Lord, Constance!"

"I couldn't move. I just watched. I . . ." her voice broke.

"You couldn't have done anything in weather like that."

"I know. The fishermen couldn't, and they were close. He was just . . . gone."

"Constance . . ."

"It was a nightmare, Elizabeth. I didn't know what to do, I felt like it was my fault. I should have known what he had in mind. I shouldn't have gone with him. I mean, what if he said to himself something like, 'If Constance won't go with me to the Chutes, I won't do it today,' and I said yes, I said, in effect, 'Okay, David, kill yourself today.' "

"No. I won't let you take the blame for what David did. He was sick; we all knew it. We knew before he tampered with the prescriptions he was filling. Before Ellen disappeared. He should have been institutionalized. There's no other way he might have been alive today. Even then, I doubt it."

"You're right, I know you're right. But it's on an intellectual level. Emotionally it's another matter."

"You should have talked with someone."

"That's good, Elizabeth, coming from you," Constance said, and it was hard suddenly, and brittle.

"What did you do?"

"Nothing. Virtually nothing. I left the car and started walking. I think I must have been in shock. It was hours before I got home, and I was frozen. I told my parents about it. Father advised me to keep quiet. You may remember how image-conscious Father was. As if it could make a difference, my coming forward. David was dead. David wanted to be dead."

Elizabeth pressed her fingers to her lips. She was

the last person to act as someone's conscience, or sort out the rights from the wrongs.

"Do you know what Damon thinks?" Constance's voice was rough with tears and memories. "He thinks David's ghost is stirring up this old pain. That he's restless because he'll be declared legally dead in April when the seven years have passed. That's Damon, our boy genius, the mathematical wizard. He's totally lost it."

"Is he capable of murder?"

There was a long pause. And then Constance said quietly, "I don't know. He's crazy like a fox, not a lunatic. Not like David. Who knows?" The diamond hardness returned to her voice. "Stephen says you're getting a divorce. Is that true?"

Elizabeth winced.

"It must be," she retorted bitterly. "I'm the liar, not he."

"I'm not blind. There's still something between you."

"I know," Elizabeth said quietly. There was no point in being hurt. In being angry. "But it's just the past. It doesn't let go easily."

"Do you know that he doesn't drink, Elizabeth? He quit when you left him. I don't get it."

"Maybe he didn't have a reason to drink anymore," Elizabeth managed. She hung up the phone.

She went to the window and looked down on the tops of the eucalyptus and date palm trees. She was at the Cascades now. She had left the lunch that Detective Sibben had interrupted and gone straight to the Royale and packed. She couldn't help but wonder why she'd bothered. Tomorrow she would be back home again, and everyone knew where her home was. Someone even knew how to open the door. She shivered.

And then finally she called her office at Everhold. Bill Eliot, her boss, came on the line.

"I heard what happened, Elizabeth. I'm sorry as hell. Why don't you come stay with Barb and me and the kids for a few days? Bring that ugly horse you call a dog. We'd love it."

"Thank you, Bill. I appreciate it. But I'm pretty well settled, and my 'ugly horse' is staying with a friend. The police will clear out soon and let me go home."

"Ugh! I can't imagine how you do it. I always said you were tough."

"I think you said I was hard, but we'll let it go. Is everything falling apart without me?"

"You know it. And speaking of hard, allow me to show my true colors. I've expressed my sympathy, so check that off. The next question is, have you been working on your designs? It's getting close enough to deadline to start me sweating."

"I'll have them."

"I know you will, love. I just get a little tense."

"Too much coffee. It'll get to you."

"Yeah, that's what they tell me. They making any progress on the killing?"

"Not that I know of, but I'd probably be the last to hear."

"Well, you can scratch me off as a suspect. The last thing I would do at this point is interrupt your layout on the card designs. It must be some art critic."

"God, Bill!"

"I know. I'm sick, right? I've heard that. Hey, you

check on your calls? From what I hear, the switch-board has melted down. You're going to have to hire your own operator to handle the flow."

Elizabeth could feel herself tense.

"You wouldn't have a record of them, would you?"

"Why the hell not? I'm not doing anything. Just hanging around acting as my number one artist's secretary." Elizabeth could hear the squeak of his old-fashioned swivel chair. She could imagine him waving his arms in silent mime for the list of her calls, and someone, probably Reba, dashing to bring it. "It took a stolen grocery basket from Frye's Supermarket to hold the damn thing. Let's see . . . your friend Constance called a half dozen times. Hmmm. A couple calls that pertain to work . . . I don't know why we bothered to fit those in. Collingswood & Booth. A couple from a man by the name of Baille. You know him? He wouldn't leave a number. And a Mary Rhinehardt. They don't say how many times she called. A Stephen Kenwood. He takes first place for number of calls. And a Detective Sibben, about you-know-what. Sounded like a ghoul, Reba thought. And an unidentified woman. She called twice. Didn't leave her name or number."

Elizabeth sat down slowly. Oh, Lord, it couldn't be. It was probably nothing more than a telephone salesperson, a wrong number. The silence spun out, but Elizabeth didn't hear it.

"You there, Elizabeth? An impressive list, don't you think? You're worse than my teenage daughter."

"Thanks, Bill. No idea who the woman was?"

"I've got theories, love. I've got my money on

113

Jackie O., but hell, it could be Liz. The office pool is favoring Liz."

"Very funny, Bill. Maybe my dog and I *will* come to stay with your family. It would serve you right."

He laughed.

"Anytime, Elizabeth. I mean it. And don't come in to work until you're ready. But, ahem . . . keep hitting those designs."

"I'll be in tomorrow. After I see Sibben. He has some notion that the world revolves around his schedule. Something like you, Bill."

"Sure, I'm a slave driver. See you tomorrow."

Elizabeth hung up the phone. She stood looking at it for long moments, as if she expected it to ring. As if she *knew* it would.

It did. It filled the artificial atmosphere of the hotel room with its urgent scream.

"Elizabeth?"

She'd have thought that one could not recognize a voice heard briefly so long ago. She'd have been wrong. The distinctive, well-modulated tones were as familiar as if she'd heard them yesterday.

"Yes," she said chokingly. She wanted to rage and weep, to hold back this moment from happening. But there was no breath in her, and time stopped for no one.

"I'm frightened, Elizabeth."

Elizabeth drew herself together, muscles and sinew and mind. She asked.

"Where are you?"

"In Phoenix."

Oh, God!

"Grace, *why?* You know the danger!"

"We live here." There was a muffled sob, the ghost

114

of some impossible, ironic amusement. "Can you believe it? It's been so many years. And now here we both are, in Phoenix, of all places. Twelve hundred miles from home."

"It was too dangerous to keep track of you. I didn't dare." Elizabeth's throat closed up and she swallowed a sob. "Everyone comes to the sun belt. It's the thing to do."

"I'm being watched, Elizabeth."

Elizabeth could feel a shiver run over her flesh. He was close. Oh, God, he was close. Nearer than she had ever dared fear.

"Don't panic," she said sharply, as much to herself as to the other woman. "There's a dozen possible explanations. You've got to be sure."

"And then what? Tell Randolph?" A tremor ran through the woman's cultured voice. "I'm sorry; I'm sure you're right. I'm panicking.

"I know the last thing I should have done was call you, Elizabeth, after the care you've taken. But sometimes the burden is just too much. And I feel that if I could just talk about it, talk to *you*. You're going through your own hell and can understand mine. Do you see?"

"Yes. But it can't happen."

"The police can't help."

"That was never an option."

"Oh, there *were* no options! I'm not railing against that! I wouldn't change it, I wouldn't take one step back. But I'm afraid to move forward. What if I *am* being stalked?"

Stalked. The word ran like fire along Elizabeth's veins. A predator and its prey.

"Watched, you said."

115

"Yes, watched. 'Stalked' sounds paranoid. I hope I haven't gotten to that point."

Elizabeth said tonelessly, *"I've* brought them all here. You do understand that? They've followed me. They've followed me right to you."

Grace was gathering her own reserves of strength. She said dryly, "It's a big city."

"Things are happening. Ellen's body was found in Portland a few days ago."

"I read about it in the *Oregonian*. It's a terrible thing, but scarcely unexpected. We always knew what they were capable of."

Elizabeth breathed. Grace was fine; she had her old composure back. A moment of panic, a misstep, that was all. No harm done, as Bill would say. But Lord, the timing was so crucial. Each player was taking his position on the stage and there was no margin for error now. Obviously there never had been.

"You know that you're only as safe as you are quiet, Grace. You can't afford to know me."

"I know. I panicked. It won't happen again."

"Good. You're a very strong woman, Grace."

Grace laughed softly, shakily.

"I'd like to believe I'm half as strong as you are, Elizabeth. You've been our rock. I know you won't let anything happen."

"I won't," she vowed grimly. She was probably lying even now. She was growing adept at it.

Chapter Thirteen

December 1986

Snow had started to fall in the early afternoon. It was Friday. The wet streets hissed with the heavy volume of traffic heading out of the city, heading into the city. Wind drove the snow horizontally into the windshields.

Thanksgiving was forgotten in the promise of a white Christmas. The first splash of bright lights and tinsel decked the parks and city streets. The weather forecasters warned of a cold night, and a whisper of the chill to come silvered the wind gusts. It was a bad day to die.

The dormitory was a holdover from the sturdy construction of the 1950s. The wall heaters creaked and groaned, but they worked, and the bare rooms were as warm as their perseverance and the dorm supervisor would allow.

Elizabeth turned off the light and crossed to stand at the window. It was nearly midnight, and the snow was beginning to drift. It fell in mesmerizing slow motion in the glow of the street lamps.

The cold came through the windowpanes. Elizabeth wrapped her arms about her body and leaned against the wide painted sill. Only the main streets were running now, and they weren't visible even from the top floor, where Elizabeth was. The cars in the parking lot had long since lost their individuality beneath a white blanket of snow.

She would see Stephen at Christmas. After nearly six months of being separated by more than half the continent, they would be together. And he wasn't going back to Chicago when the holidays were over. He would be continuing his undergraduate studies in Seattle.

That would be better. She wouldn't feel as if she were marrying a stranger.

If they *did* marry. Stephen seemed like a memory with the snow falling and the cold stealing into her bones.

Ellen had only a few more minutes to make curfew. She usually came in as the door was being bolted for the night. Tonight she might claim the storm as a delaying factor, she might even call in that she was stranded, and spend the night somewhere. She was a resourceful woman and the strictures of college life were rarely allowed to interrupt her other pursuits.

But she came. A car pulled to the curb and Ellen climbed out. She wasn't hurrying. She talked a moment with the driver, the car door open and the snow blowing in. And then she stepped back and slammed the door, and the car pulled away.

Ellen glanced up at their window. There was no light in the room but the glow of Elizabeth's cigarette, and she didn't know if Ellen could see her, but she raised a hand.

They weren't friends. They would never be. But Elizabeth was struck suddenly by how small her roommate looked against the snow piled along the walk. Ellen seemed to move with difficulty, stopping every so often to catch her breath as if the path were a long uphill incline instead of a brief, level stretch of relatively clear concrete.

When Ellen disappeared from sight under the portico, Elizabeth closed the drapes and flipped on the light by her bed. Ellen had had too much to drink or she was ill, and in either case she wouldn't welcome any intrusion.

Elizabeth went into the bathroom and washed her face and brushed her teeth. She thought of living with Stephen and what it would be like to have all the time she could ask to get to know him. It was hard to imagine. He was a complicated man. Knowing he loved her was not as difficult as knowing why.

She didn't hear Ellen come in, but she was sitting on the bed when Elizabeth came out of the bathroom. She still wore her outdoor things, and her boyishly square face was drawn and pale. Her short blond hair stuck wetly to her forehead, as if she'd been sweating, and her eyes looked almost glazed.

"I couldn't remember if you were going to your sister's or not. I couldn't see a light up here," Ellen said tersely.

"I'm not. I figured they could use the time together before the baby."

"Yeah, the baby. That must get old." Ellen's eyes glittered oddly in the dim bedside light. "It sure has for me."

Elizabeth was a private person. She rarely spoke of her sister, so it wasn't likely that Ellen was accusing her of wearing out the subject. But Ellen was often enigmatic. She wanted people to believe that she was a hard-case, and it was probably true.

"Are you going to bed now?" Ellen asked jerkily. "Or are you going to prowl all night?"

"I'm going to prowl," Elizabeth said mildly. She was used to the edge in Ellen's voice. "I'll keep the light covered."

"My luck. I thought you'd be gone. I hoped . . ." Ellen's voice trailed off. She put her hands on her knees and seemed to hold her breath. Her eyes were closed tightly.

"Are you ill, Ellen?"

Ellen gave her head a shake. After a moment she let out her breath and brushed the damp hair from her forehead with a coat sleeve. There was a line of perspiration along her short upper lip.

She began to struggle out of her coat and scarf. She kicked off her boots, and getting to her feet with difficulty, went into the bathroom. Over the roar of the washbasin filling came the unmistakable sound of her being sick.

Elizabeth waited ten minutes and when Ellen didn't come out, she knocked on the door.

"Ellen? Are you all right?"

There was no answer. The water continued to run full blast into the sink.

Elizabeth opened the door.

Ellen was on her knees beside the stool. She clutched the edge of the basin, and she didn't seem to notice that her hair was wet from the force of the faucet's spray. A deep, wrenching groan came from her throat. The baby slid out onto the cold linoleum of the floor.

120

It was that which shook Elizabeth from her paralyzation, the tiny infant lying in blood and amniotic fluid on a floor too cold to touch. She rushed into the room, dragging towels from the rack to wrap around the baby. He was slippery, and her hands were trembling so badly she could hardly pick him up.

He wasn't breathing.

Elizabeth tried to think what to do. She swallowed tears, hysteria. She held the infant upside down and began clumsily to rub the tiny back with the towel.

The chest gave a convulsive jerk, like a sob.

It echoed Elizabeth's own. She murmured under her breath, she pleaded, she prayed. The chest shuddered again.

Oh, God! He wasn't a whitish red any longer. He was turning blue. He was dying.

There was no running for help. The white ropelike cord connected him to Ellen, who still clung weakly to the basin, her eyes tightly shut, her face contorted with pain. And Elizabeth couldn't put him on the floor, even wrapped in towels. A minute might be too long.

There was no one to hear her if she called. The dorm was virtually deserted for the weekend.

Elizabeth shivered violently. She ran a finger inside the baby's mouth. She didn't know if she should try to breathe life into him. Even in the extremity of the moment she was terrified she might hurt him. That she might do the wrong thing.

His tiny chest heaved again, but this time it was very nearly a gasp. Mucus gurgled in his throat.

Elizabeth was crying. She lowered his head again and wiped his nose, his mouth. A thin, weak cry came from his throat.

"Oh God, yes, please, please, love. Breathe." She murmured the words, mindless words, like a litany. She rubbed his back, his head. His circulation had to be almost nil, she had to warm him.

His chest sank and then expanded, another cry lifted, a little stronger.

"Yes, that's it, love!" He was breathing! He was! He drew breath and the gurgle of mucus in his throat couldn't prevent the air coming in, a tinge of pink spread beneath the ashen pallor of his skin.

"Stop it, Elizabeth!"

Ellen's voice was devoid of expression. She was pale, but she had delivered the placenta now, and the contractions had stopped. She sank back onto her heels as if she were weak, but her voice wasn't. "Stop it," she said again.

"Ellen, are you all right? He's breathing, do you see? He's breathing."

Ellen gave the infant a cold glance. His feet and hands were a deep blue still, but his face and torso were beginning to assume a natural hue.

"What do you think I'm talking about? I want you to stop."

Elizabeth looked at her in shock.

"What are you saying, Ellen?" Every nerve was on end. Her scalp prickled as if there was danger. The baby was crying in earnest now, and she gave Ellen all of her attention. "What are you suggesting?"

"Quit trying to get it to breathe."

"He *is* breathing."

"Stop it, damn it! I want it to die!"

"No," Elizabeth straightened, stiffened. "You don't know what you're saying."

"Why don't we argue about it? Yes, I do, no, I

don't! While the little bastard gets stronger and no medical man will believe it was a stillborn."

Ellen grabbed the infant's ankle in a rough clasp.

"Give it to me! I'm not afraid to do it!"

Elizabeth didn't dare move. Ellen was deadly serious. She wasn't excited or out of her senses with the moment. She knew exactly what she was doing. She was killing her child.

Elizabeth knew that her legs wouldn't work. She had been kneeling too long, and they had lost all feeling. The baby was still attached to the placenta. She couldn't move out of Ellen's reach with him even were her legs to cooperate. There was nothing she could do but attempt reason.

"You don't want him to have a bruise on his leg, do you?" she asked coldly.

"No." Ellen let go. "No, you're right. The press and the police love that sort of thing. He's got to be unmarked when they find him."

Elizabeth inched back slightly. Ellen might be bleeding heavily, she might collapse or go into shock. She needed medical attention; God, she needed psychiatric attention. She dared to think the baby's only danger at the moment was from Ellen.

"You need to see a doctor, Ellen."

"Sure. That's what I need. Bring the whole damned world in here. Let everyone know." Ellen hesitated, then she seemed to pull herself together. She said quietly, reasonably, "Listen, Elizabeth. This is my life we're talking about here. I can't afford to screw it up. Do you know what would happen if it came out that I'd had a kid? It would ruin everything. My parents, my granny that's financing my next two years and setting me up in business? They'd dump me. I'd be thrown out of here, I'd lose my scholarship. My life wouldn't be worth shit."

"What about an adoption agency? Some family would be overjoyed to have your little boy."

"Christ! I'm wasting my time talking to you! I'm supposed to waltz into an agency with the kid under my arm, I suppose, and say, 'Here, I've got something for you.' Sure. And what do I do with it in the meantime? Pretend I'm babysitting an infant that isn't even half an hour old? In a dorm that doesn't allow kids in here after hours? Christ, Elizabeth!"

She moved quickly. Her hand came up like a streak and she slapped Elizabeth across the face a stunning blow. Elizabeth's head rocked back, striking the panel of the door, and Ellen was on her. She dragged the infant from Elizabeth's arms, and staggering to her feet, thrust the baby's head under water in the overflowing washbasin.

Elizabeth threw herself forward. She pushed Ellen hard, unbalancing her. Ellen reeled.

The baby dangled upside down in her hands, his tiny fists flailing, water dripping from his hair and face. Elizabeth held her breath. Ellen had only to open her hands, to let him fall.

She didn't. Perhaps she was still thinking of the bruises she didn't want the police to see.

"Get back, Elizabeth," she hissed. "I mean it! Get out of my way."

"Give him to me, Ellen."

"No." She stepped back to the basin. She kept her eyes watchfully on Elizabeth as she plunged his head deep into the icy water.

Elizabeth was sobbing. She flung herself at Ellen, grasping her hair and dragging her head back, forc-

124

ing her away from the water. She was strong. Ellen's strength was adrenaline and resolution, but hers was terror. She brought a forearm across Ellen's throat and pressed hard. She cried brokenly.

"Let me have him, Ellen. Don't make me hurt you."

But the strength was going out of Ellen, not the breath. Her knees began to fold up. She slid slowly to the floor. Elizabeth eased her down, taking the baby from her arms.

"Damn it, you are an idiot!" Ellen rubbed her throat. "You're determined to ruin me, aren't you?"

Elizabeth wrapped dry towels around the baby. She studied him anxiously, looking for signs of harm, but he still breathed, and made fitful small sounds of discontent.

"You need a doctor, Ellen. God knows how much you're bleeding. It won't do your scholarship any good if you bleed to death, with or without a baby."

It sounded hard. It *was* hard. It was difficult to care what happened to a woman who would kill her own child.

Elizabeth put the baby down on a pile of linen and began to rummage through the cabinets, keeping an eye on Ellen. She tore off strips of clean cotton sheets.

She looked anxiously at the infant. And then she wrapped a ribbon of sheeting around the umbilical cord a few inches from the navel. She tied it as tightly as her trembling fingers would allow.

"What in the hell are you doing?"

"I don't know," Elizabeth admitted flatly. "I've got to tie off the cord. I've got to get him out of here."

Ellen laughed. She leaned against the wall, and her

strength may have been spent, but her mind was absolutely lucid.

"He'll bleed to death when you cut the cord."

It froze Elizabeth's fingers. What if Ellen was right? What if, after all of this, she killed the baby through her own ignorance?

"That's not possible," she decided. "He's self-sufficient now. He doesn't need the placenta."

But still she was very careful. She took another strip of cloth and tied the cord off again, this time a few inches above the first knot.

There was antiseptic in the medicine chest. Elizabeth poured it on the razor blade. She could feel her blood congealing. She was about to cut through flesh and blood. She had to be right.

"You're in the wrong major, Elizabeth. You should be in medical. In fact, I'll donate him to the science lab when you're done there. They can put him in a jar." She snickered. "What's the matter, Elizabeth? Maybe you'd like to give *me* the razor. I can do it."

Elizabeth drew a deep breath and let it out slowly. She looked at the tiny scrap of humanity. She said some line from a forgotten prayer over and over in her head. She cut the cord between the ribbons.

He didn't bleed. Only a drop or two welled from the thick white rope. Elizabeth sank back on her heels and wiped sweat from her forehead with one arm.

"It's a laugh," Ellen observed caustically. "All this fuss. If he lives, you'll have more grief than I will. Want to know why?"

"No," Elizabeth clipped.

She was busy. She was fashioning a clumsy diaper, tying it at the corners.

"It's more than *my* life being screwed up. There are people besides me who won't dare let him live. Do you hear me, Elizabeth? They'll kill him if I don't."

"Shut up, Ellen. You're very transparent."

"Am I? Did you suspect I was pregnant? No, you didn't. Nobody did. I've done a damned good job of covering it up. Even from you, my roommate. You'd never believe it if you hadn't seen it, would you?"

Elizabeth tore the sheet, fashioning a makeshift gown for the infant. She didn't know what he needed, how cold it was outdoors. But it was an awful night. The worst night this winter.

"They'll kill him. When they find out about him, they'll kill him. Do you hear me, Elizabeth? Are you listening to me?"

"Who will?"

"You've got no clue, have you? Good God, Elizabeth! Do you ever stop and wonder what's going on around you? There's more to life than your fiancé, believe it or not."

"Tell it to the police."

"Damn you, Elizabeth! Don't you hear what I'm saying? You can't go to the police!"

"Sorry. I can. It's exactly what I am doing."

"You want the little brat to live? He doesn't have a chance if you go to the police."

"You don't, you mean."

"You turn him over to the police, welfare, whatever, you're drawing a map with a big red arrow for these guys. The kid's dead."

"Right, Ellen. A conspiracy."

Ellen laughed.

"Yeah," she agreed. "You're damned close."

That was the irony, that somehow she got through to Elizabeth, struck a nerve, when she wasn't even trying.

"What are you talking about?"

"Haven't you been listening?"

"Someone will *kill* him?" Elizabeth's hands had stilled upon the small, wriggling bundle. She whispered, demanded, "Who?"

Ellen let her head fall back against the wall. She smiled at the ceiling.

"Who, Ellen?"

"Figure it out," Ellen sneered. "You're the A student."

Elizabeth sank back. She looked at Ellen and she knew that, ludicrously enough, Ellen was speaking the truth. It meant that there was no way out of this. There was no one she dared entrust the baby to.

"What about the baby's father?" she asked at last.

Ellen laughed, a short, hard burst of sound that was devoid of amusement.

"I suppose you haven't figured that either," she taunted. "It's Stephen, of course. Your dear, devoted Stephen. It kind of makes you think, doesn't it?"

Chapter Fourteen

"Of course," Elizabeth said sarcastically. "You have no reason to lie, do you?" She gathered the baby in a dry towel and held him against her. She looked down at Ellen.

"I'll help you into bed."

"Don't bother."

Ellen got to her knees. She reached for the towel rack and pulled herself to her feet. She swayed slightly, but then she laughed, and it was as cold as the look in her eyes. "I really *am* all right, you know. You're probably hoping I'll hemorrhage, but I won't. I've had time to learn something about this, read up at the library. I didn't just burst in on the whole idea like you did."

"If enlightenment was all it took, I don't suppose doctors would ever get ill."

Ellen pressed her fingers into her belly inches below the navel.

"I'm okay. As long as the uterus is a tight knot that I can feel in the lower abdomen, I'm not hemorrhaging. It's when it gets flaccid that there's danger." Ellen laughed. "God, does that sound good! I should be a damned medical professional. I should be a midwife!"

"I'd certainly ask for you," Elizabeth said dryly. She tightened the wraps around the baby. He was sleeping now as if, through all this, he was trusting her to care for him. An unfamiliar thrill ran along Elizabeth's flesh.

Ellen opened the cabinet under the sink. She took out a large shoebox that contained newspapers and string and a plastic bag. "I saved this to make it easier to dump him down the trash chute," she offered conversationally. And then she moved lightning quick. She came around with the razor blade Elizabeth had cut the cord with in her hand.

"No!" Elizabeth staggered back, instinctively twisting away from the razor as Ellen slashed at her face. She lost her balance and went down, the baby still in her arms. Ellen flung herself upon her.

Elizabeth threw up an arm to ward off Ellen's attack. She managed to get a grip on Ellen's wrist, and locking her elbow, Elizabeth pushed the baby awkwardly behind the stool.

She clasped both hands on Ellen's wrist. She held back the razor blade that strained toward her face in taut, bloody fingers. Ellen was rigid, bent over Elizabeth in grotesque concentration, her expression scored with lines of furious determination.

Elizabeth was the stronger. She forced Ellen's arm up, but as Ellen felt her advantage being lost, she abruptly relaxed her hold and twisted to the side. Elizabeth's momentum carried her with Ellen and they rolled, each scrambling for the razor.

Ellen was underneath now. She had lost the blade.

She didn't hesitate. She brought up her free hand and dragged her nails down Elizabeth's face.

Elizabeth flinched and jerked her head away, but she maintained her grip on Ellen. She pinned her arms while Ellen struggled and tried to lash out with her feet. The baby began to cry.

It was impossible, this, Elizabeth holding her roommate down in the middle of the night while the scratches on her face stung and trickled with blood. Her long dark hair coming down and every muscle trembling with fear and fatigue. Ellen a mess of blood and madness, and an infant crying in the corner. It was impossible.

Elizabeth let out a ragged breath. She looked for the lost razor blade, but it must have flown some distance. Ellen's hands were empty.

Ellen had quit struggling.

"Come on, Elizabeth," she panted. "It can't matter to you if he lives or dies. Be reasonable. There's too many kids in the world as it is. Nobody's going to miss one more. You know I can't let you take him out of here."

She was in no position to object, but Elizabeth shivered. It was as if her determination to see the baby dead was greater than the limits of Elizabeth's physical endurance.

"You don't have to do anything, Elizabeth. Just leave him in here with me and go to bed. Pretend tonight never happened.

"I have the box. I'll just tie it up tight and drop it in the trash chute. It goes to the incinerator. Our problems are over. My life is normal again, and you don't have somebody stalking you. Because that's what will happen. Until they get their hands on the kid and see him dead, you won't have a minute you can call your own. And once they get the kid, you're next. Because you'll know too much.

"I'm talking sense, Elizabeth. You don't want to screw up. Do you think Stephen will stand by while you play hide-the-kid? Hide *his* kid? He won't. He won't want you to have anything to do with the brat. I swear to God, he would give the nod on it. He'd want you to leave the kid in here with me. It's the answer to everything."

Elizabeth felt ill. She said grimly, "You have all the answers."

"Sure I do. It's simple. You're the one who's making it complicated."

"Why would someone want to hurt a baby? Besides his loving mother, of course."

"Oh, for Christ's sake! Figure it out! I don't care. Why should I? Let me get up, Elizabeth. I'm getting a backache."

"I'm taking the baby," Elizabeth said tautly. "And if you give me any more trouble, I'll take him downstairs to the supervisor so fast you won't know what hit you. And I'll have the police up here before your head has stopped spinning. Got it?"

Ellen laughed.

"I must not be hearing right. You're threatening me?"

"Yes," Elizabeth agreed. She came to one knee and then to her feet. She moved deliberately and kept her eyes on Ellen. "But that's hardly a big deal compared to kidnapping, is it? That's what I'm doing."

Ellen rolled to her elbow. She drew up her knees and brought herself to a sitting position.

"Oh, *I'm* sure to squawk about it! Keep your

mouth shut, and he's all yours. I'll make you a present of him. But don't expect it in writing. My lawyer wouldn't approve." She got to her feet. She was a little stiff, but lord, she was an Amazon for not being in a hospital somewhere, being fed glucose through her veins. "Who's going to clean up this mess?"

"I guess you are," Elizabeth said coldly. "You're the one with all the energy." She took the baby past Ellen and went out into the bedroom, bringing the torn sheet with her. She put him on the bed and began to tear long strips of cloth about six inches wide.

She watched the bathroom door. The razor was still in there somewhere.

Elizabeth dressed in warm trousers with heavy socks and snow boots. She stripped down to her bra above the waist, and unwrapping the baby from his toweling, she balanced him with one hand against her body.

She didn't know what she was doing, but obviously the infant would need body heat, her warmth, against the freezing cold of the night. His own ability to stay warm had to be very limited.

Elizabeth held the baby, his head below her breast, his chest and drawn-up knees against the flesh of her belly. She began to wind the strips of sheet around the both of them, cocooning his small, vulnerable body into as much contact as possible with her own. She supported his head with the strapping, his face turned to the side, his tiny balled fists trapped in warmth between them.

Ellen came out of the bathroom.

"The cold is going to kill him," she observed nonchalantly. She sat down on her bed. She had washed

133

and her short blond hair was brushed, and she had changed into pajamas.

Elizabeth couldn't deny the possibility, but she didn't know what else to do. She was afraid to ignore Ellen's oddly sincere persistence that someone was out to harm the baby. Nor could she keep the baby here till morning. If she dozed off, Ellen would see her chance to kill him.

Elizabeth drew on a light sweater. She was terrified that she would suffocate him, and she paused, alert to any change in his breathing, his small sounds. She put on another sweater, listened. One more. His greatest immediate threat to survival was surely the cold.

Ellen shook her head.

"If you could just see what a mistake you're making. He's going to die anyway. If not tonight, then as soon as they find out about him. And they will, Elizabeth. No matter what you do.

"Give me two minutes. *Two minutes,* Elizabeth. And I can spare both of us this mess.

"Sure, I admit to self-interest. I won't deny it. I want the tidy answer. But you walk out of here with him alive and there won't be any tidy answers left. There won't be *any* answers."

Elizabeth dumped the contents of her purse onto the bed. She took her wallet and a pack of cigarettes. That would have to do. She had $40 in cash and a couple of credit cards, and she needed to have her hands free, not tied up with a purse.

She shook out a cigarette and put the others in the pocket of her coat. She found her scarf, her gloves were in her coat. She looked at Ellen.

"One last time," she said. "Who will want to kill him?"

"Oh, *please!* I can't believe you! I'm not exactly on your side of the fence in all this, or didn't you notice when you were holding me down and sitting on me? And by the way, your face is a mess." She lay back on the bed.

Elizabeth had forgotten the scratches. She went into the bathroom and washed them with soap and water. It brought tears to her eyes. The baby made small fussing sounds. He probably didn't like being bound so tightly, or the insecurity of her leaning over the basin as if he might fall.

Elizabeth blotted the red streaks dry and applied a light layer of makeup. She looked around the room.

The razor blade had caught under an edge of the linoleum, and she retrieved it. She put it in the wastebasket under used cosmetic puffs and a cigarette pack.

There was one other detail to consider. Elizabeth took a roll of cloth adhesive tape from the cabinet.

Ellen was still stretched out on the bed.

"Swear you won't tell where you got him, Elizabeth. Promise me."

"We're not exactly on the same side of the fence in this, or didn't you notice when you were trying to use a razor blade on my face?" Elizabeth reminded her harshly. She took a felt-tip marker from her briefcase. "I don't owe you anything, Ellen. But frankly, I'm not likely to tell, am I? I can't afford to, if the baby *is* in danger. Do you want someone sent up to check on you?"

"No. How are you going to get past the alarm?"

Elizabeth shook her head. She went out the door and closed it behind her.

The dorm was quiet. The baby's cries hadn't been the lusty volume of an older child, but still they could have penetrated the thick plaster walls if there had been anyone at this end of the wing to hear.

But this was the weekend, classes had closed early at the threat of the approaching storm, and most of the women had headed for home before the streets had frozen.

Mrs. Rasmussen wasn't at the front desk. She made rounds on the hour, checking and rechecking every outside door. She was certain the night would come when only her keen eye would prevent them from all being murdered in their beds.

Elizabeth went behind the desk and shut off the alarm. She tripped the electronic eye that gave the image at the front doors to the television monitors.

She tore off a long strip of tape, and put the felt-tip marker between her teeth. It was going to be very close if Mrs. Rasmussen was on her swing back to the desk.

Elizabeth pressed the tape over the buzzer that activated the front doors. The loud, raucous buzz seemed to fill the building.

She ran to the door, shoved it open, and stuck the marker into the crack to keep it from closing. She dashed back and tore off the tape, and mercifully the buzzer fell silent.

Elizabeth sped back to the door. She pushed it open with her shoulder and kicked the marker free.

The cold hit her like a blow. The door slammed and latched at her back.

Elizabeth stood a moment on the frozen step. She was locked out. There was no turning back now.

Chapter Fifteen

Elizabeth's resolve hardened with each step. She couldn't worry now that the air was too thin for the baby, strapped so close against her beneath the layers of clothing. She couldn't think about the cold stealing in. She had to concentrate with everything that was in her.

It took twenty minutes of struggling through snow and ice to reach the Circle K. The lights and the warmth looked more like coming home than the best Christmas she could remember as a child. She stamped her feet and blinked in the commercial gleam of her shelter.

"Hey, some night, huh? You must be crazy to be out. You can bet I'd be home if it was up to me. But it ain't."

The clerk wasn't particularly interested in having customers. He had a cozy game of solitaire going in the little room back of the counter. But he liked the sound of his own voice, and the college kids were a steady part of their trade.

Elizabeth shook snow from her scarf. She could

feel the infant begin to wriggle. She prayed he wouldn't start to cry.

"I could use a cup of coffee." She looked around her. "And the paper. Is it on the newsstand?"

"I got coffee, but you're out of luck on the news. Truck brings it around, oh, maybe four A.M. That's a couple of hours yet. And I can't even guess how late it'll be with the weather shot to hell."

"What about yesterday's paper?"

"Nope. Sold out by dinner. There's the coffee. Help yourself." He motioned with his head toward the coffee machine and styrofoam cups along the wall.

Elizabeth stood helplessly. She could see the telephones, protected halfheartedly by the overhang of the wide, flat roof. They weren't any good to her without the number.

"Do you have a telephone book?"

"Yeah, I got one. You ain't going to try to talk me into a long-distance call on my phone, are you?"

"No. I just need to see the book. I'll call from the pay phones."

He slung the books onto the counter.

"Yellow pages or white?"

"White."

"Yell if you need anything," he told her, and went back to his card game.

Elizabeth scanned the columns. It wasn't there.

"I'm sorry," she said. "I've got to have a newspaper. An old issue is fine."

She felt desperate; she *was* desperate. Her face was starting to sting again.

"Yeah, well, maybe you should have thought of

that a little earlier in the day. What's so important? They got a sale or something?"

Elizabeth forced herself to walk across the room and pour herself a cup of coffee. She mustn't appear agitated. She didn't want to stand out in his memory later, if it came to that.

She said mildly, "It seems like you would have an old issue of the *Oregonian* around. Under the coffeemaker? Maybe at the back door, to wipe your feet when you come in? In your parakeet cage?"

He was starting to get annoyed at her persistence, but that last struck him as funny. The boss would die of apoplexy at the notion of him keeping a bird in the little office that three shifts a day had to share.

"Right," he agreed. He got up and came around the counter. "I got nothing better to do than watch a bird fling seeds and feathers and crap all over my desk. I'll ask Santa Claus for one." He reached under the counter and rummaged around. *"Playboy, Penthouse.* I suppose they ain't going to cut it. Hey, here's something. But it ain't the *Oregonian.* It's one of them local rags. This one's out of Gresham. Will that do?"

Elizabeth took it with fingers that shook. She didn't know. But God, please God, it was possible.

"Thank you," she muttered. She wanted him to go back to his game, but now he hung interestedly over the paper as she spread it out.

She found the classified ads, but the entries were disappointingly sparse. It wasn't there.

"Hey, you want ads? Why didn't you say so? I got the want ads from yesterday." The clerk went back into his office and came out with a section of newspa-

139

per folded clumsily so that the crossword was exposed.

Elizabeth fumbled with the pages.

"Thank you." She feigned calm. She took a sip of the scalding coffee and spread out the pages. She willed him to go back into his office.

"You any good at crosswords? It beats the hell out of me why they put in stuff that you'd have to be a damned Einstein to figure." He turned back to his card game.

The baby began to squirm again. It felt as if he was beginning to struggle in earnest now. He must be all right, he must be gaining in strength and vigor. God knew what his cry would be like now.

Elizabeth scanned the columns. She took the paper and walked to the far end of the store. The baby was making small sounds of discomfort, of anger, and any minute the clerk was sure to hear him.

He put his head around the door.

"You say something, miss?"

"Er . . . I may have been thinking out loud. I'll need a couple packs of cigarettes, but there's no hurry. I'll let you know."

"You got it. Give a yell."

Elizabeth couldn't believe her eyes that it was there. She read every word as if she had never seen it before.

"I'm going out to use the telephone," she called. "I'll be back to pay for the coffee."

"Sure, sure, make your call."

Elizabeth went out into the snow. She wasn't thinking about the cold now. She didn't even hear the baby's fitful sounds. She took off her gloves and dialed the number, and it was as if she was in a vacuum, hearing the ringing of the telephone in some giant hall that was beyond her reach. She tensed toward the sound, she willed a voice to answer at the other end.

"Hello?" A woman's voice, cultured, mature.

And there were no words. Elizabeth had gotten no further than this in her mind. She was suddenly staggered by the necessity for absolute coherence, total lucidity. She had to catch the listener with the desperate urgency of the situation without frightening her away.

"Is this . . ." Elizabeth cleared her throat of huskiness. "Is this 649-2251?"

"Who is calling please?"

That was a good question. It was 2:30 A.M. by Elizabeth's wristwatch.

"My name is Elizabeth Purdin. I work with your husband's brother at Royce Pharmaceuticals."

She was probably out of her mind. The woman hadn't identified herself. Elizabeth was hoping—no, *praying*—that she had Grace Royce on the line.

"I'm sorry, Elizabeth, I'm afraid I don't remember you. Did we meet at one of David's parties?"

"We haven't met," Elizabeth managed. She closed her eyes and reached for words. It *was* Grace Royce, and she hadn't hung up. She was waiting for Elizabeth to speak, as if she didn't find it incomprehensible that an employee of David's would be calling at this appalling hour.

"Is something wrong, Elizabeth?"

It was an unlisted number. It ran every day in the paper, but without the owner's name. Perhaps that was why Grace Royce didn't put down the phone. Why she was listening.

Where were the perfect words? Elizabeth said starkly, "Are you still looking for a baby?"

There was silence on the line. Elizabeth could hear her own ragged breathing, see it in the air before her face.

"Mrs. Royce? Are you there?"

"Yes, yes. I'm sorry. Elizabeth Purdin, you said, didn't you? This is an unusual call, Elizabeth."

"I know, Mrs. Royce. It's outrageous, and the hour is, too. But it's God's own truth. If you're still looking for a baby to adopt, I have one."

This time Elizabeth could hear her shaken breath. It came distinctly over the line.

"Perhaps you can understand my shock. Yes, we are still looking for a child to adopt. But I . . . you took my breath away. You don't mean a black market infant, do you, Elizabeth?"

"No, it's nothing like that." Elizabeth shivered. "He was born tonight, less than an hour ago."

"Oh, my heavens! My husband is out of town for several days . . ." And then she said briskly, "I have a pencil. If you could give me the name and number of the hospital where the baby is. I don't suppose you know yet what agency will be handling the adoption?"

"I'm sorry," Elizabeth said. She *was* sorry, dreadfully sorry. People like the Royces believed in agencies and bureaus and red tape to be gotten through by the proper channels. They didn't understand that life wasn't necessarily like that. It was something Elizabeth was only now learning.

"Elizabeth, are you there? Don't hang up."

"I'm here, Mrs. Royce. But there *is* no hospital.

142

There's no birth certificate, and there won't be any adoption papers."

There was a long silence. And then, "Where is the infant?"

"He's here with me." Elizabeth took a deep, steadying breath. "This is nothing like what you've thought or planned, I'm sure, in looking for a child to adopt, Mrs. Royce. It's not orderly or neat or legitimatized by legal approval. I'm sorry. But it's a tiny baby, and no one could need you more."

She was crying quietly. It was too awful, begging for kindness for this poor little scrap of humanity who had everything against him. Absolutely everything.

"I'll come," Grace Royce said resolutely. "Where are you?"

"I'm at the Circle K, on Brighton. Listen, Mrs. Royce. It's more complicated than I can go into on the phone. And I don't want to frighten you, but it's imperative that you not tell anyone where you're going, or let us be seen together. The baby's life could depend on your secrecy."

Grace Royce gave a muffled choke of laughter that was almost a sob.

"Forgive me, Elizabeth. I'm not taking you lightly. I'm mocking myself. After the thousand times Randolph has warned me of the danger of being kidnapped for ransom, and I'm doing exactly what I shouldn't. If you're a terrorist, Elizabeth, you are *very* good. You've found my Achilles' heel."

Elizabeth leaned her forehead weakly against the phone box.

"There's nothing clandestine about this, Mrs. Royce. I want you to understand that. The baby isn't stolen, he's not connected to anything illegal. But he may be in danger."

"Is the baby well?"

"He seems to be. But he was born under unsanitary conditions and without medical care."

"It's a boy?"

"Yes."

Elizabeth heard the shudder of the other woman's deep breath, and then Mrs. Royce said briskly, "I'd like to bring Edith with me. She used to be my nurse. I would trust her with my life. The baby should have medical care at once."

Elizabeth nodded wordlessly. She was doing the right thing. A woman who kept a nurse on her staff, who had the money and the connections to pick up a telephone and summon anything she wished to her door. Except a child. She and her husband had been running a discreet ad for an infant to adopt for the past year or more. And it wasn't only in Portland, or even in Oregon. According to David, the ads ran in many of the major cities across the country.

"A nurse would be wonderful. He seems fine, but I can't claim to know anything about it. Be sure she doesn't talk to anyone."

"Give me twenty-five minutes. The roads may delay us a little longer. But please, Elizabeth—wait for me. Don't leave."

"I'll be here."

"Elizabeth?"

Elizabeth had been almost to hang up.

"Yes, Mrs. Royce?"

"The mother doesn't want the baby?"

"No. She would kill him if she could."

There was the hiss of Grace Royce's breath being drawn in.

"And the father? Do you know who he is?"

"Yes," Elizabeth said tonelessly. "I'm afraid I do."

Chapter Sixteen

Present

Elizabeth placed her hand on the cold glass of the police station door, but before she could push, it opened out. Stephen took her arm in hard fingers. She could feel his anger through the fabric of her coat.

He walked her away from the entry hall. They were in the giant concrete valley that separated the parking garage and the lesser brick buildings of the precinct. The mammoth parking garage cast long, cold shadows over them, blocking out the sunlight.

"I thought you'd run out on Sam," he said tautly.

Another time she might have reminded him with spirit that she would never leave Sam, that she had taken the dog when she'd taken nothing else, when she had walked out of their home and disappeared two years ago. But now she was tired, drained. She didn't feel a match for his anger.

She said quietly: "Constance says you want a divorce."

He dropped her arm.

"What does Constance know about it?" he grated. "Do you?"

He shoved his hands down into the pockets of his car coat. His eyes were dark and hard.

"No, God damn it! If it were up to me, we'd still be struggling along in our own particular hell, unable to reach each other for the secrets and the lies! It wasn't I who left!"

"Even though you think I killed Keith?"

"You didn't," he said flatly. "Christ! You can't even watch a dog get a shot! You're capable of a lot of things, Libby, but hurting a person isn't one of them. Not physically, at any rate."

"Than you've changed your mind since yesterday."

She would never forget the way he had looked at her, the shock and horror. As if in an instant he had known the truth, and it was terrible.

"Yes," he admitted. "I got a shock. A large block of my life . . . hell, if you will, fell suddenly into place. I looked at you and I couldn't believe it. That you could have spared me *that,* and you didn't lift a finger. It knocked me out."

Elizabeth's nerves tensed, her muscles. She was terrified of where this was leading.

"It wasn't your baby," he clipped.

Elizabeth stared at him. She was speechless.

"When you were so ill, delirious . . . God, there were times when it looked like you would die, Elizabeth! You talked. There wasn't a lot of sense to it, but you kept coming back to the baby. I thought it was yours."

"You thought . . . ?"

"Yes," he said harshly.

147

"That I . . . that when you . . . when you were in Chicago those months . . . you thought I had your baby and gave it away without telling you?"

He laughed derisively.

"Not mine," he said.

Elizabeth closed her eyes and stared into the past. Every misunderstood word, every guilty lie. She could hear him asking, his face closed, so closed, "Was it mine?" and she, thinking that he was talking about his baby with Ellen, retorting, in some kind of bitter self-mockery at her misplaced constancy, "You tell me." She could remember how he had looked, the blow that she had thought was guilt.

Elizabeth shivered violently. The truth, or part of it. All these years too late.

"And then, when you were finally well, you were so wary. You wouldn't touch the subject. It was obvious you didn't want to talk about it." He let out a short, hard breath. "And *I* couldn't."

"Ellen said the baby was yours."

"Ellen was a troublemaker."

"That's it? That's all? 'Ellen was a troublemaker'?" She sounded half-hysterical. She was. "Are you denying you slept with Ellen Glover?"

"Categorically." He shook his smooth dark head in exasperation. "Why would I, for God's sake? I can't remember a time when I wanted anyone but you."

Elizabeth closed her eyes on the pain. Dear Lord, what had she done? What had she done to them, with her image of betrayal, her damning fragile self-esteem?

She had believed in his infidelity for so long. While he had believed as badly of her.

After a long moment she looked at him, and asked, "Whose baby did you think I had?"

"Every man I met," he clipped. And then, "That's what that sneer was about, me knowing all the hotels, wasn't it, Elizabeth? About me having an affair with Ellen."

Elizabeth nodded wordlessly.

"You thought I had an affair with her while I was engaged to you, that I got her pregnant and then abandoned her. And still you married me. You had to have thought you were making the mistake of your life, but still you married me."

She made mistakes. She never stopped making them. But marrying Stephen hadn't been one of them.

"You married *me*," she countered raggedly. "You thought I was sleeping with God-knows-who. Having a baby and giving it away like so much merchandise while you were in school in Chicago. Lying to you with every breath. But still you married me."

"There was a difference," he said shortly. "I loved you."

Oh heavens, he *must* have! Logical, clear-headed Stephen Kenwood, who never put a foot wrong, who never spoke a word without considering it first. He *must* have loved her.

She pressed cold fingers to the hollows of her eyes. She was so tired. Soul-weary.

"Who killed Ellen, Stephen?"

He said between his teeth, "I suppose you think I did. And Vanfossen, too."

"Did you?"

"Of course, I didn't!" he bit out.

Elizabeth looked at him for long, long moments.

149

And then she opened her purse and took out the closed lockblade knife she had washed clean of Keith's blood. She held it out to him.

His glance went from her set, pale face to the knife that she offered.

"It's not mine," he said.

Oh, but it was! She knew it was! She felt like the breath had been knocked from her body. He was lying. And there was only one reason for him to lie.

Her fingers trembled as they tightened around the bone handle of the knife. She had to think of something to say, something to gain time, distance, to walk away. She let it drop back into her purse.

His hand came up. He was very quick. His fingers closed around her wrist and he drew her hard against him.

"So help me God, Elizabeth!" He flipped open her purse with his other hand and took out the knife. He looked at her, their faces almost touching, his etched in granite. "You found this at the murder scene, didn't you? You hid it from the police!"

"Stephen . . ."

"Say it!"

"Yes."

He swore.

"You little fool! Do you know what you're playing at? You must have a death wish!"

He released her abruptly, looking at her with the hardest eyes she had ever seen.

"It's not mine," he said again.

Elizabeth shivered. She was on a skyride and she didn't know where the next drop was, or if the brakes were going to hold. Everything pointed to Stephen, shouted his name. But if he had done it, if he did kill

Ellen and now Keith, then she might just as well give up. She wasn't going to win. She didn't *want* to win.

Elizabeth let out her breath. It was white in the cold air. She held out her hand for the knife.

"I'm sorry," she said. "It's a lot like one you used to have."

"Identical, in fact," he agreed. "Royce Chem gave out half a dozen of them one Christmas." He put the knife in her hand and closed his lean, strong fingers over hers.

"This thing is dynamite, Elizabeth. And it's not just a matter of tampering with evidence, which is damned serious. The killer must know you have it. It scares the hell out of me, the risk you're taking, carrying it around."

"I know," Elizabeth admitted. "But as long as I have it, at least I know that no one will come up behind me . . . use it on me. I can't leave it home. They could be waiting for me . . ."

"Libby," Stephen said tautly. "You told Sibben you weren't in any danger. Have you changed your mind?"

"Yes . . . no." She ran a hand across her eyes. "No. I'm sure I'm safe for now. I'm just unnerved at going back to the house.

"I know I'm being a fool. It's been completely cleaned and painted and all new locks and deadbolts installed. And heavens, you should see the outdoor lights. It looks like a football stadium. Not to mention the squad cars Sibben will have cruising by to see that I don't take off."

"Don't go back."

"I have to."

"Why?"

151

"Because it's the only way I can get over it. I'm afraid it will never go away if I run."

His voice was quiet. He breathed, "Did you care so much for him?"

"No," she whispered. "Don't you see, that's the worst of it? He was caught up in this and died horribly because of me. And I can't even say that I loved him."

Stephen put his arms around her. She buried her cold face in the fabric of his coat.

"You don't love easily, Elizabeth. No one can blame you for that. Not even me, who has been waiting around for, what? Eight years? You've never made promises you didn't keep."

Elizabeth closed her eyes against the sting of tears. She said raggedly, "I want to see Sara. I want to see her little boy. But I can't, Stephen. I don't dare go near them."

"She'll wait for you. Sisters do."

"But what if I can't ever go back, Stephen? What if this nightmare never ends?"

His arms tightened.

"It has to end."

He was the logical one. For everything there was a beginning and an end. If one could survive to see it.

"It's one of us. One of us is a killer."

"No," he said flatly. "It's one of them. You're not a killer, and neither am I. It's Damon or Constance or Mary."

"It can't be Constance or Mary, Stephen. And I don't want it to be Damon. He really cared about Ellen. I'm sure of it."

"Which doesn't necessarily clear him. More people are killed by a lover than by a stranger."

"Yes, in a rage. Not in cold blood. Not by tying her hands behind her back and cutting her throat."

He asked quietly, distinctly,

"Where did you get *that?*"

"I . . ." Elizabeth straightened away from him. "Sibben said it, didn't he?"

"You know he didn't."

"Stephen . . ."

"Don't bother." He looked tired suddenly. "That's what it's really all about. Things you know that you have no business knowing, and have no intention of sharing. I should be used to it. Particularly since you never asked me to understand, or cared if I didn't. It's an old song. I should know all the words by now."

"Don't you know I would tell you if I could?"

"Like you told me that the baby wasn't yours?"

"It's a little difficult to deny something you don't know you're accused of," she said coldly.

"Right," he bit out. "I've noticed." And then "Okay, let's back up, Libby. We almost had a conversation going there without fighting, didn't we?"

"Yes," she said wryly. "When we were accusing our friends of murder."

"One of them is a murderer. Two of them aren't."

"You sound like Damon. Judge and jury." Elizabeth passed a hand wearily over her eyes. "I don't want to see Sibben. Was he as nasty as usual this morning?"

"More or less. He's looking into alibis."

"I don't have one."

"Neither do I. I don't know when she disappeared."

Elizabeth knew. She knew exactly.

"I tried to call you in Chicago," she said.

Stephen searched her face.

"From Constance's?"

"No." She didn't want to lie any more. Not to Stephen. "I was never at her house. I . . ."

"Don't!" he interrupted sharply. "I shouldn't have asked. If you've ever needed the cover of that myth, you need it now."

"I don't know if I have it. I don't know what Constance has told the police."

"She'll stick to her story."

"She's really upset with me, Stephen."

"She may be, but you're forgetting something. You're her alibi."

"Yes. But it's likely that she was with someone and asked them not to talk so she could cover my absence from the dorm. Lord, I don't know! Is Sam all right?"

"He's moping, but you can't fault his appetite. I think he wants to go home."

"I *want* him home. I'm not going into that house without him!"

"You won't have to. Tell me when you're going and I'll pick him up and meet you there."

"After work. I should be there about 5:15."

"Right." Stephen looked past her at the door. "Nichols has seen you. Sibben will probably be out here himself in a minute to be sure you don't change your mind and leave."

"It's a wonder he hasn't arrested all of us."

"He can't. It's been too long. They'll never solve the case."

"You sound very detached. Don't you care?"

154

"I've known for a long time that Ellen was murdered. So have you."

"I told you when I was delirious with pneumonia, didn't I?"

"Yes. You were very agitated and didn't know what you were saying. But you knew that Ellen was dead. You knew how she died."

"It's ironic," Elizabeth said bitterly. "I put everything I had into building walls around what happened back then. And I had already told so much of it while I was ill. It seems such a waste, doesn't it?"

"There will always be walls, Libby," Stephen said gently. "You'll always build them and stand behind them. And there'll be half as many answers as there are questions. Some things can't be changed."

"Like Ellen."

"Like Ellen. Like us." He ran a hand over his smooth dark hair. "But if it helps, you never betrayed anyone."

"Not even you?"

"Least of all me."

Elizabeth bit her lip. She said at last:

"You must have thought I killed Ellen."

"I thought the killer told you about her murder while you were delirious in the hospital. I still do."

Elizabeth could feel a chill run through her. She could imagine it, herself drugged and vulnerable, someone leaning over her, whispering to her. Telling her about Ellen. Threatening her.

"And Constance, Mary, and Damon all visited? I thought ICU was off-limits to visitors."

"It is, except for immediate family. As your fiancé, I stayed with you. Since your sister was across town in St. Mary's, having a baby, someone—Constance,

155

I suppose—talked the doctors into letting them visit for a minute or two. They were only allowed in one at a time, and I stepped out to cut down on the congestion. I should never have left you.

"You had been very quiet until then. Alarmingly quiet." He ran a hand sharply across his hair. "All I knew was that you had disappeared for several days and come back ill. Ellen hadn't been reported missing yet. I didn't know I was leaving you alone with a madman."

Elizabeth shivered.

"No one could have known. And anyway, the killer didn't want me to die then. Not until he knew where I had been those missing days."

The "he" hung between them in the still air of the concrete canyon.

"You think it's Damon?"

"Oh, God, I don't know!" It was wrung from Elizabeth. "How can it be? How can it be any one of them? It's insane to think we know a killer. That yesterday we sat at a table with a killer."

"We did, though," Stephen said hardly. "Don't doubt it for a moment. If you lose sight of that, then you lose your edge, and you're damned well going to need it!"

"I know." She *did* know. She couldn't afford to crumble now. She took a deep, steadying breath. "I became agitated after they had all visited me in the ICU. I started talking about Ellen being killed. Is that right?"

"While the last visitor was still with you."

"Damon?"

Stephen nodded grimly.

"Damon," he agreed.

156

Chapter Seventeen

"Well, well. If it isn't Miss Purdin. Now, why am I surprised to see you? All those unreturned calls to your office. Nobody having the slightest idea where you were. And me thinking, of all things, that you'd skipped. I should be ashamed."

"But you're not." Elizabeth took one of the chairs he indicated. "You're disappointed."

Sibben grinned wolfishly.

"It would have made things interesting. Nothing like flight as an admission of guilt." He nodded at Stephen. "Kenwood, I appreciate your coming back in. We've run across something that you just might get a kick out of."

Elizabeth's nerves tautened. She wondered what Stephen was thinking, if he was half as apprehensive as she was. He didn't look it. He didn't look like a man who knew that his wife had a missing murder weapon in her handbag at a police station.

"Let's get on with it," Sibben began. "I'm sure you have an alibi all figured out for the time your friend was killed in Portland. Run it by me."

"Are you sure you want to bother?"

"Not really," he admitted lazily, but his eyes were sharp. "I'd rather cut right to the part about you hiring someone to waste your boyfriend. But it'll keep. We can get the paperwork out of the way first. Your alibi, Miss Purdin."

"I don't know when Ellen died. Just when she disappeared. Is it the same thing?"

"We'll say so, okay? The coroner is working on the finer points. And by the way, I let the Portland P.D. in on your pal Baille's theory. They'll be letting us know if she was pregnant. Not that it's going to come as a surprise to you either way, is it? She was *your* roommate."

"We roomed together. We didn't share confidences."

"And you worked together. In fact, you got her her job. But she never told you anything, right?"

"I didn't get her the job. I mentioned to her that there was an opening at Royce Pharmaceutical, where I worked, and she applied for it. I didn't recommend her. We weren't friends. We hardly knew each other."

"Sure, sure. And where were you the night she disappeared?"

"I was at the home of a friend, Constance LeMirre. I was in the early stages of pneumonia, and was eventually hospitalized. I'm sure Constance has told you the same thing."

"Are you?" Sibben taunted. He leaned forward in his chair and rummaged through the stack of papers on his desk. He drew one out. "There's a Dr. Henry Tomson who is going to confirm that you were ill in bed, right? But guess what? There's no record of it in the old boy's files. And he's been dead for years.

"Miss LeMirre's parents were there. They could confirm your story. But they're dead, too. Everybody's dead. Ellen Glover is dead."

"Everyone's mortal," Elizabeth said caustically.

"Now, that's a good point, Miss Purdin. Everyone *is* mortal. And fallible. They make mistakes."

"Even you, Detective? You surprise me."

"Sure. Even me. I'm making a mistake right now, not booking you."

"For murdering Ellen?"

"Oh, please, Miss Purdin. You know as well as I do that I'm talking about Vanfossen."

"You've found his body?"

"No. Sorry about that. You want to tell us where to look?"

Elizabeth let out her breath. It was going to happen; it had to. But she dreaded the final reality of Keith's death.

"I thought you were satisfied with my alibi."

"Yeah, that was a beaut. I have to hand it to you. That touch with the slashed tires. A poor little female who's just naturally frightened of a mouse. Where *would* she go, bless her, but to the nearest police station? Where all the big brave policemen can protect her. But you know what, Miss Purdin? If I had to lay odds on who could best take care of themselves, you or five of my top boys, I'd put my money on you. I'd put it on you every time."

"You think I had Keith killed?"

"You bet. You knew you needed an alibi, and you knew when. You just didn't know it was going to happen in your own house. You didn't like that. It wasn't supposed to lead straight back to your door."

"I guess this is where I'm supposed to break down

159

and admit it. Shouldn't you read me my rights? Advise me to call my lawyer?"

Sibben snorted. "I'll leave that to Kenwood. He doesn't seem to be worried that you'll talk too much."

"I'm not. Any more than I can figure out why you called me back. If there's nothing else, we'd like to go."

"I'm coming to it, Kenwood. I have a few more questions for Miss Purdin. For instance, what line of work was Vanfossen in?"

"He said he was an insurance broker."

"He said?"

"That's right."

"But he wasn't?"

"No."

"What was he?"

"*I* think he was a private investigator."

"Bingo!" Sibben slapped the desk with an open palm. "A private investigator, nosing around your place, *your* place, Miss Purdin, just happens to wind up dead. Because he *is* dead. You said so all along, and we've as good as confirmed it.

"The prelims indicated it was AB negative blood, and our follow-up lab tests verified it. And it's a rare type. Add that to the fact that Vanfossen is missing. That he was *your* boyfriend, and that it was *your* house. You figure it."

"I'm trying to," Elizabeth said dryly. "Why am I supposed to have had him killed?"

"I wish I knew. Maybe he was getting too close to something you didn't want him to know. Maybe he was talking too much. Maybe you were just plain spiteful about breaking up with him."

"Who was Vanfossen working for?" Stephen cut in.

"Good question. It'll be interesting when we figure that out. Miss Purdin was obviously his case.

"It makes you think, doesn't it? Who would be so curious about what Miss Purdin is up to? And what *is* she up to, that somebody will pay big bucks to have her followed? Something that she felt strongly enough about to have a man killed just for asking too many questions."

"It's all conjecture," Stephen said. "You have no case. You don't even have a victim."

"The body will turn up. It always does."

"Are those my keys?" Elizabeth asked sharply. She leaned toward the envelope Sibben had just emptied on the desk. "Did you learn anything?"

"There was no wax residue, clay, anything someone could have used to make a mold. The only prints were yours."

"No one has access to my keys," she agreed.

"Ah, but there you're wrong. Someone *did* have access. A copy was made off one of them."

"A copy . . . ?"

"That's right. I'm not talking about some sophisticated replica here. This was nothing more than someone tossing the key on the counter at your corner hardware store and having them make a copy. It took two minutes."

"That's impossible."

"Is that right?" Sibben mocked. "How do you figure?"

It *was* impossible. At work Elizabeth kept her handbag in her possession or in a locked drawer. Away from the office she was just as cautious. Even

161

staying with Constance, Elizabeth had kept her handbag with the keys in it in a locker bag with a combination lock while she slept at night. It was the care she had always taken, had had to take.

"I'm not careless with my keys."

"I'll just bet you're not," Sibben agreed. He pushed the keys across the desk. "They're all yours. The lab's done with them."

"So am I," Elizabeth said tautly. She swept them into the wastebasket.

Sibben shrugged.

"You've got the money to throw around. And you might not quite trust those, all right. Especially if you didn't pay off your man after he did the job."

"Is that everything, Detective?"

"Sorry. I'm afraid it's not quite that simple. There's the little matter I wanted Kenwood to hear. He's going to get a charge out of this. Assuming, of course, that he doesn't already know."

Elizabeth straightened in her chair.

"I can't wait," she said tautly.

Sibben selected a sheet from the file. He slid it across the desk so that Elizabeth and Stephen could both read it.

"We found your stash," he drawled.

It was a copy of a bank statement in the name of Elizabeth Purdin. The current balance was $450,000.

"If I'd known drawing Christmas cards was so lucrative, Miss Purdin, I'd have listened a little more closely to my art teachers in school. But then again, what do I know? Maybe the money came from some-where else. Care to comment?"

Elizabeth glanced at Stephen. She didn't know what she read in his eyes, but it wasn't accusation.

She knew what accusation looked like. She managed a faint smile.

"Now I see why you don't want a divorce."

His lips twitched.

"No, you don't," he denied. And then to Sibben, "Do you have the signature on this account?"

"Sure do." Sibben slid it across as well.

"You stay busy, Detective," Elizabeth observed dryly. "While investigating me, did you also find my account at Bank One? You might have noticed a little discrepancy with this."

"I did, as a matter of fact. Something like $2500, $2600 in it." He leaned toward Elizabeth and said nastily, "You really should try to put a little something aside every paycheck, Miss Purdin. Plan for a rainy day."

Elizabeth tossed the sheets of paper back across the desk.

"This isn't mine."

"It's your signature."

"It's very close. But it's not mine."

"Oh, come off it, Miss Purdin. It's your name, it's your signature, it's your money. Why deny it?"

"Because it's the truth? Or is that passé?"

Stephen leaned forward.

"Freeze the account, Sibben. Whatever they're playing at, they need that money. Someone is going to feel it. They may get careless."

"You act like it's not her money, Kenwood. It has to be. It's how she could afford to hire a professional to hit Vanfossen. And why she needed to. It makes sense."

"Where did the money come from? Does the bank claim to have seen Elizabeth? Who signs the deposits? Have there been withdrawals from the account, and how were they transacted?"

Sibben thumbed through the file until he found the papers he wanted.

"The account was transferred from a Portland branch about a month ago. The balance at the time was $400,000. It was done by phone.

"An automatic deposit was made October 9 at a local branch. That to the tune of $50,000."

"There haven't been any withdrawals? How do you explain that, if Elizabeth used the account to hire a killer?"

"I *don't* explain it, Kenwood. She can hardly write him a check, can she? Not that it matters. The point is, she has the money. She has access to *big* money. If some guy's depositing dough in her account, he can just as easily drop her a bundle in cash."

"You've got no proof of any of this."

"Not yet, Kenwood. Not yet. But I will."

"Who made the deposit?" Elizabeth managed. Her throat was dry. "Whose account was the deposit drawn on?"

"It wasn't a 'who.' It was a 'what.' A pharmaceutical company in Portland."

Oh, Lord! She sent Stephen a tortured glance.

"Royce Pharmaceutical?" Stephen asked.

"You got it. The company you both used to work for. The company Ellen Glover worked for. Is that a coincidence, or what?"

"Who signed the check?"

"Your old boss at the company. David Royce."

164

Chapter Eighteen

It was all right. The house *wasn't* haunted. Sam had forgotten or dismissed it in his delight at being home, and there were no ghosts to follow Elizabeth from room to room. It might never have happened.

Elizabeth went into the backyard with Sam and threw the tennis ball for him. The sun was just beginning to set, and long shadows fell across the brown grass and the few hardy iris stalks along the fence.

A car drew up on the street, and although Elizabeth couldn't see it, she knew the sound of the engine. She told Sam to wait, and went in and opened the front door just as the chimes of the doorbell rang.

"Hello, Constance."

"I know I'm early," Constance apologized quickly. "I thought about calling to ask if it was okay, but then I chickened out. I was afraid you'd say no. We need to talk, Elizabeth."

"I know." Elizabeth stepped back and Constance came into the room. She closed the door, but she didn't lock it. It was not yet night, and she wasn't going to be spooked and paranoid and driven to hide behind drawn drapes. "Can I get you something to drink? I didn't know what Damon would want, or even if I should have hard liquor on hand. Don't drink and drive, et cetera."

"He's coming with Stephen. But if you didn't have anything to drink, he'd clean out your furniture polish and nail polish remover. It's a little late to try to rehabilitate him." Constance looked around the room. "This is nice. You've done some pretty things with it. I'd still like to help with the decorating, if you want me." Her restless glance settled on Elizabeth, and she said softly, "I've been a bitch about all this, Elizabeth. About you and Stephen. I'd like to say I'm sorry."

Some of the tension went out of Elizabeth. She put down the glass she had been filling with ice.

"I'm sorry too, Con. I shouldn't have hung up on you. It was rude, and I'm sorry. We've been friends too long to fall apart now."

Constance laughed. There was suddenly a sparkle in her lovely blue eyes, and she came across the room and put her arms around Elizabeth and gave her a quick, hard hug.

"God, yes. We do go back. Lies and alibis, that's us. Here, I'll fix my own drink. Are you glad to be home?"

"Very. I hate living in a hotel."

"And what about Sam? I hear he stayed with Stephen. Did that work out?"

"Sam was delighted to see Stephen and, curse his fickle heart, went off without looking back. My feelings were hurt. But now he's just as thrilled to be home. He's an easy-to-please dog."

"Yeah, and you're a sap. I always said so." Constance took her drink and went to stand at the arcadia doors. She tapped the glass where Sam leaned against it, as if he could feel her fingers. "I was way out of line suggesting I knew what Stephen wanted, Elizabeth. I was shocked and hurt to learn that he was married to you, and I spoke out of turn. But that doesn't mean I don't still want him."

"I know," Elizabeth said gently.

"Do you?" Constance turned, her body as tense as a coiled spring. "Do you know how angry I am? You've treated him rotten, Elizabeth. He wouldn't take it for two minutes from anyone else. But you can walk all over him. He just keeps waiting for you to get your head straight. And meanwhile, he defends you and picks up the pieces, and sets you back on your feet. I don't understand it. Why can't it be me?"

Elizabeth shook her head helplessly.

"Why is it *me*?" she asked raggedly. "I've never done anything right. I'm drowning now in mistakes I've made. Oh, Con, I don't want to hurt you. I don't know myself what's going to happen to Stephen and me. This could finish it."

"You just don't see, do you, Elizabeth?" Constance blinked away tears. "You just don't see. It doesn't matter what you do, what happens. You could have murdered that poor guy, murdered Ellen, and he'd still be there for you. He'd defend you. There's nothing I can do against that."

Elizabeth pressed her sleeve to the dampness in her eyes. The sun had gone and cold was beginning to come through the glass where they stood.

"I don't want to lose you, Constance. I need you."

"I know. I've been lost myself." Constance sniffed and took a sip of her drink. "Let's dry our eyes, love.

The ghoul twins would enjoy seeing us at each other's throats. We can't give them the satisfaction."

She meant Damon and Mary, of course, and she was probably right. They should be along any minute, with Stephen driving Damon so he wouldn't run down some luckless pedestrian.

Elizabeth felt wrung out and the evening hadn't even started. She wished she could take an aspirin and go to bed.

"You don't like Mary much, do you, Constance?"

"Yuck. Who does? Her dermatologist husband? I doubt it. He probably married her for her organizational skills. She's hell on polishing the glasses and cutlery, even when we're in one of the nicest restaurant in town. Talk about embarrassing! I was sorry I wore my mink."

Elizabeth hadn't noticed. She had hardly taken her eyes off Damon.

"You're a snob," she said lightly.

"Oh, God, I hope so! I do my best. If I ever go Howard Hughes like her, shoot me. She's one paranoid, pathological cookie, our Mary Prill."

"She's not that bad. A little obsessive-compulsive. Aren't we all?"

"Speak for yourself, kiddo. Do you know she folds her tissues into little squares and puts them in a plastic sandwich bag before they go into her pocket? Tell me you do that."

"Maybe she thinks she'll catch something sitting by Damon."

Constance's beautiful golden head went back and the laughter bubbled from her lips.

"Elizabeth, you're worse than I am!"

"He *does* look ill."

"Christ, wouldn't you? Heroin and gin. Or heroin and muscatel, depending on his circumstances at the moment. He never eats . . . can you imagine what his liver looks like?

"I see car lights. It's got to be them. How lucky can we get?" Constance went to the bar and topped off her drink. "I'll play bartender, if you don't mind. I'm going to need something to occupy me as this lovely evening unwinds."

"You're welcome to it," Elizabeth said, and went to the door. She stood in the doorway and watched Damon and Mary and Stephen come up the walk.

Everyone's here, she thought. Everyone. And one is a murderer.

"Where's the booze?" Damon demanded. He made a face at Elizabeth and went past her to where Constance stood. "Well, well. Look who's drinking like a sailor. Stir me up something, Con."

His rough dark-blond hair was wild, and he wore a lightweight shirt, as if he didn't notice the chill in the night air. He looked around the room with interest. "This is it, huh? Right where the body dropped?"

"Shut up, Damon," Mary said sharply. Her face was white and pinched, emphasizing the long, unattractive line of her jaw. "We just heard on the car radio, Elizabeth. The police have found a body in Roosevelt Lake. They're working on the identification."

Elizabeth's eyes went to Stephen. She felt like Mary looked. Scared, and without the wind to run.

"Don't look so stricken, Elizabeth," Damon drawled. "You can hardly be surprised."

"Excuse me. Constance, will you be hostess? I've got to make a phone call." Elizabeth went into the

169

kitchen and let the door swing shut. She had to call Sibben, she had to know if it was Keith.

She fumbled with the phone book. She couldn't find the number. Her fingers were trembling and she felt ill.

Sibben might have given her his number. Her purse was in the bedroom, but not her keys. Her keys were in her pocket.

Stephen came up behind her. He reached across her and dropped Sibben's card onto the counter. He was still wearing his overcoat. She could see the sleeve and smell the cool evening air on him, and perhaps a whisper of Damon's cigarette smoke.

"It isn't Keith," she said raggedly. "It can't be. Sibben would have called."

"Do you want me to call him?"

"No. Thanks. I'm fine." And then, "Do you think it's Keith?"

"Yes."

Elizabeth took a deep, shuddering breath. She could hear the other three arguing in the living room.

"I'd better find out." This was steadier. She turned around and looked up at Stephen. He looked like he could weather anything. "Is Sibben going to want to talk to me tonight?"

"He'll want to talk to all of us."

"Only those who knew Keith."

Stephen tilted his head. It was the slightest gesture toward the other room, where the others waited, or waged war, but it spoke volumes.

"Ask them," he said.

Elizabeth shivered. She picked up the phone and dialed, and when the dispatcher answered, she asked for Detective Sibben. He was going to have to work

170

all hours for her to reach him now, but apparently he did. He came on the line.

"Sibben here."

"Yes, it . . . it's Elizabeth Purdin. The news reported a body was found. Has it been identified?"

"Now, that's a funny thing. I was just thinking about calling you. Yeah, it's him, all right. Vanfossen. The little fishies made a mess of him, but not mess enough. It's a positive ID."

Elizabeth closed her eyes. She pressed her fingers to her lips to keep from making some sound, a protest. She hated Sibben in that moment.

"You there, Miss Purdin? He was a mess, okay? But it was obvious what killed him. Just like your college pal, your roommate? His throat had been cut."

Elizabeth wasn't going to give him the satisfaction of breaking down. She said coldly, "Next you'll be ordering me not to leave town."

"You got it. You see that you're nice and handy when I come looking for you."

"I'm not going anywhere," she clipped. She dropped the phone into the cradle.

"It's Keith," she managed. "His throat had been cut."

Stephen put his hands on her shoulders and she leaned against him. Her mind was reeling. She had to think. She had to go back out there with these people who were her friends, *had* been her friends. She had to consider every word before she said it, and still hear everything both spoken and unspoken around her.

"I hear Sam singing for you," she said at last.

"Do you? I hear Damon getting drunker."

"That too. He doesn't drive, does he?"

"I don't know. I hope not. Why?"

"He could hardly have called a cab to help him take Keith's body away. If it *was* Damon."

"Mary claims he's not always as stoned as he would have us think. It's hard to recognize the college whiz kid when you look at him now, isn't it?"

"But he's there," Elizabeth said tautly. "He's watching every one of us, and he's not missing a thing. This is all some kind of a logic game to him. Half the time I'm certain that he set it up like this. The other half I'm convinced he's just grasping at straws like the rest of us."

"That's rich," Damon drawled. He held the door open with one hand, and there was no guessing how long he'd been standing there. "When it was *you,* Elizabeth, who killed Ellen. I saw you do it."

Chapter Nineteen

It froze them. Five seconds, ten. And then Mary said furiously into the well of silence, "Damon, you ass! Do you know what you're doing? You're shattering your own alibi!"

"Another country heard from," Damon mocked. "What am I supposed to need an alibi for, Mary dear, if they hang the murder on Elizabeth?"

"You don't know *where* Elizabeth was! None of us does. But you're stupider than I think you are if you claim you saw her with Ellen. All Elizabeth needs to do is give the police a story they buy, and guess who's left with good old Ellen? You, you staggering fool!"

"Ouch! Mary, Mary, this all seems to be getting under your skin. About to go crackers, are we?"

"*I'm* not. Take a good look at yourself."

"A little nervous about them finding Vanfossen's body, Mary?" Damon taunted. "Wondering when the police are going to start wanting to know where *you* were the night he died?"

"Don't worry about me," Mary said grimly. "*I* didn't kill him."

"Do the police know that?"

"We don't know that it *is* Keith Vanfossen," Constance cut in. "Maybe you two could shut up long enough for us to find out. Elizabeth?"

"Yes," Elizabeth said softly. "It was Keith."

"Oh, God!" Mary wrenched out.

Constance went across to the bar. She stood looking down at the various bottles as if she had never seen them before. After a moment she tossed over her shoulder with her customary edge, "What's it to you, Mary? Do you see this as your chance to win an Oscar, or are you admitting, ever-so-carelessly, that you knew the guy?"

"I didn't sleep with him," Mary spat. "You can't claim the same distinction."

Constance laughed.

"Jealous, Mary? But just as a matter of record, I didn't sleep with him, either. What a waste. He was just my type."

"God, Constance! You make me sick! You're worse than Damon. He can claim inebriation, at least." Mary sat down heavily on the sofa. Her lips were twitching.

"We all knew him," Damon said. He joined Mary on the sofa, stretching his legs and propping his feet on the coffee table. His shoes were surprisingly expensive calfskin. "He's been dogging us forever."

"Speak for yourself," Constance demurred. "I never saw the man before he came by my place looking for Elizabeth. Disappointing, Mary, but that's the extent of my carnal knowledge of him."

"Change the face. You can't remember all the men you've slept with," Mary snapped.

"Now I *know* you're jealous. Worried about your dear boring husband? I'll put you out of your misery.

174

I don't bother with men old enough to be my father."

Mary gasped and went white with rage.

"You pretentious bitch! You're no better than Ellen! And look what she got!"

"Are you threatening me, Mary dear?" Constance purred. "Who would think a little mouse like you would have such a nasty temper? You look like you might just hurt someone if you had the chance. I had better watch my back, hadn't I?"

"Maybe you had," Mary gritted. She fought to control her ragged breathing, her fury. "In case you haven't noticed, it doesn't pay to know too much. And you consider yourself such a bright, clever girl. Maybe you *had* best watch your back."

"Cat fight!" Damon jeered. "We've got a live one! Drag up your chairs, but mind the blood spattering!" He looked around at Elizabeth, and his face was alight with the same kind of manic excitement he had demonstrated at the restaurant when they learned about Ellen. "Apologies, and all of that, Libby, my love. I wouldn't want to be in bad taste here."

"Don't be such a bore, Damon," Constance adjured him. She took a chair and leaned back, crossing her long legs. "Lord, don't you just love these friendly little get-togethers? It makes me wonder how we ever took the chance of losing touch."

"What chance? Damon was manipulating us every minute. He knew where we were. And you can bet there was never a moment when he considered giving up his little game of cat-and-mouse. Calling me at work, scaring my babysitter, taunting me that he was going to show up when James was home."

"Poor Mary," Damon jeered. "You don't get it,

do you? You were closer to the truth when you were making the same wild accusations about Elizabeth.

"Elizabeth is the mainspring here. She's the pivot. She sits here without saying a word, and she waits to see what we're going to say, and she already knows what we're trying to figure out."

"Sure," Constance said coldly. "Because she killed Ellen. You saw it. You're a broken record, Damon."

"Yeah. I was getting somewhere with that until Mary flew into hysterics. Why do you think Elizabeth wrote us a message in Vanfossen's blood? Because she knows what's going on here, that's why. She sent for us."

"Somebody play me a few bars of the theme from *Twilight Zone*. Damon is sliding into another dimension."

"Cute, Constance. Almost as cute as you hiring Vanfossen to gumshoe around and dig into our personal lives. It had to be you. It showed your distinctive touch of class."

Constance's laugh was laced with contempt.

"Sorry," she said. "You'll have to look elsewhere for your class. But something does occur to me. You're systematically attacking each one of us. I guess Stephen will be next, and then you can start on the phone book. Do me a favor and skip the L's. I'm already sick of you."

"You don't think Stephen's involved in this?" Damon grinned, the skin of his face stretching taut across his bones like a death's-head as he looked from Constance to Stephen. "Stephen is up to his neck in the cover-up at Royce Pharmaceuticals. The little matter of David Royce tampering with drugs in his lab, and half a dozen senile old fools turning up unexpectedly dead.

"I've often thought about it. The big money must have been relieved to have someone of Stephen's caliber there to sweep things under the rug for them. Too bad we didn't have that kind of pull with the backhoe man who ran across Ellen's body."

Elizabeth came around the sofa and looked down at Damon. Her arms were clasped around her body, and she looked fragile with strain. Leaning toward him, she gritted, "Is that what you think this is all about? That people are being murdered over a seven-year-old drug-tampering charge against a dead man?"

Damon's thin body straightened. He looked cold sober now.

"You tell me, Elizabeth. Is it?"

Elizabeth didn't retort for long seconds. She put a hand to her temple where the dark hair curled damply, and her fingers trembled. Stephen must think she'd lost her mind.

"It's about Ellen's baby," she said grimly.

"Ellen's *baby?*" Mary echoed. She sounded stunned, like a person with a chasm opening at her feet.

"I took the baby," Elizabeth said.

They all stared at her. Perhaps they couldn't believe she was admitting it after all this time. Or perhaps they hadn't known. All of them but one.

Constance tossed off the last of her drink. She looked strangely at Elizabeth.

"Because it was Stephen's?"

Elizabeth's glance touched Stephen's, a flicker.

"It wasn't," she denied.

"You did *what?* Are you saying you kidnapped a child, Elizabeth? That's a serious crime."

Elizabeth ignored Mary. She was frozen, she was carved from marble or from granite, something cold. She looked at Damon.

"Okay," Damon said. A tumbler fell into place in the lock in his mind, the final tumbler. "Okay!"

"Elizabeth, for God's sake!" Constance said sharply. She came close and put a hand on Elizabeth's shoulder. She gave her a small, tense shake. "Listen to yourself, love. You may be admitting to something that you'll wish you hadn't. Kidnapping is a federal offense. You wouldn't want Sibben to get hold of anything like this."

"It wasn't Stephen's baby," Elizabeth said again. "But I thought it was."

"What are you saying? That you killed it? That you killed a baby?" Mary's voice rose to the verge of hysteria.

Damon laughed. It was a thin, chilling sound, almost as high as a wheeze. His face contorted in some caricature of amusement.

"Mary, you stupid cow! Don't you get it? She didn't kill the baby! She hid it. Right, Elizabeth?"

Elizabeth nodded.

The tension went out of her, flowed through her fingertips, her flesh. She looked at Mary, hunched defensively in the corner of the sofa, Constance standing tautly, Damon tensed on the edge of the sofa like a wild animal. And at Stephen.

He met her eyes with the same dark, unreadable glance that she had never understood.

"So where *is* the baby?" Mary demanded.

"Don't you just wish you knew, Mary, my dear?

Either you're too dense to catch on or too clever to admit it." Damon shook his head and laughed without sound. "Who did Vanfossen begin investigating first, Mary? It was you. I find *that* interesting."

"How do we know he went after her first?" Constance said. "Because you say so? I'd as soon believe Mary as you, Damon, and that's not saying much."

"You're a born charmer, Constance," Damon mocked. "And you're right, you *don't* know. *I* don't know. But he went after Mary before me. It was only a few months ago I met him."

"Then I win," Mary said bitterly. "Because it's been a year, close to it, since he began hanging around. I thought at first he was investigating the doctors I work for. My luck."

"How about you, Stephen? You must have been checked out too."

"I never met Vanfossen," Stephen retorted. "But he came to the company in Denver where I was working six or eight months ago. He claimed to be an insurance adjustor for the company, and tried to get access to personnel files."

Damon laughed beneath his breath.

"I admire his instincts. He knew he'd get further with the files than with you. You got to hand it to the guy."

"What was he looking for?" That from Constance.

"Elizabeth, of course," Damon drawled.

"No. He was looking for Ellen's baby."

"Why?" Constance demanded. "Why did someone care what happened to the baby? It certainly wasn't going to say who killed its mother!"

"I imagine you can answer that, Baille," Stephen challenged.

179

"Sure. They want to kill the baby. Or should I say, 'We want to kill the baby'? It's one of us, of course."

"Of course."

"The baby died," Elizabeth said hollowly. "It didn't survive the first few days."

"You're all out of your minds!" Mary shrilled. "Sitting here talking about a poor dead infant that I'm not even convinced existed! Suggesting I would harm a baby! I have two kids of my own! I would never hurt a child!"

"You *say* you have kids. How do we know they aren't laid out in the icebox or something? You don't seem to be in a big hurry to get home," Constance taunted.

"You're sick!" Mary hissed. "Trying to impress the detective with your big talk about going to Portland to comfort Ellen's family! I knew you didn't have any intention of going."

"You know everything, Mary. You should wrap your head in a silk turban and predict how many utensils in how many restaurants you're going to have to polish before your guilty conscience is satisfied. How many charts on how many patients with a rash you're going to have to fill out before James decides he can find someone who does it better."

Mary came off the sofa as if she were thrown. She flew at Constance, her hand raised in a fist. She froze like that, trembling with rage.

"You disgusting tramp! I swear, I could . . ." she stopped herself with an effort.

Constance's laugh tinkled with derision.

"Oh, my! I'm being threatened again. This is almost getting monotonous."

Mary swung violently away. She marched into the bathroom and slammed the door.

"Imagine that," Constance mocked. "Somebody remind me to tell Sibben about Mary's nasty little temper."

"You'll remember, Con," Damon offered dryly.

"You can just bet I will. Who needs a refill besides me?"

"I'll get it." Damon took Constance's glass and went to the bar. "What are you drinking?"

"Oh, I think I'll try a rum-and-Coke this time. Mary seemed to mellow out on hers. I'll see if it does for me what it did for Mary."

"You're a bitch, Constance," Damon drawled.

"Thanks, Damon. I love you, too." Constance glanced at Stephen and smiled faintly, tautly. "I *do* love you, Stephen. I seem to remember telling you that before. Isn't life hell?" She dropped her glance, tore her eyes away. Elizabeth was close enough to touch and she touched her, she patted her hand. "Don't hate me, Elizabeth. I never had very good manners. And I *did* tell you I still wanted him."

"Your manners *are* bad," Stephen agreed shorty. "Suppose you help Damon mix your drink. Or try to talk Mary out of the bathroom."

"I'll talk to her," Elizabeth said quickly. She started to rise, but Stephen caught her wrist. It was gentle; he didn't hold her with force, but he held her.

"Wait, Libby."

She always would. She'd been waiting since the first time she'd seen Stephen.

"It's always Elizabeth," Constance said bitterly. She went to the bathroom door and pounded on it.

181

"You can come out now, Mary. Nobody cares whether you slit your wrists in there or not. It would be a hell of a waste with no audience." She joined Damon in the dining room.

"Are you all right?" Stephen asked gently.

Elizabeth let out her breath on a sigh.

"Yes," she said. She looked at the strong fingers encircling her wrist and she wished that time would stop right here. "Somebody always gets hurt."

"But it doesn't always have to be you."

She sniffed. She could feel the tears behind her eyes, but she blinked them back.

"I'd rather that it wasn't," she admitted wryly.

"Good." Stephen smiled. "I'd rather it wasn't you, either."

Mary came out of the bathroom. Her lids were swollen and red, but she seemed to have gotten control of herself.

"I've made a decision," she said. "I'm going home."

"Too late, old girl," Damon offered cheerfully. "The police won't let you. They'll want to talk to you about Vanfossen."

"I know. I'll see them first thing in the morning, and then I'll fly home."

Constance laughed.

"Can't play hardball, Mary?"

"No. Not by your rules, Constance. Not by the rules the four of you seem to want to play. You're all as hard as nails. I don't belong here."

Suddenly there was a horrible, deep, menacing growl.

Elizabeth gasped. Sam had come close to the glass

182

doors. His legs were stiff, and the hair on his neck was up. He was the gentlest of a nonaggressive breed, but now he looked through the glass with wolves' eyes.

He looked at Damon.

Chapter Twenty

The house was quiet. Outside the wind blew the bare arms of the mulberry and chinaberry trees in wild abandon, and rustled the dry fronds of the palm against the black of the night sky. But inside the house the wind was just a whisper.

Elizabeth worked in silence. Her fingers flew over the sketch pad. She could count off the minutes of the night by the audible tick of the kitchen clock.

This was the worst. When everyone on the planet slept but Elizabeth. When there was no one to call, no one to talk to, no one to touch. She should be used to it.

The designs blossomed beneath her fingers. Her mind was free to wander, and she went over each word spoken tonight. She struggled with the words that had not been said.

Everyone knew about the baby now. And whether she was confirming a killer's knowledge or shattering a bystander's innocence, there was no way of knowing. Who was shaken and who only pretended to be? She couldn't begin to guess.

There had been no advantage in silence any longer.

She had been forced to act, and she had taken the only route that looked as if it might bear her weight. Ironic that it was almost the truth, after all this time.

Sam had been stretched out sleeping on the cool tile of the kitchen floor, but suddenly he reared up. His head turned toward the front door, and his ears pricked forward as if he had heard something.

Elizabeth felt the hair stir at the nape of her neck.

"Don't start that, Sam Gamgee," she admonished him. "You've behaved strangely enough for one night."

It chilled her just to remember how frightening he had seemed, staring at Damon through the glass of the arcadia doors. He had looked as a dog might when staring at a man whom he had seen commit murder.

Elizabeth shivered and drew her robe more closely about her.

God, it *had* to be Damon. He had to be the madman behind this unending horror. The evil had come to Phoenix with Damon. It had been only a shadow, a waiting presence, until Damon came.

Immediately Keith had died. Immediately. Didn't it make sense that he had urged Mary so persistently to come as well to cloud his own arrival?

No one *knew* that Damon had received a letter. He said he had, he said it was from David Royce, and God knew that was impossible.

Impossible. As impossible as the signature of a dead man on a check for $50,000. The current automobile registration in David's name. The envelope from Royce Pharmaceuticals with clippings about women having their throats cut. Impossible.

Damon had known Ellen was dead. He had known

how she'd died. He had been the last person to talk to Elizabeth in her delirium. God, was there any doubt but that it was his words that had echoed in her head all these years?

He had known that Ellen was pregnant, something Ellen had claimed no one knew. Was he surprised to learn that it was Elizabeth who had taken the infant, or was it part of a game he played? A game that must include the death of the child itself?

Sam leaped to his feet. He struggled for footing on the tile floor, got it, and came around the corner full speed. He slid to an abrupt halt at the front door and stood frozen, every muscle poised, listening.

Elizabeth shivered.

It's the wind, she told herself. Animals are always disturbed by the wind. They can't hear as well when the wind blows, and it distorts their perception. He just hears the wind.

Sam whined softly.

Elizabeth's heart lurched. It's Stephen, she thought. She got up and rushed across to the door. She could hear the wind now. She could hear something that was not the wind: footsteps on the porch.

Elizabeth leaned against the door. She looked down at Sam for confirmation, her fingers upon the lock. Her heart beat in her throat.

The hackles rose on the dog's back. A growl began deep in his chest.

Oh, God! She backed away from the door. She should flip on the outdoor lights, she should call the police. She couldn't move.

He can't get in, she told herself hysterically. He could have a key, a dozen keys, but he couldn't slide the bolt that she had secured from inside.

The doorknob stirred. It didn't turn, the door would have to be unlocked for that, but it moved. A hand rested upon the cold metal and tried the lock.

Sam's growl deepened. He was tensed expectantly. He knew the door would open. He probably knew who would be standing there.

And then he moved, *it* did, the murderer. Elizabeth could follow his slow, deliberate progress along the front of the house by watching Sam's movements. There was a slight rattle at the window.

Elizabeth could imagine the sound of dried leaves crunching underfoot, but she didn't know if she heard them or not. Her heart was pounding too loudly.

He was at her window now, her bedroom. Sam knocked the door back and bounded into the room. He looked up at the draped window as if he were trying to see what was there, what he could hear. Someone trying the lock on the window.

There was nothing else.

Elizabeth had been wondering about the backyard. He would have to go over the high wooden fence to check the windows and doors in the back of the house, and she had wondered if she would be able to shake loose from her paralysis by then and hit the switch that would flood the yard with light. But she wasn't going to find out now. He was gone.

Sam continued to listen for long minutes. Finally he went back into the kitchen and flung himself down, but he didn't sleep. He kept his eyes on the front door.

Elizabeth was trembling violently, as if the chill wind outdoors blew across her unprotected flesh.

Now, too late, she mustered the strength to pick up the phone.

She had thought it was Stephen. At 2:30 in the morning, alone and witless, she had almost opened the door to a murderer. She had been that close. That close to death.

Perhaps she was overreacting. She took a deep breath and let it out slowly, struggling for steadiness.

She hadn't believed she was in danger as long as she had information the killer wanted. But what if she no longer had?

She remembered Grace Royce's call. Grace had thought she was being watched. What if it *had* been the killer? What if it was already over? Everything but Elizabeth's death.

"Police department."

"I heard someone outside my house . . ." The police must get a hundred calls like this a night. Lonely, frightened people, nervous insomniacs anxious for the sound of another voice. She was wasting their time. "I'm sorry. I probably should call Security. Thank you." She hung up.

She knew why she hadn't turned on the outside lights. She'd told Stephen they looked like an athletic field, and they did. They would have lit up the shrubs and the yard and exposed her to the eyes of a murderer when she drew back the drapes to look. It would have let the killer in. Violated the cocoon of safety that was only as good as her security system. And the last time it had failed.

The telephone rang.

Elizabeth jumped violently, feeling the shock of the sudden, piercing scream upon the silence. Sam looked at her. He got up and went to listen at the front door again.

The last time the phone had rung in the middle of the night it had been Keith. The night she had told him she was leaving the condominium they shared. And Keith was dead.

The telephone continued to shrill. Elizabeth got up slowly, gathering herself, and went in to take it in the kitchen. She wondered how long it would go on ringing if she didn't pick it up. She knew she was making a mistake to lift the receiver.

"Hello?" she managed.

"Hello, Elizabeth." Damon laughed, a kind of muted, mad sound, as if he knew he had scared her and was pleased. "Surprised to hear from me?"

"Not exactly." She let out her breath on a ragged sigh. "But most people would consider the hour in bad taste, don't you think?"

"But you're not most people, Libby, my dear. I knew you wouldn't be asleep. I'm right, aren't I?"

They all knew she slept little, but this sounded sinister. As if he had seen the lights on inside while he prowled about in the shadows.

"Were you outside my house tonight?"

"As a matter of fact, I wasn't. Boogeyman out there?"

"Someone. I thought it was you."

There was a pause. When Damon spoke, his voice was harsh and deadly serious.

"Don't open the door, Elizabeth. It's something more terrible than you can imagine."

A shudder ran down Elizabeth's spine.

"What do you want, Damon?"

"I know who it is," he said flatly.

189

"You know . . . you know who the murderer is?"

"Yes."

Elizabeth pressed her fingers tremulously to her lips. She managed, "You know who killed Keith?"

"Yeah. And Ellen. Both of them."

Her heart pounded so loudly in her ears she could hardly hear him over it. She had to concentrate, to lean toward every word.

"Tell me," she whispered.

"Why?"

Oh, God, he was only playing games again. She had dared think he was going to tell her . . . what? That he had done it?

"Goodnight, Damon," she said with finality. She reached to cradle the phone.

"Wait!" Damon cried. "Don't hang up, damn it! Are you there, Elizabeth?"

"I'm here."

"Okay, listen. I've figured it out. Most of it. I didn't know you took the baby. It answered a lot of questions."

He sounded like he meant what he was saying. He sounded for the moment like Damon Baille, the mathematical genius, moving chess pieces across the board with the audacity and skill that had once been his trademark.

"I'm listening."

"You've got to do more than listen. You've got to level with me on a couple of things. I want the whole picture."

Elizabeth stirred. This was madness. He was mad. She was encouraging his wild, drugged flight from reality.

"Damon, are you sober? No, I mean it. If I'm

190

going to hear you out, I've got to know if you're so stoned you can't stand up, or if you know what you're saying."

Damon laughed.

"I'm off of H. I went through a rehab program a few months ago. Now, if you want to know about me and old Jim Beam, that's another story. Knowing half of what is going on is plenty for me."

That sounded straight. Mary had suggested he wasn't as strung out as he pretended to be.

"All right," Elizabeth said. "I can't promise I'll tell you what you want to know. But I'll hear you out."

"That's confidence-inspiring. No soppy stuff about how proud you are and all that crap?"

"Sorry. I'm a cynic. You'll go back on it as soon as you have the money. Liquor is cheaper."

Damon chuckled.

"No flies on you, love. I always said you were the hardest of the lot. And you're going to need to be. This isn't over. Not by a long shot."

"Why don't you just tell me who you think it is?"

"Who I *know* it is, Elizabeth."

"All right. Tell me."

"You've got to meet me somewhere. We've got to talk."

"You *don't* know."

"Hell's bells, woman! I know who it is! You said you would listen. I want you to meet me at my place. It's a dump, but so what? It's the Aloha Apartments, and I'm in number three. At 3842 N. Woodbine. Got it?"

"Sorry."

"What? You won't come?"

"You got that right. I'm supposed to meet a crazy

man in a dump at three in the morning? You're kidding. In the bright light of day I wouldn't trust you as far as I could throw you."

"Take it or leave it."

"I'll leave it, thanks," Elizabeth said. She started to put down the phone again.

"Okay, okay, Don't hang up. Hear me out. We have to meet, but some of this I guess we can discuss on the phone. I don't care for the idea that somebody could listen in."

That was the Damon she knew—paranoid.

"I have a private line."

"Yeah, this one is, too. Okay, listen up." He paused; perhaps he was considering what he would say. Perhaps he was casting a glance over his shoulder to see that no one was there. "Do you know about any big money changing hands? It wouldn't necessarily have to be a safe deposit box. It could be right out in the open. A bank, a savings-and-loan. Do you know of anything like that?"

Elizabeth leaned against the kitchen cabinet. Something was happening here. This wasn't a drunken lunatic trying to scare her. This was a computer at work.

"Yes," she said finally.

"Okay! Now we're cooking! Give me the details."

"The police came across an account in a local bank when they were investigating me. It's in my name. The ID card contains facts pertinent to my birth, etc. The signature is very close to mine."

"Beautiful! Big money?"

"Very big—$450,000."

Damon chortled.

"I knew it! I knew it! Where's the money coming from?"

"The last deposit was signed by David."

"Christ!" Damon breathed. "That gets you, doesn't it? But it makes sense. It was off the Royce Pharmaceuticals account?"

Elizabeth couldn't pretend to follow the racing of his mind. She nodded her head slightly, and said, "That's right."

"Okay. I got it. The company's gone belly up, we know that. With David dead but no body to prove it, everything is in receivership until the waiting period is over. Yeah, it'd work."

"Wait a minute, Damon. We know David is dead. We know the company was liquidated, dismantled, dissolved. Even if David were alive there would be no account to write checks on. This makes no sense."

"Sure, it does. Now, the second question. You're not going to like this one, Elizabeth."

"I'm sure you're right," Elizabeth said dryly. "I told you I may not answer."

"Yeah." His voice lowered, the words seemed to hiss along the wires. "What did you do with the knife?"

Chapter Twenty-one

Elizabeth froze. The soft hairs on the back of her neck stirred as if a cold wind blew through the house.

"Did you lose it?" she asked.

"Oh, hell, Elizabeth, let up! Quit jumping at your own shadow. I didn't waste the guy. Neither did you. It seems like we could put our heads together on this."

"You seem to know *I* didn't do it. I don't know the same about you, Damon. How do you know there *was* a knife?"

He hesitated a moment.

"I *don't* know," he admitted. "But it figures. It adds up."

"No, it doesn't. God, you scare me, Damon."

He laughed thinly.

"I'm flattered, Elizabeth. I really am. I'd have to say there aren't many people who can scare you."

"It wasn't a compliment," she said bitterly.

"Elizabeth? Tell me about the knife."

"What makes you think I know?"

"I told you," he said impatiently. "It's logical."

Maybe it was. Something had to be. And he

couldn't harm her through a telephone wire. She fed one more bit of information into the computer.

"The knife was on the floor when I came in."

"Yes! Good girl! Whose knife was it?"

"I don't know."

"You don't know? You took it and threw it in the river for no reason? The police don't know about it. That means you got rid of it."

Elizabeth smiled faintly. She ran the sleeve of her robe across her damp forehead.

"That's an Oregon native talking. Do you know how far it is between rivers in Phoenix? And the canals are cement. Anything that goes in will show up when it's drained."

"Okay, you didn't chuck it in the river. You *did* take it. Why? Because you knew whose it was. And you didn't want the police to know."

"It wasn't Stephen's," she denied flatly.

"Yeah, that's where we're heading. Who else would you take that kind of a risk for? You thought it was his, but then you decided it wasn't. What changed your mind?"

What *had* changed her mind? Elizabeth gave her head a slight shake. Distrusting Stephen, fearing Stephen, left her with nothing. Nothing to fight with, nothing to feel. She had known, standing in the cold morning air outside the police station, that if Stephen was the killer, then she was already lost. She was going to break. She was going to die.

Maybe she should tell Damon that it was because Stephen had said the knife wasn't his. Damon would laugh over that. He would enjoy the image of her, as insipid as Mary, waiting to be told what to think.

"You have to believe in someone," she said at last.

"You had better watch yourself, Elizabeth. You're breaking your own number-one rule."

"What rule is that?"

"Don't trust anybody."

He was right. But he was wrong.

"Are you saying that Stephen murdered Keith?"

"What if I am? Would you believe me?"

"No."

"Sure," he said sharply. "You'd rather believe it was me."

"You cared about Ellen."

"Yeah. And Stephen cares about you. That makes you about as safe as Ellen was, doesn't it?"

"Damon?"

"Yeah?"

"How did you know Ellen was dead?"

There was a silence. Perhaps he was considering his retort. Perhaps he wasn't going to answer at all. Finally he said, "You told me."

"When I was in Intensive Care?"

"When else? You don't go around blabbing your secrets to the world, in case you haven't noticed."

"That's why you said you saw me kill her? Because you believed that I had?"

"Nothing else made sense. I came all the way from my cozy little Portland slum to see you hang. No, that's passé, isn't it? I think it's lethal injection now in Arizona. But you get the picture. I was anticipating some long-delayed vengeance. Let's make that 'justice.' It sounds nobler."

Elizabeth shuddered. There was no mistaking the bitterness, the pain. He wasn't playing games now. Elizabeth could almost believe in his innocence.

"Why did you change your mind?"

He laughed raggedly.

"It's as basic as learning that you didn't do it. I told you I know who the killer is."

"Tell me."

"Describe the knife to me."

She might as well. Perhaps she was learning as much as he was. If he was getting a glimpse into her mind, she was seeing into his as well.

"It's a lock-blade," she said succinctly. "Three inches long closed, twice that when the blade is open. The handle is a pale beige, with a grain running through it. Deer antler, probably."

"Yeah," Damon breathed. "And the blade says 'India' on it."

Elizabeth shivered.

"Yes," she agreed. "India."

"Royce Chemical Conglomerate gave out a few of them one year to the favored employees. Not Royce Pharmaceuticals. I'm talking the mother company. Gave them to all the fair-haired boys. I guess that's where Kenwood came by his. He worked for Royce Chem more than he worked with us at David's. He's still with them, isn't he?"

"No. He's with Execucon."

"Whatever. It's not pertinent."

That was Damon's gauge of things. Its relevance to whatever consumed him at the moment.

"Do you think the murderer left the knife deliberately?"

"You got me there. Maybe. But I have to go with it being accidental. Overlooked in the chore of getting the body out of the house."

It made a picture, a terrible picture, but not one she hadn't already confronted a thousand times.

197

"Tell me who it is, Damon."

"Meet me."

"You must think I'm crazy."

He laughed.

"Not crazy. Canny. You know you can't protect the kid if you don't know who will strike the blow."

"I told you, the baby died."

"That's the story. But it won't hold water. Every step you've taken since the night the baby was born has been with its safety in mind. Christ! Look what it's done to you. Cost you a marriage. Turned your blood to ice water. Because there *is* ice in your veins, Elizabeth. You're standing not ten feet from where a man's throat was cut, and you're not turning a hair. Every day of your life you're watched, you're followed, you're threatened in a very real sense. And you know it. You've always known it. And you don't blink an eye. I wouldn't take you on in a game of poker if I held four aces. Tell me you don't know what I'm talking about."

The stiffening had gone out of Elizabeth's knees. She slid down the cabinets until she sat upon the cold tile floor.

"Damon," she said raggedly. "You know too much. The more you know, the more you frighten me."

"But you'll meet me."

"No."

Damon cursed under his breath.

"Okay, don't come to my place. There's got to be some well-lit, confidence-inspiring all-night laundromat where we could meet at this hour."

"What about the police station?" she taunted.

198

"Ha! Forget it! They'd roust me for the color of my socks. No way."

"All right," Elizabeth said with resignation. She was a fool, she *was* crazy. "There's a Safeway on 40th. It's open all night. There's a small cafeteria and the coffee's hot."

"Sure. And the lights are bright and there are employees everywhere keeping an eye out for unsavory types like yours truly. I'll be there in half an hour. Oh, and Elizabeth? One other thing."

"Yes?"

"You couldn't happen to get your hands on a few of those bills in your phony account, could you?"

"That's all I need. The police would love that."

"They couldn't do anything about it."

"You must be joking. First off, it's not mine. Second, it's illegally obtained."

"Who is going to complain? The murderer, using your name? Or the guy paying in the money? People who are being blackmailed don't talk about it, love. That's the beauty of the thing."

Blackmailed. Elizabeth drew her knees to herself, wrapped her arms around them. Blackmailed.

"No, Damon," she said tiredly. She *was* tired. "I don't have the access codes. I guess you'll have to earn a living the usual way."

"That's a woman for you. Make them a few promises and they start nagging you to get a job."

"Half an hour, Damon."

"Yeah. Half an hour. You have a gun?"

If she said yes, he'd laugh. If she said no, he'd know she was defenseless.

"Why?"

He laughed anyway.

199

"That's what I mean. Wary. If you're scared now, it's nothing to what you're going to be. Don't be late, Elizabeth. I hate to be kept waiting." He hung up.

Elizabeth looked at the phone. She slowly became aware of how cold the floor was. She got up stiffly, and put the receiver back on the hook.

She stood a moment and then picked up the phone again. She dialed Stephen's number.

It rang on empty air. Fifteen times, twenty. Elizabeth looked at the clock. She shivered.

She turned on the outside lights, the one in the garage where her car was. She had to get dressed. Wear something warm against the windy night chill. She took a moment to lift the curtain and look out.

Sam watched her, but he didn't stir from his place by the door. There was nothing for him to hear.

Leaves tumbled and spun on the dry front lawn and ran across the cement driveway. They had piled up against the closed garage door, and it looked undisturbed. Trees lashed in the wind, but the light chased the monsters away.

She was almost to turn away when she saw something fluttering from the mailbox. The wind tugged and tossed it, but it held fast in the grip of the latch.

It hadn't been there when she'd come in this evening. She had collected the mail then. It hadn't been there when she was saying goodnight to Damon and Constance and Stephen. Goodbye to Mary.

It was twenty yards away along the street. Perhaps she was mistaken. Perhaps it wasn't the pale blue shade of an envelope from Royce Pharmaceuticals. And perhaps, please, Lord, the murderer hadn't put it there as he paced outside her house, trying the doors and the windows.

Elizabeth let the curtain fall.

"You're going to wait here, Sam."

The dog was the lucky one, the smart one. She was the fool, going out alone into that wild, terrifying night.

Elizabeth dressed hastily. The thick coil of her hair was beginning to come down, and the wind was sure to finish it, but she didn't dare take the time to rebraid it. She had to see what was in the letter, she had to get to the Safeway before Damon did. She had to have the advantage of choosing the safest table. She shivered at the thought of walking across the parking lot of deserted cars where Damon could be waiting for her.

Elizabeth flung on her coat and took a minute to dial Stephen's number again. It rang on silence.

The light was on in the garage. Elizabeth looked through the peephole in the door to see that no one was there, that her car was empty. She took a deep breath and opened the bolt.

Nothing sprang at her. There were no shadows in which anyone might hide. She got into her car and locked the doors behind her. She wasn't brave tonight. She was running for her life.

She opened the garage door with the remote and backed out. She turned at the street and continued backing until she was alongside the mailbox. She rolled down the window.

She hadn't been mistaken. The letter didn't say "Libby Purdin" this time. It said "Libby Kenwood." It was someone who had sat at the table in the restaurant and heard Detective Sibben challenge her name.

Elizabeth's fingers trembled. She looked along the street. She couldn't seem to stop searching for a blacker shadow among the dark, bobbing shapes cast by the trees.

There was one more house after hers on the dead-end street. She wondered what they must think of her. Bringing death to their quiet, secure neighborhood. Turning on enough lights in the middle of the night to make them protest to City Hall.

Elizabeth looked again at the envelope. Perhaps she should take it to the police station. She might have time before she had to meet Damon. They could analyze it, x-ray it, whatever they did. They might be able to turn up something.

But in that case, she wouldn't have access to the contents. Not now, immediately, and it might be nothing but a threat, but it might be more. It might tell her something that she had to know to survive. A glimpse into the most deadly of minds.

Elizabeth tore open the envelope.

It was a clipping, as before, but it was yellowed with age.

Tonopah, Nev. Police here have reported the discovery of the body of a newborn infant. There are no leads as to the identity of the child. The cause of death has not been determined.

Elizabeth bit her lip. She folded back the brief clipping and looked at the photostatic copy stapled behind it. The letterhead was from the office of the medical examiner of that Nevada county.

Tonopah, Nev. Dec. 12, 1984. The recent news-paper account of the discovery of the body of an infant in this county is unsubstantiated and

202

without basis in fact. The conclusion of this office and of the police department is that no such body exists.

Elizabeth smoothed the sheets of paper beneath her trembling fingers. She folded them back into the envelope, and drew the car jerkily away from the curb.

They knew the child was alive. The killer knew. There was no mistaking it now. She *had* to talk to Damon.

Even if he was the killer.

Chapter Twenty-two

December, 1986

Sometimes Elizabeth was alone in the small, drab motel room. Sometimes Ellen was there with a razor blade, slashing at Elizabeth's face, struggling to wrest the baby from her arms. Or Stephen. Or Grace Royce, trying to talk to her, the roaring in her head so loud she couldn't make out the words. Sometimes the baby-killer was there.

Elizabeth had traveled by bus for three days. Three days and nights. She was in Nevada now, and she had to keep going. The baby's life could depend upon it.

By Reno, Elizabeth knew she was ill. Very ill. She found a motel somewhere in the outskirts of the city; she didn't know how. She told herself she would rest and then go on, but in actuality, she barely made it home. She could have died there.

She couldn't recall when she'd first become ill. There were fields there, stretching forever. It was as if she sat unmoving, and the same scene was unfolded around her time and again, like the background in a child's cartoon.

It was just as well, because she could scarcely move. Her arms and legs felt like lead and her head was light. She was going to have to remember to eat more often, and to try to sleep while the bus shuddered its way across the unending miles.

She had left the infant with Grace Royce. She couldn't regret it. The Royces would give the child all the love and security that he'd never have found otherwise. But sometimes Elizabeth put her arms around her body where the baby had rested and there was a hollowness there, as if she had lost something vital. Her head ached.

She didn't know, couldn't even imagine, where all this was taking Grace Royce. Through hell, perhaps.

Grace had believed in the danger to the baby. She was afraid not to. Between the threat to the infant and her own fear that a flawed adoption could jeopardize her claim on him in the future, she had before her a monumental task: creating on paper an infant who existed only in the flesh.

Without the Royces' political and financial influence, Elizabeth doubted it could be done. It would take a rich man to buy a child's safety, the contrived birth certificate, the doctor's oath. And a biological family, if it came to that.

The Royces had powerful connections. They could get things done. They were accomplishing the impossible now.

Grace Royce was.

She had undertaken the task while her husband was still in Albany on business. As the head of Royce Chemical, one of the largest chemical-manufacturing plants in the country, Royce was often away from home. But the timing now was perfect. Randolph and his team of lawyers would test the fabric of the child's safety net.

Elizabeth pressed fingers to her hot, aching forehead and tried to think. She tried to follow in her mind the path Grace and the infant, accompanied by the nurse, would be taking as Grace had described it. Had anticipated it to be.

Elizabeth didn't know where their route would lead. Away from Nevada, that was certain, that was what she was doing here. Creating a blind trail. Lying on a sagging mattress somewhere in Nevada, too ill to lift her head, while perhaps behind her a killer retraced her steps. At times it was more than she could do to remember why.

Grace had left town with the infant the same night as Elizabeth had stepped on the bus. She was creating the existence of an adoptable infant as far from Portland as the fingers of her influence could reach. She couldn't risk that a killer might link her tiny new son to Portland, to Ellen Glover, to Elizabeth Purdin.

The room smelled musty and dank, but Elizabeth didn't notice. She was too hot, but the blankets at times weren't warm enough to keep out the chill. And the visitors never stopped. Or rarely stopped. Perhaps there were moments when she slept quietly. Or perhaps they were dreams, not delirium. It didn't matter.

Stephen was silent. She didn't know what went on behind his dark, quiet eyes. She never had known. She couldn't see deception there. She couldn't see lies.

He didn't look away. Elizabeth tried to call him

closer, talk to him, but when she would reach out, he would fade away. Her fingers closed on air.

Ellen slashed her with the razor. Sometimes it would bite deep into her chest, and she would wake coughing. And even then Ellen would mock her, threaten her. Ellen would ask over and over where the baby was, and she would wander around the room looking for him. Or she would ask about Stephen.

Elizabeth tried to warn Grace Royce. She would be talking to her on the telephone, and the next instant she would be lying in the snow, freezing to death.

Or she would be riding in the car, the nurse's car, going up the long, frozen stretch to the nurse's house beside the river. Grace would ask about the baby's father. Elizabeth couldn't speak, she couldn't form the words. She would wake coughing again.

The killer who stalked the baby was faceless. Sometimes it would be Ellen, with long, dripping nails like razors. At other times it was a man with a gun. Once it was Stephen.

She woke gasping and coughing. Some tiny thread of sanity told her she was sick enough to die. She should call a doctor, an ambulance, get to a hospital.

But that would never do. She had to go on, she had to leave a trail that showed credit card receipts, erratic flight, a suggestion that an infant accompanied her.

She was forgetting what she had to do. She had bought a few things, a can of formula, diapers, to leave in an occasional motel room or restroom. But she had forgotten to do that here, wherever here was.

Elizabeth sat up on the side of the bed and told

herself she had to go on. That she had to get back on the bus and travel for another day. Then she could rest. She could go home.

But there was no strength left in her. She had to consider the danger of collapsing now, being hospitalized, and leading the killer immediately to her. He would recognize a ruse.

Elizabeth tried to call Stephen. She shouldn't have. What if he knew she had been missing from the dorm since Friday? What if he demanded to know where she was? What if she couldn't stop herself from asking about him and Ellen?

He didn't answer. She had enough left of her sanity to know that it was the best thing, but she wept as she struggled into her coat and shoes. She needed him.

Somehow, Elizabeth got home.

There were times when she knew she was in a hospital. When the white bed and stark walls didn't swing around her so violently. She could feel Stephen's hand holding hers then, surprisingly tense, and she could hear his voice telling her that she was going to get well.

The tears came so easily, so uselessly. She couldn't look at Stephen, but he was there, he was touching her, he was offering the will she lacked to save her life.

Eventually she knew the others. Constance, telling her not to worry, that she wouldn't let the board expel her. Mary, complaining of the trouble Elizabeth had caused them, disappearing as she had without a word. And Damon, laughing over her nerve at standing the school on its ear the way she had done, walking out without a backward glance.

Damon was the one who mentioned Ellen. He said

she had been gone since Monday, two days after Elizabeth's disappearance had been discovered. She was still gone.

Elizabeth's recovery faltered. The dreams came back. She knew now where Ellen was, and even in the dreams she no longer wielded a razor. She lay quiet, her hands tied behind her, her blood drained away. Elizabeth would never forget it.

Stephen was always near. She could reach out in the middle of the night and he'd be there, taking her hand and holding it comfortingly to his chest. She could feel his heart, the steady rhythm that willed her to strength. It was something else she would never forget.

It was Stephen who told her that her sister's baby had been born. Sara had a baby boy.

It was useless to rail against fate, against timing, but that was the cruelest blow of all. Losing Sara. Ellen's death ruled out any hope that the danger to the infant was imaginary. Elizabeth knew that going to her sister now would be to lead a killer to her door.

It almost broke her.

Constance fought the Board of Regents on Elizabeth's behalf. She assured the members that Elizabeth had been under her roof, too ill to consider the problems created by her unauthorized absence from the dorm and her classes. She assured them that Elizabeth had been under a doctor's care, and that if his verification of Elizabeth's illness was demanded, it would be duly provided.

Elizabeth was put on temporary probation, but her permanent reinstatement followed within a few weeks. Something of her life was salvaged. Something.

Chapter Twenty-three

Present

Elizabeth drove fast. She didn't know how long she had sat in the car, reading and rereading the yellowed clipping. She hadn't seen a copy of it before, but she had always known of its existence. An effort to reach the killer, if indeed there was one, as he followed Elizabeth's trail into Nevada. Telling him the infant was dead.

But it wasn't working any longer. The killer knew the baby hadn't left Portland with Elizabeth. How close was he to figuring out where the baby *had* gone?

Elizabeth glanced at her wrist, but she had forgotten to wear her watch. She circled the parking lot slowly. Once, twice. She drew into a space as close to the light as she could find.

There was no one in the parking lot. The wind tugged at her hair and distorted sound so that she hurried toward the light. She hated the thought of someone hurtling out of the darkness at her, with her unable to hear their approach until it was too late.

It was bright inside the store. As she approached

the delicatessen, Elizabeth could see that Damon hadn't arrived yet.

She let out her breath on a sigh of relief, and chose the least secluded table. Her back was to the wall, literally as well as figuratively.

It began to rain suddenly. The wind flattened icy drops against the glass, and steam from Elizabeth's breath formed on the inside of the panes. She used a tissue to clear a small area, but it did no good. She couldn't see the parking lot or the street that flanked it.

Damon might walk, or he might catch a cab and be dropped close under the awning. Or, knowing him, he might find his way in through the back of the store, and bluff his way through the employees-only warehouse.

Elizabeth was haunted tonight. The murderer outside her window, the obituary notice on the baby. Reliving the hell of her flight into Nevada and her illness.

And calling Stephen, the phone ringing on dead air. Like that night she had lain ill in Nevada, and she had called him because she needed him. Like she needed him now.

Damon knows who the killer is.

She repeated it over and over to herself. *Damon knows who the killer is.* She clung to it. She prayed he wasn't playing some bizarre game, or worse, setting her up, as perhaps he had set up Ellen and Keith.

Oh God! *Was* it Damon? Was she meeting a killer in the middle of the night? If she was, her flimsy precautions to ensure her safety were less than useless. He could overpower her in an instant and walk away, unscathed and unhurrying, without even drawing anyone's attention. It would be that simple. Child's play.

She began to shake again. She had thought she was past that, that she was as close to steady as she could ask of herself. Maybe she was. Perhaps she would be like a victim of shell-shock, always trembling.

Elizabeth thought about trying Stephen's number again. Surely there was a phone nearer than the ones outside, under the eaves. She saw none. She glanced at her wrist again. It was unnerving not to know how much time had elapsed since she'd left the house.

Where was Damon? Was he waiting until the rain let up to venture out? The minutes were ticking slowly, but there had to be some passage of time. Surely it was close to an hour since they had talked.

Damon must be the killer. Mustn't he? When she was talking to him, listening to him, she couldn't believe it was he. His frenetic energy, assembling order out of a fragmented collection of facts. Arriving at killer and motive as if it were nothing more than a parlor game.

Was that what it was to him? Had drugs and liquor and his own personality deficiency made the taking of life nothing more than a macabre joke? She wished to God she knew.

If Damon wasn't the killer, it was conceivable that he could work out who it was. She remembered his uncanny accuracy about the knife, the blackmail money. Even the fact that the baby was still alive. Like some obsessed hacker finding his way into a virtually inaccessible computer system.

Unless it was not genius at all, but simply madness. Offering her bits and pieces of information that he already knew. Trying to build a case for his innocence in her mind so that he could lure her out into the open. As he had done.

Elizabeth shivered. It looked as if it had stopped raining. Damon should be along any minute.

But he didn't come. Elizabeth got up at last and walked to the back of the store in search of a clock. She was shocked when she saw the time. It was 4:30. He was over an hour late.

Elizabeth went back to the table. She stared into her styrofoam coffee cup and tried to think. Was he setting her up? Was he deliberately trying to bring her to his apartment? Or had something happened to him?

She tossed off the rest of her coffee and drew on her coat. She ran through the light sprinkling of rain to her car.

She would drive by his place. That was all . . . drive by. See if she saw him on his way to meet her. She wouldn't get out of her car. Then she would go straight home.

It was a dark street. A narrow alley ran along a wall of high grape stakes to parking in the rear, but Elizabeth had no intention of driving down there. It would be too easy to be trapped.

The sign was old and peeling and swung drunkenly in the wind. The apartments lay back behind a stand of battered garbage cans and irregular rows of old citrus trees.

Elizabeth stopped on the street. Nothing stirred. Rain dripped off the eaves and was lashed away before it could hit the ground. It wasn't a place she would consider approaching at night under the best of circumstances.

The man erupted out of the darkness, his head

down and his feet flying. He almost ran into Elizabeth's car. He had to slow momentarily to negotiate the unexpected obstacle in his path.

He looked straight into Elizabeth's eyes. And then he ran, disappearing in a second into the shrubbery that faced the street front.

It wasn't Damon. For a moment Elizabeth had thought it was, looming out of the damp shadows to scare her, or worse. She was trembling with the shock of it.

She had never seen the man before, and yet for a second there had been something, a whisper of familiarity. A nameless moment of recognition, quickly gone.

Elizabeth forced herself to move. She uncurled her frozen fingers from the steering wheel and unlocked the car door. She got out.

Rain spit icily into her face. She walked carefully, deliberately, past the battered garbage cans. Her coat wasn't warm enough. Chilly needles of cold went through the fabric and into her flesh. She moved as skittishly as a young colt through the staggering bank of shadows.

The door to apartment 3 stood ajar, rocking gently in the wind. Elizabeth steeled herself. She stood as far back as her arm would reach and pushed the door open.

She had known. Almost known. Damon was dead.

It *isn't* one of us, she thought wildly, and she was crying. Crying for Damon's lost genius, crying because it wasn't someone she loved who had wrought this horror. Not Stephen, not Constance, not Mary. And not Damon. It was him, the man she had seen flee. Somewhere in her subconscious she could almost put a name to him, to the killer.

Elizabeth went inside.

There was a low candle burning on a folding table. It was the only light in the shabby studio apartment.

Damon was leaning forward, his left arm extended. A tourniquet still bit deep into the flesh of his upper arm in some obscene parody of life. Stopping the blood that was flowing nowhere, that was growing cold in his veins. An empty syringe protruded from the inside of his elbow.

Elizabeth swung the door gently shut. Suicide? Had Damon killed himself? She went closer. She was in a nightmare and she could wake up whenever she chose. One can die in a nightmare and wake up unscathed.

An accidental overdose? He had said he was off heroin. Had he misjudged what his body could tolerate after his withdrawal?

There was a note beneath his bent arm. She didn't touch him, she knew death when she saw it, but she wanted to. She wanted to put her arms around him now, too late. Mad, tormented Damon Baille. She wept as she read the note.

Elizabeth:
I'm compelled to tell you that you were right. I killed Ellen and Vanfossen. You'll appreciate that I remembered your number-one rule: Always leave yourself a way out.
D.

Elizabeth was shaking violently. It wasn't suicide. It wasn't an accidental overdose. It was murder.

And the murderer had seen her. He could be coming back. Couldn't she hear something above the whistle of the wind?

And then she knew what it was: footsteps, running footsteps, coming fast. She shoved the door shut and closed the flimsy lock. An imitation of a lock, it wouldn't hold out a hard gust of wind.

Elizabeth backed up. She was locked in here with a dead man, with Damon, and it *was* a nightmare! Please God, her terror would roll back the tortured blanket of sleep and let her wake, gasping and damp with sweat, in her own bed!

The footfall stopped outside the door.

Elizabeth made no sound. She crouched low behind the shabby cabinets and reached up to draw the telephone down beside her. She began to dial.

The door rattled. It flew backward on its hinges.

There was silence.

Elizabeth closed her eyes tightly. She willed the operator to pick up the phone, but it was already too late. She wouldn't have time to give the address before she was struck down.

"Elizabeth? Elizabeth, by all that's holy, answer me!"

She hadn't thought that she could move, had thought that she was paralyzed. But she came to her knees, her feet; she flung herself upon Stephen.

"God, you're all right! Elizabeth, thank God!" His arms were so hard they took away her breath. She wept against his coat that was already damp with rain. "Libby, thank Christ!"

"I saw him, the murderer! I *saw* him! He ran. I thought . . . I heard footsteps . . ."

Stephen pressed his face against her damp hair.

216

"Dear God, you scared me! I saw your car. I was scared to death I was too late."

"I'm sorry," she whispered. She clung to him. "I'm sorry, Stephen."

He lifted her chin. She could feel his hands shaking as he smoothed the wisps of wet hair back from her face.

"You take chances," he said raggedly. "You can't do that. Don't you see you can't?"

"I know. I didn't mean to. I thought I was being careful. I didn't mean to come alone." Elizabeth took a breath and put her hands over his where they touched her face. "Damon said he knew who the killer was. I tried to call you. How did you find me?"

"It wasn't difficult," he said grimly. "I tried to call you from work. When you didn't answer, I came as fast as I could to the last place on the planet I would want you to be. I thought . . . I was scared to death I was too late."

Elizabeth pressed her face against his coat. They had to talk about Damon, they had to call the police. But she held it back for a minute more, the horror of reality.

"Do you usually call me at four in the morning? I must be a sound sleeper."

"I don't," he denied. "But I almost do. I imagine that you're awake and that you need me. It might be imagination, but it certainly doesn't help me sleep, I can tell you. And anyway, tonight was different. We had reason to believe Damon was behind all this. Even Sam indicated it. Near Damon was the last place you should be."

"He called me tonight and said he knew who the

murderer was. He wanted to meet somewhere and talk.

"I know what you must be thinking, Stephen. I'm not crazy enough to meet him here. We were supposed to get together at the Safeway on 40th. But when he was over an hour late, I decided to drive by here, to see if he was on his way. I wasn't going to get out of the car.

"I had just stopped on the street and turned off the lights when a man came running from the direction of Damon's apartment. He almost ran into my car. And then he disappeared along the street.

"Stephen, I had to check on Damon, didn't I? I had to know if he was all right, if I had just seen a murderer."

"No, love, you didn't. You should have gone to the nearest telephone and called the police. Not the nearest, on second thought. Somewhere out of this neighborhood." He looked at Damon, Damon's body. "We'd better call them now."

Stephen went around the counter and retrieved the telephone from the floor where Elizabeth had dragged it. He began to dial.

While he waited for the connection, his dark eyes rested hungrily on Elizabeth's white face. He reached out toward her where she stood, staring down at Damon's bent head.

"Come here, Libby," he said.

Elizabeth went to stand within the circle of his arms.

"There's a note," she said raggedly. "But it wasn't suicide."

"How do you know?"

"It was what he said tonight. Something like . . ." she paused. She could hear a mechanical voice announce the police station.

Stephen gave their names, the street address and apartment number. In her mind Elizabeth could hear Damon saying the same address tonight, calling her to come, to meet the same fate as he.

Stephen put down the phone.

"They're on their way. You were telling me why Damon didn't commit suicide."

"Yes, it was something he said tonight. He said I was forgetting my number-one rule, something like that. Like he says in the note. But it wasn't anything about leaving a way out. He said my rule was to never trust anybody."

Stephen went across and read the note, reread it.

" 'I'm compelled' ", he quoted. "That sounds like Damon's droll version of 'I'm forced.' It could be. The killer could have stood over him with a weapon. A knife, no doubt. He could have ordered Damon to write a suicide note and then overdose."

"And then the police would be convinced that the killer was dead. We'd all believe it was safe."

"And you would get careless."

He looked at her. He could have said "like you were careless tonight," but he didn't. She was too thin in her damp coat, her face white and scored by dried tears.

He couldn't believe he'd let himself think for one second that she might not have survived. He couldn't imagine the world without her in it. If she didn't want him, she could say so, but he would still need to know that she was all right, wherever she was.

219

He reached for her and drew her away from the frozen horror of the room.

"I'm going to take you home. Sibben can find us when he's ready."

Chapter Twenty-four

Elizabeth couldn't stop trembling. She put her face into her hands and the tears seeped between her fingers. Stephen drew the car into the curb.

"Sorry," she murmured. She pressed her sleeve awkwardly to her wet eyes.

He reached out and drew her into his arms.

"It's shock," he said gently. "You've been through too much tonight. God knows how long it's been since you slept. You're running on nerves."

"I want to tell you about the baby."

He went very still. And then he smoothed back her wind-tangled hair.

"You think you do now, love. Your defenses are down. Tomorrow you'll wish you hadn't."

Elizabeth took a ragged breath and closed her eyes tiredly.

"I don't want to go home."

"You're not. I'm taking you home with me. I imagine you need a strong drink or a sedative, but I'm afraid I don't have either."

"Constance says you don't drink anymore."

"Does she?" he drawled.

Elizabeth opened her eyes. She wanted to read his face, although she knew she never could.

"It's not true?"

"Oh, it's true enough."

"But I'm intruding?"

"No, love, you're not," he said emphatically. "But I have to admit to being a little wary of information coming through your sources."

Heavens, that was true enough, that was fact. Look what Ellen had done to them, Ellen and her lies.

"Was the drinking a problem?"

"A problem?" Stephen repeated, and there was irony in it and self-derision. "I'd have to say it was a problem. Problem enough for you to leave me over it. But if you mean was it hell to kick it, then no. I didn't miss it. It didn't matter."

Elizabeth stared at her clenched hands. She wanted to touch him, to take the bitterness away. All this time too late. She whispered, "I've made a mess of things, haven't I?"

"No more than I have. I let it eat me up. Thinking of you with another man. Having his child. It was easy to let liquor blur the edges a little. But it didn't really help. It only made the wall between us higher.

"What I didn't realize until it was too late was that the only thing that mattered was having you there. Even if you weren't all that I saw when I looked at you, at least you were there. I could touch you and I could hold you, and if there were shadows in your eyes, at least I could help you to live with them. I never dreamt you might take it all away."

Elizabeth shook her head mutely. Her throat ached with tears.

222

"It wasn't your drinking. It was me. I couldn't stand it any longer."

"Living with me?"

"Lying to you. It was destroying both of us."

"When I realized you weren't coming back, I left everything. I just walked away. I thought I'd go crazy. I eventually wound up in Denver. It was as good a place as any. When I found out you were in Phoenix, I came here. Sounds fairly obsessive, doesn't it?"

"I'm sorry I left the way I did. It was terrible. I knew it, but I couldn't see any other way."

"It was the only way you could have left me, Libby. Because if I had known, I wouldn't have let you go."

"Wouldn't you?" she murmured. She wished he had caught her packing the few things she had taken with her. Stopped her. However wretched and determined she had been, she would have stayed if he'd asked her to. "I couldn't stop thinking about Ellen. You and Ellen. I couldn't talk about it, Stephen. Not to you. Least of all to you. I was afraid you might tell me the truth, and I couldn't bear it."

"This is the truth," he clipped out. "There was never anything between Ellen and me. Since the first time I saw you, there was no one else. Even when I could see in your eyes that you thought I was a murderer. I figured I could live with it."

She pressed her sleeve to her eyes and asked through the tears that shook her voice, "Do you think the man I saw killed Damon?"

"It's either that, or Constance or Mary, isn't it? The last of the circle. And Mary was spooked enough last night to already be gone home. Sibben will have to look into it. Don't think about it." He took his arms away. He reached out and pressed the ignition. The engine sprang to life and he turned the heater on high. "You're still freezing, aren't you? It's not much farther."

"I left Sam in the house."

"He'll be fine." Stephen switched on the headlights and windshield wipers and drew out onto the nearly deserted street.

Elizabeth leaned back and closed her eyes. The approaching car lights lit up the back of her lids, invaded the dark world behind her eyes. She hoped she was finished crying. She didn't want to cry any more.

"Do you remember when I was in the hospital, Stephen?"

"Distinctly," he clipped.

"I thought I was going to die."

He glanced at her, her closed eyes, the weariness in her too-thin face. She almost *had* died. The doctors had considered her status very grave. He had fought for her life then like he was fighting for it now, with everything that was in him.

"You were very ill."

"You were always there. Whenever I reached out, you were there."

"Where else would I be?" He took her hand, closing his fingers around the coldness of hers. "Where else would I be?"

"Stephen?"

"Yes?"

"I want to tell you about the baby. I may be in shock, I probably am. But I'm sane enough, composed enough, to known what lies can do. What they've done to us." Elizabeth's fingers tightened on his. She opened gray eyes that were startlingly bright and lucid. "No more lies, Stephen."

"All right. You can tell me about the baby. But not yet. You're all in."

They drove in silence for several miles. And then Elizabeth said tiredly, "Poor Damon. I still can't believe it. I mean, I almost do, and then the impossibility of him being dead burns through me like acid. I can't believe it."

"I know. If there's any comfort, he went the way he would have chosen. With a needle in his vein."

It sounded cold, but it was a fact. He had lived his life determinedly stoned.

"He told me tonight that he had gone through a rehab program and was off heroin."

"I believe it. His arms were scarred, but there weren't any recent needle marks."

Elizabeth sighed heavily. This was unreal, driving through the dark, wet streets and talking about Damon's death. It couldn't be happening.

"He said the money in the account under my name was blackmail money. He wanted me to get some of it for him."

Stephen grinned.

"It wouldn't have been Damon if he didn't."

"I know. I told him to get a job."

"Good girl."

"Good callous girl," she amended dryly.

"Don't be hard on yourself, Libby. You didn't bring him into this any more than you brought Vanfossen in. They knew what they were doing and knew the risks. Neither's motives were anything but self-serving. I've known Damon for a long time, but I can't claim to have liked him. He was a singularly unlikable bastard."

Damon would have enjoyed such an epitaph. Elizabeth smiled faintly.

"You're right," she admitted. "But I'm sorry he's dead."

"I'm sorry, too. But it was simply a matter of time. He'd pretty well used himself up.

"Possibly the only decent thing Damon did in his life was to have a genuine affection for Ellen, and I'm not even sure about that. He seemed to care more about her after he knew she was dead. The whole thing may have been some distorted identification of himself with the victim, knowing Damon. On second thought, there *was* one other decent thing he did: he tried to warn you. That must have appealed to his macabre sense of humor."

"At least it's not one of us. I thought it had to be someone out of our own mad little circle. It made it all so much more horrible, if that's possible."

"Did you see the man well enough to describe him to the police?"

"Yes. I think I can sketch him." She looked wryly at her hands. They were trembling too violently to hold a pencil. "I almost *knew* him, Stephen. He looked so familiar. And yet I could swear I've never seen him before."

"It will probably come to you when some of the shock has worn off. Don't try to force it."

"I can't force it," she admitted tiredly. "At least, not without a cup of coffee. That's all that's kept me going the last few days."

"We're almost home."

Almost home. Elizabeth turned her face toward

the darkened car window and blinked away the wetness in her eyes. She touched the cold glass.

"It's still dark," she said huskily. "But it must be past five."

Stephen glanced at his watch.

"It's a quarter to six. Another hour till daylight."

"Will we be in trouble for leaving before the police got there?"

"I doubt it. Sibben will be too pleased to have the case wrapped up so neatly. He's not going to be very open to the idea that Damon is another victim and not the killer."

"Except that he'll be disappointed I wasn't involved. It may give him the motivation he needs to keep the case open." Elizabeth pressed her fingers to the tension in her forehead. "Are you sure Sam will be okay?"

"Yes. Stop worrying. He's probably on the sofa by now."

"That's what I'm worrying about," Elizabeth said.

"Too late. We're here."

The car lights swept over leaded glass windows and a massive oak front door partially screened by a trellis covered with trailing ivy.

"Stephen, this is lovely! You *live* here?"

He smiled faintly.

"Do you like it?"

"It's beautiful. It reminds me a little of Portland."

"Me, too. That's probably what attracted me to it."

"Do you miss Portland?"

"No. There's nothing there." He cut the lights and came around the car to open her door.

"It's a beautiful house. I just thought . . . I don't

know. That you were a transient, I guess, like the rest of us. Renting a place and trying to figure out what it was you wanted."

"I've been there," he demurred. He touched her face. "I know what I want."

Chapter Twenty-five

"You let Sam Gamgee come in here?" Elizabeth marveled. She stood beneath the skylight in the vaulted ceiling of the living room. Champagne carpeting set off the cool native stone of a corner fireplace and the built-in hardwood and glass bookshelves which flanked it on either side. A low leather sofa faced the exquisitely worked tile of the hearth.

"Sam likes it."

"I'll just bet he does. It's a wonder he ever came back to me."

Stephen crossed to the fireplace and struck a match and fire began to curl around the logs.

"Sam would like to live here," he said softly.

She went very still. She looked at him, the light and shadow from the fire playing across his lean, enigmatic features.

"You wouldn't try to take my dog away from me, would you?" she managed.

"No. I'm talking about a package deal. You and Sam."

"Stephen . . ."

"Never mind," he said quietly. She was too shattered, too spent. Today had been difficult enough. "Come over here by the fire and get warm while I put the coffee on. You'd probably better take off that wet coat."

Elizabeth struggled obediently out of it.

"Maybe we can forget the coffee, Stephen. I'd like to talk, if you don't mind."

"About Ellen's baby?"

"Yes." She bit her lip. She had spent years trying to forget so that even in an unguarded moment she wouldn't somehow jeopardize an innocent child's life. She had promised herself she would never tell.

"Are you sure?"

"I'm sure," she said tightly. She walked into his arms.

He held her safe. She had been lost without him. She could hear the steady thump of his heart as if it were her own, as vital to her survival as her own.

"All right, love," he said softly. He drew her to the sofa, close to the warmth of the fire. "Tell me."

She hardly knew where to begin. Even her memories were disjointed.

"I always remember the snow," she said bleakly. She stared into the dancing flames, but she could feel the snow, it went through her flesh and into the bones. "It was so beautiful. And so terrible. It suffocated me. I thought it would suffocate the baby." Elizabeth ran a trembling hand across her forehead. The past came out of the shadows and stood before her. Ellen did. "It was a Friday. The snow began to fall early, and classes were closed. The dorm had emptied out for the weekend, of course. The only reason I was there was because Sara and Tom's baby was so close, and I didn't want to be in the way at their place. I thought they should have the time together.

"Ellen came in just seconds before curfew. She made a few typically cryptic remarks, but I could see she wasn't feeling well. I thought she'd had too much to drink.

"Lord, I wish it had been no more than that! She was in labor, Stephen! I hadn't so much as suspected, living side by side with her. I don't think anyone had. Damon, I guess. She told him, didn't she? He said she did."

Elizabeth shook her head and tears glittered in her eyes. "She had the baby on the bathroom floor. I thought . . . I don't even remember what I thought. I was staggered.

"I coaxed the baby into breathing. Or maybe he would have breathed anyway, I don't know. But he was all right, he wasn't blue, that horrible shade of death he had been. He was crying. I'll never forget how good his thin little spidery cry sounded.

"When Ellen saw that I was helping him, she told me to stop. She said she wanted him to die, Stephen. Her eyes were hard, but they were . . . sane, if you know what I mean. It was as if her determination to destroy him was stronger than I was . . ." Elizabeth gulped on a sob. "She fought me for him. She held his head under water in the washbasin."

"God, Elizabeth!"

"She was insane, Stephen. Her behavior was insane. I swear she knew exactly what she was doing. I didn't think I could prevent her doing it.

"We struggled. She wasn't strong physically, of course, and I was able to get the baby away from her. I tied off the cord and cut it while she taunted me that

I was killing him." Elizabeth shuddered. "I could have been. I didn't have a clue as to what I was doing. But I had to get him away from her. She tried to cut my face with a razor blade."

Stephen was as tense as she. She could feel him wince, the irregularity of his breathing, but he didn't interrupt her. He let the words, the anguish, pour from her.

"She would have killed me to get the baby. She would have. He was in the way of her plans. That was what she said, as if I was being unreasonable to stop her. She had a shoebox and some string she'd saved to put his body in. To throw it down the garbage chute." She wept softly. "She scratched me."

Stephen's fingers touched her face where the scratches had been.

"You had the scratches when you were in Intensive Care. Mary was wandering around talking some rot about you trying to poison Ellen. She stuck with it, more or less. I thought about strangling her."

Elizabeth laughed shakily and wiped her eyes.

"Mary's awful. I hope she goes home to Portland and stays there. And I hope it snows every day."

"Tell me about the snow," Stephen urged her.

"It's really nothing. I'm fixating on it, I guess. I just remember it in association with that night. The days that followed. It wouldn't have been half so bad if it hadn't been cold. I doubt if I would have gotten sick if I hadn't been half frozen. And then thinking about it all these years. Trying *not* to think about it. Ellen's body in the cold, frozen earth. It's a nightmare.

"The snow was deep. The roads were icy. It was as

232

if the world had stopped dead, nothing was moving or alive, and the storm had stopped it.

"Anyway, I tied the baby to me with strips of cloth, so that he'd have my warmth. I watched Ellen, and I tried to plan, to figure what I would need to get him safely to someone who could give him care. That's when Ellen began to talk about the danger to the baby. She said something like, 'Do you think *they* will let him live?' and, 'When *they* find out about him, they'll kill him anyway.'"

"Who?"

"I wish to God I knew. When I tried to get her to tell me, she just laughed. But I had to believe it was the truth. Only a few days later, she was dead. I *had* to believe in the threat then." Elizabeth's voice wobbled. She said tiredly, "It was only later that I realized I had asked the wrong question. I should have asked 'Why?' rather than 'Who?' She might have said. She might have been less wary and said more. If I knew *why* someone wanted to kill the baby, I'd *know* who, wouldn't I?"

"She gave you no idea?"

"None. I've spent years considering every word that she said. But now we know she was telling the truth, Stephen. Someone *is* stalking the baby. They've killed Ellen and Keith, and now Damon. They've been following me. They want me to lead them to him."

Elizabeth was shivering. The fire was warm and her hair and clothing were nearly dry. Stephen's arms were hard about her. But she couldn't stop shivering.

"I gave him to Grace Royce."

Just like that she destroyed the walls and the secrets. She made him a gift of her trust. She put the life of the boy, her life, into his hands.

"Good for you," he said approvingly. He traced the line of her jaw with the backs of his fingers. She couldn't imagine that she had ever thought his eyes were hard.

"There was an ad in the *Oregonian* about a couple looking for a baby to adopt. David pointed it out once. It just gave a phone number, but he said it was his brother's ad.

"I called Grace Royce from the Circle K near the dorm. She came right out in the middle of the night." Elizabeth sniffed raggedly. "She hoped I wasn't a terrorist."

"She sounds like you," Stephen said gently. "Taking insane chances."

"She took a chance, all right. About everything. But she loved the baby on sight. She was wonderful. She and the nurse began to make plans to obtain a phony birth certificate, adoption papers. They were going to create an adoptable infant in some other state, and travel there and appear to pick up the baby. She planned to cover every detail, even biological parents and a doctor in attendance at his birth. Whatever it took to protect the baby from the danger it was in being Ellen Glover's child.

"Grace planned to have her husband's lawyers go over every detail of the adoption with a fine-toothed comb. If they couldn't find any flaws, then she could rest fairly easy that the killer couldn't find any, either. He couldn't trace Ellen's baby to them, and the child would be safe."

"Grace is married to Randolph Royce?"

"Yes. David's older brother. I guess you and I, as

well as Ellen, Constance, Mary, and Damon, all worked for him when we were at Royce Pharmaceuticals. David was the head of it, but the major stockholder was Royce Chemical Conglomerate. You probably know Randolph Royce."

"I've met him. He spent a lot of time at the Seattle plant." Stephen said softly, "I've seen the boy."

"Have you?" Elizabeth breathed. A light flared behind the gray eyes.

"He came into the plant a few times with his father. He's a nice-looking little boy. Very self-assured."

"He's the same age as Sara's little boy. You can't believe the times I've wanted to see them both."

"You were afraid the killer might think you'd given Ellen's baby to Sara?"

"God, yes! However irrational that may be. It wouldn't be difficult for the killer to get hold of medical records that prove the baby Sara has is her own. But what if he didn't, Stephen? What if he killed Toby and *then* realized his mistake? I just couldn't take the chance.

"I broke off contact with Sara. You know that. I've never seen her little boy. Not even a picture of him. And maybe he wasn't in any danger and I've hurt Sara for no reason. Maybe the killer always knew I had a sister and knew her little boy wasn't Ellen's. I just didn't know.

"But, Stephen, someone *does* go through my mail. The apartment manager where I lived when I first came to Phoenix discovered a bug on my phone. And I've been followed." Elizabeth sighed. "You've seen Sara's boy, haven't you? What does he look like?"

235

Stephen brought his thoughts back from the dangerous picture her words had painted.

"Toby? His hair is dark. He has your gray eyes. He probably looks a little like our children would look."

Our children. As if there would be a tomorrow and the sun would shine.

Chapter Twenty-six

"I want to see my nephew. I want to see Sara. I even want to see Tom."

Stephen smiled faintly.

"Don't get rash."

"You're right. Don't let me get crazy." She fumbled in her purse for a Kleenex and her fingers touched the clipping. She unfolded it.

"The night I gave the baby to Grace Royce, we planned that I'd take the bus and go as far as I could into Nevada, directly away from the direction Grace would take. It was supposed to look like I still had the baby with me, just in case someone was looking for him. Meanwhile, Grace would put this article in a paper somewhere in Nevada, so that if anyone was following, they'd think the baby had died.

"If the ruse worked at all, it wasn't for long. See the second sheet."

"Sweet Christ!" Stephen gritted between his teeth. He wasn't looking at the papers she offered, he was looking at her. "You were in Nevada . . . excuse me, *somewhere* in Nevada, critically ill and alone and with no one but a murderer knowing where you were.

Good God, Elizabeth! Wasn't there something in you, *something,* that wanted to send for me? To let me help?"

Elizabeth didn't look at him, at his exasperation and anger. No, not anger. Pain. She kept her eyes on the papers in her hands.

"There was everything in me," she admitted raggedly. "Everything in me wanted you there."

"Oh, Libby," he said on a sigh. He put his arms around her and rested his face against her hair. "I'm sorry, love. It was my fault if you didn't trust me. It was something I said or did, or failed to do. I was never good at words with you. You mattered too much."

She wept against his shirt, holding him, aching.

"I never meant to hurt you, Stephen. It's the last thing I wanted. I left so I wouldn't hurt you."

He laughed softly, unexpectedly.

"Good thinking," he said, and it was laced with irony, but no sarcasm. He could have been bitter.

"You'd better not be laughing at me, Stephen Kenwood," Elizabeth warned darkly.

"No, love. But don't do me any more favors, all right? I hardly survived the last one."

Elizabeth closed her eyes and rested against him. She wanted to stay in his arms. The hell before her and the hell behind couldn't reach her here. But after a moment she let out her breath on a sigh, and straightened away from him. She was tired, so tired.

Stephen read the clipping, the sheet behind it. He glanced at the envelope.

"I had no idea any of the Royce Pharmaceutical inventory still existed." His eyes touched her face, the shadows beneath her eyes. "Where did you get this?"

"It was on my mailbox tonight when I went out to meet Damon."

"I don't suppose you saw anyone?"

"No, but I know it was the killer. He walked around the house and tried the doors and windows."

"God!" He grated. And then, "I should have given you my work number." He took a pen from his breast pocket and wrote the numbers across the Royce Pharmaceutical envelope. "If I'm not in the office, they can reach me."

"Good," she said. She folded the envelope and it wasn't threatening any more. It was just an envelope. "Thank you."

"Tell me about Nevada," he clipped.

"I took the bus, like I said. I was trying to leave a trail away from the baby. I didn't make it as far as I'd hoped.

"By the third day I was too ill to go any farther. I got a motel room and tried to wait out the illness. I thought it was the flu and that I'd get better if I could just rest awhile.

"But I got worse. I was afraid I would have to be hospitalized there, and the killer would discover that the baby had never left Portland with me. So I started home.

"You know the rest. I guess the doctors sent for you. I don't remember making it back to Portland."

"Constance called me on Sunday evening," Stephen said briefly. "She was upset over your absence and thought I should know. I took the next plane out of O'Hare. You didn't get home until Wednesday."

He had been out of his mind with worry. He would like to say he didn't remember it, either, the days not knowing where she was, what might have happened to her. And then the long, long days and nights, waiting beside her bedside while each tortured breath she drew seemed like it might be her last. He would like to, but he couldn't. It was seared into his brain.

"Do you know what the real irony is, Stephen? The Royces are here in Phoenix. They've lived here for several years. I must have led the killer straight to them.

"Grace found out I was here. She called me a few days ago and said she was afraid someone was following her. I told her not to panic, that she had to be sure. I've been scared to death since that I may have helped the killer. I may have played right into his hands."

"Royce must have twenty-four-hour security around her and the boy."

"No, that's just it—he doesn't know anything about the boy being in danger. As far as *I* know, he doesn't. Grace planned for him to believe the child was born where the adoption papers claim. She didn't think he'd go along with getting a baby under such murky circumstances. Or that if he did, he might not believe there was a threat to the little boy. The only way to protect the baby was with her secrecy."

"It still seems probable that Royce has security around his family. He's an important man, powerful in political circles. His family would be an ideal target for kidnappers or terrorists, as Grace mentioned to you.

"I can't believe Royce leaves them exposed even to the possibility of threat, Elizabeth. Maybe Grace has refused a bodyguard, thinking it would scare the boy. Who knows what the circumstances could be? But I would have to say that if she's being followed, it's for her own safety. After all, we know the killer is right here. We saw what he has done. You probably saw him."

"That's true. He may be a madman, but he can be in only one place at a time. But who is he? How did he get his hands on a knife from Royce Chem?"

"That's a good question."

Stephen went across to the open bookcase and took down a familiar terra cotta bowl, retrieving the contents. A lock-blade knife with a stag antler handle.

"I used to keep my rings in there," Elizabeth said tautly. "When I was washing the car or working in the garden."

Stephen paused. He said dryly, "Yes. And when you were leaving me." He came back to the sofa and offered her the knife.

She barely touched it before handing it back to him. Her fingers were trembling too badly to open it if she had wished to, and there was no need anyway. It was identical to the one she had found on the bloody floor of her house.

"Do you think David Royce owned one of these?"

"I don't know. It's possible. Are you suggesting David isn't dead, after all?"

"He's dead. Constance saw him drown."

Stephen's brows rose.

"Did she?"

"She just told me recently. After Damon's spooky talk about David's spirit getting restless, remember that? Damon claimed he'd come to Phoenix because he'd gotten a letter from David. But last night he told me a different story. He said he came to see that I was executed for killing Ellen."

241

"That sounds like Damon," Stephen said shortly. He returned the knife to the bowl. "Are you ready for that cup of coffee?"

"Yes, please. May I look around?"

"I hope you will. The bathroom's the second door to the back."

That was probably a kind way of saying she looked terrible. Elizabeth went down the hall, opening doors and looking inside. It was a beautiful house, exquisitely appointed.

She found a den done in elegant hardwoods with a desk and personal computer and a pool table; a guest room in pale shades of blue that looked out on a deck and a landscaped back yard with a sparkling diving pool; a large ivory-and-gray bathroom with a skylight and gleaming tile mosaics on the floor.

Elizabeth brushed out her hair and clipped it back. She patted her face with icy water, but it was going to take more than that. It was going to take a miracle. A miracle, and a good night's sleep.

Neither was likely to happen. This was Saturday, but Sibben was probably in his office already, poring over the paperwork on Damon's death. He would be gratified to learn that Elizabeth had discovered the body. She would probably be at the police station most of the day.

Elizabeth hung up the towel. She was pale. There were shadows beneath her eyes, but there were none in them. She was experiencing the weightlessness that went with sharing a burden. Sharing it with Stephen.

Elizabeth paused by the bookshelf. She recognized

some of the books. Her leatherbound copy of the *Lord of the Rings* trilogy. A volume of *The Three Musketeers* she had given Stephen. She went around the corner into the kitchen.

Stephen glanced up and she smiled faintly.

"I see you didn't leave everything. You took the books."

"Some of them. And you may have noticed the Charles Russell painting we bought at the art auction on the wall in the den. The watercolor you liked so much is in the bedroom."

"Your bedroom?"

"Yes."

"I didn't go in there. I thought you might show it to me."

His hands paused on the coffee cups. He searched her face and there was something in his eyes. Warmth and waiting.

"Are you being deliberately provocative, Elizabeth?"

"I love your house. Did Constance decorate it?"

"No." He was certain about that. He grinned. Elizabeth had almost forgotten how the creases along his mouth deepened when he was amused, when he smiled. "Do I look like a fool? The wife of a chemist I work with is a decorator. She did it."

That was good, that was wonderful. She was jealous. She loved Constance, but she didn't want her here, she didn't want her near Stephen.

"I'd like to see the bedroom. I'd like to see if it's our bed."

He came very near. His fingers touched her face.

"It can be," he said softly. "Is that what you want?"

Elizabeth had never wanted anything else. She went into his arms. She could feel the uneven crash of his heart.

"Yes," she breathed.

Chapter Twenty-seven

"Elizabeth?"

Stephen sat down on the bed beside her. He hated to wake her. She was worn out, and today was going to be bad. He touched her face.

"Wake up, love."

She stirred. He could feel his heart beating thickly in his chest as he waited for her to waken. He waited to know that what he had seen in her eyes last night, this morning, had been real . . . that she was coming home.

It was real. She smiled before her eyes were open and she cradled his hand against her face.

"Did I dream you?"

If she had, it was some dream. It had taken their breath away. He leaned over and kissed her and she wound her arms around his neck.

"Good morning," she said.

Stephen chuckled.

"Good morning. I was wondering if you were going to wake up this morning."

"I think I won't, thank you." She yawned and smoothed her hair back from her face.

"Sibben is on the phone."

That brought reality rushing in: Sibben and Damon, and Keith's body in the lake.

"He would be. He can wait, can't he?"

Stephen grinned. He said wryly, "Sibben can probably wait. I'm not sure Sam can."

Elizabeth sat up. She looked for the clock.

"Oh, poor Sam. He's going to need to get out of the house. What time is it?"

"Don't worry, it's still early—9:30. But I think we'd better go. Shall I tell Sibben we'll be there in about an hour? We can let Sam out and pick up your car by then."

"All right." Elizabeth looked for her clothing. Stephen had apparently found everything while she was sleeping and put them at the end of the bed for her, but it must have taken some searching. She gave him a look, she said, "I don't suppose I can claim intoxication?"

He had been about to go back to Sibben on the phone, but he stopped. He came back and kissed her hard on the mouth.

"No, you can't." His eyes soft, he said, "I hope you don't think you need an excuse."

She chuckled. She ran her fingers down his face.

"I'm so glad you're real."

He had been thinking the same thing. He had needed to know it was him, not just loneliness and fear and someone to cling to in the face of death. He knew now. The room was filled with sunshine.

"This conversation deserves more attention than we can give it. Let me get rid of Sibben. Don't go away."

"I think you're forgetting Sam." She pressed her

lips against his neck and it was heaven, but it was amusing, too. It had been so long since anything had been amusing.

"You're right. Poor Sam. Too bad." He kissed her one more time, ran his hand down her bare arm.

"May I use your shower, Stephen? I'll be quick, I promise."

"*My* shower? I thought it was our shower." He looked into her gray eyes and he was very near. He wasn't teasing now, or distracted by the feel of her body in his arms. This was serious, this was everything, this was life. "You *are* coming home, aren't you, Elizabeth?"

"Yes," she said simply. She leaned into him, her face into his chest, and he could smell the faint herbal scent of her hair, the sweet warmth of her skin.

"When?"

"Today?"

"Perfect answer." He kissed her again. "Damn Sibben," he muttered. He laughed. He got up and went back out to the phone in the living room.

Elizabeth smiled. She thought of picking up the extension on the bedside table. She would like to hear Sibben sputtering with rage at how long he had been left waiting. He would probably be all set to send a police escort for them.

At her house, the bright outdoor lights of last night were colorless and weak against the brilliance of a cold, clear morning. Elizabeth unlocked the door and she and Stephen went inside. Sam rushed to meet them. He howled discordantly and bounded happily about, his toenails clicking on the tile of the foyer.

Stephen unlocked the arcadia door and let him out.

247

Elizabeth looked around her. It seemed cold inside. Standing here in the middle of the room, it was impossible to forget last night's terror. Damon's phone call.

"I need to change," she said. She tried to sound natural. She tried not to look at the kitchen, where only last night Damon had stood. The sofa, where he had sat with his feet propped up on the coffee table.

She had cleaned up afterward in the early hours of the night before she sat down to her designs. She had even taken out the garbage, the empty liquor and soft drink bottles, in the dark. She had walked out to the dumpster by the street, by the mailbox where a few hours later the murderer retraced her steps and tried the doors and windows. She felt ill at the thought.

Stephen must have been thinking along the same lines. He said abruptly, "I'm going to look around outside. I'll turn off the outside lights."

"All right."

Elizabeth willed herself to move. She went to her desk and gathered up the drawings she had been working on when Sam had begun to show alarm. Bill would be waiting for the designs. She had only three left to do.

Elizabeth walked down the hall to the bedroom. She selected clothing from the closet and bureau and tried to concentrate on changing. She brushed her hair until it shone, and then wound it into a coil at the nape of her neck.

She could hear the faint crunch of leaves outside. Stephen was looking for footprints, anything, but there would be none. She began to shake.

Stephen came back into the house. Perhaps he could feel her shattering, perhaps the horror was a tangible presence here this morning, but he came straight through the house as if she had called him.

"Elizabeth?"

He opened the door and came to her. She was white. She was sitting on the edge of the bed as if her legs wouldn't support her, and probably they wouldn't. She was trembling.

Stephen sat down and put his arms around her.

"It's all right, love."

"I'm losing my nerve," she said. "It's happening too fast. It was just last night that we learned Keith's body had been found. Everyone was here. All of us. And now Damon's dead. He can't be, but he is. I saw the killer. I *saw* him. I've got to do something, I've got to draw him." She held out her right hand. It was shaking too badly to hold a pencil. "I've got to convince Sibben that it was murder. But if he believes it, I'll be bringing his suspicion back to me. He wants to believe *I* did it. My alibi is the murderer. That's ironic, isn't it? He's the only one who knows I didn't kill Damon."

She was about to cry. She had thought she was over that. She had wept more since discovering Damon's body than she had in the last two years.

"It's not a matter of alibis now, Libby. It's identifying the man you saw. It'll pull it all together. And you're not losing your nerve." He smiled faintly. "You're gathering it."

Elizabeth blew her nose.

"Is that what I'm doing? I'm sorry, Stephen. I'm so scared I can't think straight. There's not much left between that little boy and a killer."

"There's you," he said. "And there's me. Between us, we'll convince Sibben to keep the investigation open. When the man is identified, it will all be over."

Elizabeth let out her breath on a long, steadying sigh.

"You make it sound so simple."

"It's not. It's not simple at all. We're in the eye of a hurricane. But we're together. I would rather be in hell with you than anywhere on earth with someone else."

"I know." She put her hand against his jaw. She couldn't imagine going through this without him, even facing the day. "I wish it were already over."

"Soon," he promised.

"There's so much I have to do. It's Saturday, but Bill will be in the office. I need to take my designs in. I have to pack, and talk with the manager about breaking my lease.

"There won't be a problem. They offered to let me out when . . . when Keith died. But it's still a headache. Everything in the refrigerator is going to spoil if I don't get to it right away."

"Give me the manager's number. I'll call him." Stephen grinned. "Sam and I will take care of the refrigerator. We'll hire movers for the rest."

It wasn't what was really bothering her. She said, "I've got to see Constance."

He studied their intertwined fingers.

"Do you?"

"I feel I should. I hate hurting her. We've all been friends for a long time."

"You've been friends. There's never been anything between Constance and me. Only that we both love you."

Elizabeth hadn't seen it. She must have been blind but she would have said there was strong affection

250

between Stephen and Constance. She had tortured herself that there was much much more.

"You don't like Constance?"

"I didn't say that. She's been a loyal friend to you, up to a point. She would have shattered any chance of a reconciliation between us if she could have."

"I know." Elizabeth *did* know. Constance could have destroyed them. But Elizabeth shared the burden. She had been too hurt to say, "No. Hands off." Constance would have understood that. She would have respected it. "She feels I've lied to her. I have, in a sense."

"By not telling her we're married? I don't think it's any of her business."

She said softly, she breathed it, "By not telling her you were mine."

He drew her close, pressing his face against her neatly coiled hair.

"Oh, Elizabeth. Let's go home and make love all day. It's Saturday, for God's sake."

Elizabeth chuckled.

"There are problems with that plan. But I can't think what they are."

"I can." He unbuttoned the top button of her blouse. "It's too far away."

"And Sibben will call. He'll know we're in bed again."

Stephen laughed. He leaned across her and took the phone off the hook.

"He won't *know,*" he said. "He'll have to assume."

Chapter Twenty-eight

Detective Sibben leaned back in his chair.

"You sure you got time for this?" he asked sarcastically. He had three files in front of him and there was no question they were growing. Keith Vanfossen, of course, and Ellen Glover. And now Damon Baille, and whatever had been put together on him in the few hours they had had.

"Time for what?" Stephen wanted to know.

"Your pal Baille's death, for starters." Sibben flipped open the top folder and stared glumly at the first page for long moments.

"I found the body," Elizabeth offered tonelessly. "I'm sure that's what you find so interesting in your report. Stephen came along a little later. He called your department and left our names."

"Is that so? Out for a walk in South Phoenix at four in the morning? You do that often?"

"It's not South Phoenix. And it wasn't four A.M. That may be when Damon died. I didn't get there until later, if you'll check your fact sheet."

"Oh, so you know when Baille died. That's interesting. Your famous ESP at work again, Miss Purdin?"

"We talked on the phone at three."

"Chummy. I think I'll just save myself the aggravation of pretending you don't know what the note he left said. You wouldn't have missed a chance to read it. So let's just consider it as a given that everybody has read it, okay?

"If you talked to Baille less than an hour before he did himself, why'd he bother writing you a note? You two have a quarrel? A little unfinished business that sent him prematurely on his way?"

"He was murdered."

"Baille? You're out of your mind. This isn't Vanfossen, you know. Remember Baille? The guy with the needle in his arm? And that was pure horse, by the way. A quick way to go."

"Damon wanted me to meet him last night," Elizabeth said. "He'd figured out who the killer was."

"Sure. Why not? And you just hop right out in the middle of the night. What do you have to worry about? There's somebody's blood all over your house not a week ago. Nerves of steel, right? Because you're not in any danger, right?"

Stephen leaned forward.

"It wasn't suicide."

"Convince me."

"Elizabeth saw the killer."

Sibben looked narrowly at Elizabeth. Of course she did. Of course.

"Okay," he said irritably. "Let's hear it."

"I called you last night," Elizabeth said. "You said it was Keith's body."

"Yeah."

253

"Who identified him?"

"Nobody. We matched his prints."

"Is that usually how it's done?"

"Sometimes. Why? You want to take a look at him?"

Elizabeth ignored his taunt.

"You knew whose prints you were trying to match because of the rare blood type and because Keith was missing. It was 99 percent positive that it was Keith's body. Isn't that right?"

"Not 99 percent. But pretty certain, yeah. What's the point?"

"I don't know," Elizabeth admitted. "I thought if someone had come forward to identify the body, they might know who Keith was working for."

"Nope. Purely lab work. Of course, the prints have to be on file in a case like this. Prints could be all over a murder scene and if it's some ordinary Joe who has never been printed, big deal. They have to match prints on file or a suspect."

"But you had Keith's fingerprints? Did he have a criminal record?"

"Lots of people are fingerprinted. Anybody who's bonded. Vanfossen's prints were on file for his P. I.'s license. Is this going somewhere, Miss Purdin?"

She supposed not. She wondered if Keith had family, if that was fabrication as well as everything else about him. She thanked God they had had his fingerprints, that they hadn't called her.

"We saw Damon last night. Stephen and I and Mary Rhinehardt and Constance LeMirre. We were all together at my house."

"And I wasn't invited? I'm hurt."

Elizabeth ignored his sarcasm. She hardly heard it. She was reliving last night.

"Damon was his usual self, don't you think, Stephen?" She wasn't going to mention how guilty Damon had appeared, or Sam's reaction to him. She wasn't trying to decide if Damon was a murderer anymore. She had to prove that he was a victim. "He left with Stephen and Mary; Constance drove herself. Then he called me about three A.M. No, it was earlier. We hung up at three. We talked probably ten minutes, maybe fifteen. He told me he knew who the killer was. He was very lucid. He asked if I knew of big money changing hands. Blackmail money, he called it."

"So? He already knew. He wanted to see if his account had been discovered yet?"

"Why? If he was planning to kill himself in the next hour, what difference would it make?" Elizabeth ran a hand across her forehead distractedly. "If Damon had put together a blackmail scheme that had garnered him half a million dollars, do you think he would turn around and kill himself? Would you?"

"No, ma'am. But believe it or not, I'm no psychotic killer. Baille wouldn't have done himself in, either, if you hadn't confirmed that we were on to the account. That's how he knew it was over."

From any angle, Sibben would have Elizabeth play the role of the hangman.

"Damon was theorizing about the money. He had deduced the likelihood of blackmail. He wanted me to confirm it."

"He deduced? The guy was a junkie. I've got a sheet on him as long as my arm."

255

Elizabeth leaned forward, her voice quick and determined.

"You'd have to know Damon. He was a mathematical wizard. Really. When he was in school, he'd go up against a calculator, he was a chess ace. No one could touch him for mathematical brilliance. And that while he was heavily into drugs and alcohol.

"Everything and everyone he met was a riddle to be solved. He wouldn't leave it alone until he had it. And he would. There was no confusing or distracting him."

"Okay, if you say so. He's not the first egghead to go on self-destruct. Or to turn doper, either. Frankly, he sounds like he'd make a great killer. Bumping people off for some sporting satisfaction that's lost on the rest of us. You're not making a case for his innocence, you know."

"I'm not trying to. I simply want you to consider the man involved. If Damon weren't the killer, he'd be the one who could make sense out of it. The one who'd figure out who the murderer was and the motive and the whole sick fabric of it. And that's what he did. He figured it out. That's why he's dead."

"So you just take his word for it that he's solved the murders? You go out in the middle of the night to his place? Don't you find that just a little risky? Even you, Miss Purdin?"

"We were supposed to meet at an all-night grocery store. When he didn't show up for over an hour, I drove down the street where he lived. I thought he might have gotten delayed, and that I'd see him heading toward the store."

She didn't know what she'd have done if she *had* seen him. Unlocked the door and let him get into the car with her? Rolled down the window a crack to insist he go on to the Safeway and meet her there?

Stephen stirred. He was thinking the same thing. The chances she took. It scared him to death.

"I found his apartment building and stopped and turned off the lights. It was raining. I figured I could see better out the side windows using the light from the street lamp. I wanted to see down the walkway where Damon's apartment was.

"A man came running out of the darkness, right toward my car. When he saw me, he ran into the shrubbery and disappeared. But I saw his face. I would recognize him if I saw him again. I could sketch him."

"He came out of where?"

"From the direction of Damon's apartment."

"From the direction. Not *out* of the apartment?"

"No. It was too dark. But there was nowhere else he could have come from. The walk feeds through a narrow break in the shrubbery. He had to have come from Damon's."

"He didn't *have* to. I've been there all morning. Apartment 4 is just beyond Baille's. He could have come out of there."

"And ran when he saw me?"

Sibben shrugged.

"Maybe he had been looking the place over to see what he could rip off. He was feeling guilty."

"Who lives in the fourth apartment, Sibben?" Stephen asked.

"Nobody," Sibben admitted. "That's why I think

257

it was some would-be burglar. Maybe he even stumbled on Baille's body. He's not exactly going to call the police, is he?"

"Are you saying you won't look for the man Elizabeth saw?"

"Oh, we'll look. Miss Purdin can give me her drawings and she can look through the mug books if she wants. But you've proven nothing to me. Here's one dead psycho, a known drug abuser, with some powerful stuff hanging out of his arm. And here's a note saying he killed a couple people who we just happen to know *were* killed. Why would I look any further? Do you think I'm some kind of a masochist?"

"Do you have a copy of the note?" Elizabeth asked. "May I see it?"

"Yeah, I got a copy. I got the real thing." Sibben handed her a copy. "What's wrong with it? And don't tell me it isn't his handwriting, because we're supposed to have a forgery expert in the middle of this. It would be too sloppy even for my taste."

"I think it is his writing. I'm sure it is. But it's not what he would say. It's inaccurate."

Sibben sighed noisily.

"I've seen a lot of these," he told her. "Say a guy is about to waste himself. He isn't going to say, 'I'm killing myself because I'm a loser.' He's going to go with something grandiose. Something like, 'I'm killing myself because nobody understands how wonderful I am.' You see? You might call it inaccurate. He calls it a flaming work of art."

"All right," Elizabeth said. She was beginning to get a headache. "You're the expert. But we knew

258

Damon. He's not going to say something like, 'I'm compelled.' He was playing word games. He was saying someone was forcing him to say it." She shook her head. "And that's not all. He refers to his remembering my rule. To always leave a way out."

"Yeah. I liked that. Giving credit where credit's due with his last breath. Sick, but thorough."

"Where's the grandiosity in that? You're saying it's not characteristic."

Sibben raised his hands.

"So tell me."

"It was something he said on the phone tonight, this morning, whatever you want to call it. He said I was forgetting my number-one rule. I asked him what he was talking about, and he said, 'Don't trust anyone.' Those were his words. 'Don't trust anyone.' "

"That's it, huh? It's not good enough. The guy could have been rambling. He was busy anticipating that final rush. It was a good one as pure as that h was."

Elizabeth sat back impatiently. She said:

"So that's it? Case closed? What happened to your theory that I was involved? And by the way, what was Damon's reason for killing Ellen and Keith? What made him decide he had no option but to commit suicide? You weren't exactly breathing down his neck."

"I didn't say you weren't involved. I'm not convinced. But Baille wanted the blame, and he's got it. For all I know, you could have been in on it with him. You could have talked him into pulling the plug. And be sitting here now as sweet as you please, telling some story about seeing a man come from Baille's apartment. Pointing out flaws in Baille's suicide note just to make yourself look innocent. I'm sure nobody knows where the hell you were while Baille was checking out. You could have been there."

"And if you're wrong?" Stephen cut in sharply. "If Damon *was* murdered, and Elizabeth saw the killer? What do you think her life will be worth if he knows who she is and can get to her?"

"I said I'd look at Miss Purdin's sketch, didn't I? We can get in a police artist as well. But for all intents and purposes, this case is closed. The one in Portland is closed." He picked up the phone. "That reminds me. Your boy Baille was right. The Glover girl had been pregnant. But she'd delivered the baby. Full term. They brought in a forensic anthropologist. He said there was no question about it."

Elizabeth looked at Stephen. She could feel a chill run over her skin like an icy finger. The baby could have been there, too, tiny bones to be handled, catalogued, and thrown away.

Stephen put his hand over hers where it lay tautly on the arm of her chair. Sibben finished his phone conversation and hung up. Stephen asked, "What about the autopsy? When will you have the results?"

"On Baille? They're doing it now. But there aren't going to be any surprises. Straightforward overdose. We get them all the time. Most of them are accidents, of course. Too much, too fast, too pure." He yawned. "Too stupid."

"His arms were clean," Stephen said. "A lot of scarring, but no new tracks."

Sibben grinned wolfishly.

"Yeah. How about that? But it doesn't mean anything. Maybe he was shooting himself somewhere else. Maybe he was taking a little breather to get his habit back under control."

"He told Elizabeth he'd gone through drug rehab a couple months ago."

"Haven't they all? A habit gets expensive. Maybe too expensive to support. They dry out so it doesn't cost so much to feed the monkey. Of course, it doesn't take long to be right back up there again."

"But Damon was clean?"

"Prelims indicate he was. We'll know after the autopsy."

"And when will that be?"

Sibben looked at the clock. It was eating up the day.

"Why?"

"Think about this." Stephen leaned forward. There was an electricity in him. "We have a murderer who takes a particular interest in the most grisly of blood-spilling. The throat, the jugular vein, the carotid artery. It's violent, it's messy. Christ, it's the epitome of anger! It might look cold-blooded and tidy when there's no body, when the body has been buried for years. But it's not. It's fury and it's violence."

"Sure. I can buy that. But that doesn't mean he's going to turn that kind of rage on himself. He's not going to slash his own throat when he can go more or less painlessly and with the rush he's lived for."

"Right. I agree. But if it wasn't Damon Baille, if this lunatic felt that he had to use Damon's death to get some breathing space. If he forced a suicide note with a confession out of Damon, and made Damon OD. That's not what he wants. He wants the artery open and the blood flowing. He wants, without a doubt, to cut the throat."

"Maybe," Sibben ventured. "Theoretically."

"Theoretically. Fine. Let's take it a step further. The killer had a knife. He had a weapon menacing enough that he could force Damon to kill himself. A knife, in the hand of a madman who had killed with a knife in the past."

"Okay. Where's this going?"

"There's going to be a mark on Damon's neck. Something. This is a person who was aching to spill blood. He would have held the knife to Damon's throat. At some point, he would have toyed with the temptation of using it."

"Theoretically," Sibben said dryly. He tapped the file and looked at the clock. He picked up the telephone and punched in some numbers.

"Yeah, William? Sibben here. Having a good time down there? You find anything funny about that new stiff?"

He listened. Elizabeth wished she was anywhere but here. She could hear something, a drill or a saw, in the background. It was no time to get imaginative. She closed her fingers tightly around Stephen's.

"I don't know exactly. Cuts or scratches. Bruises, maybe?"

Sibben ran a hand over his face as he listened. He glanced at Elizabeth and Stephen.

"That's great," he said sarcastically. "I suppose I have to guess where it is?"

He listened again, this time for several minutes.

"Okay. Thanks, Will." He hung up the phone. Yeah, thanks. Thanks a lot.

"You called it," he admitted sourly. "They found

a superficial cut on Baille's neck. Right over the carotid artery." Sibben looked past Elizabeth and Stephen to the glass-partitioned office door. "Let's get the artist in here," he bellowed.

Chapter Twenty-nine

The sun was so bright Elizabeth's eyes hurt. Last night's storm might never have happened. Blown-over signs and piles of dry leaves had already been righted, swept away. The cars drawing up or leaving the parking lot gleamed with new washes and polish.

Elizabeth paid the cab driver. He was supposed to take her to the door of the Olive Tree Restaurant and wait until she was inside before driving away, but he didn't. In the clean, warm sunlight it seemed absurd that danger could exist, that Stephen had insisted she take a cab rather than drive her own car because a killer had seen it. Impossible to think a threat could lurk in the busy, mundane parking lot.

Elizabeth looked about her. It was difficult to believe that there was a winter storm watch in most of the states, that snow was falling or threatening, and the roads hazardous. As difficult to believe as that Damon was dead.

Elizabeth shivered and went up the steps. Perhaps Constance had already arrived and was waiting for her inside.

The maître d' led Elizabeth through the colorfully

welcoming ambience of a Greek coffee stall to the patio in the rear. Patterns of sunlight and shadow came through the latticed arbor to fall upon the tubs of flowers, the tables of the diners. The tension in Constance's face.

She saw Elizabeth immediately and smiled, half-smiled. She knew what this was about: it was about Stephen.

"Hello, Con. Mary." Elizabeth looked askance of Constance. The last person she had expected to see sitting at the table with Constance was Mary. She had supposed Mary had already gone home to Portland before Damon's body had been found.

Constance tossed off her drink and leaned across to touch her cheek to Elizabeth's.

"I invited Mary," she stated the obvious.

"I hoped we'd have a chance to talk privately," Elizabeth said. She forced Constance to meet her eyes. She had asked Constance to come alone.

"I know," Constance said wryly. "I think I know the drill, and I didn't want to hear it. Okay?"

"No. It's *not* okay. We've been friends too long to just give up. We can talk, Con."

"I'm supposed to listen to some unpalatable drool about how sorry you are?"

"No." Elizabeth sat down. "I'm no sorrier than you would be if things had gone the other way."

Constance laughed. It sounded natural and it was. She understood this, Elizabeth's hard side.

"God, I like you, Elizabeth. You're not half as nice a person as you would like to think you are."

"Then I'm in big trouble," Elizabeth smiled. "Because I don't think I'm nice at all."

"You're not!" Mary snapped. "Neither of you!

Damon is dead! Dead! And you haven't even mentioned him. It's sick!"

Constance shook out a cigarette. She rarely smoked, but now she did, and though her moves were confident, her hand trembled. She inhaled deeply and blew a cloud of smoke from her lips.

"Shut up, Mary. I knew I was crazy to bring you."

"And you're rude. But that's no surprise. You've always considered yourself head and shoulders above everyone else. Elizabeth is as bad. She's as snobbish as you are, and twice as cold."

Elizabeth ordered a glass of wine. Constance and Mary each had another. When the waiter had retreated, Elizabeth looked at Mary.

"Whatever your opinion, Mary, Constance has been honest about wanting a third person here. What was *your* reason for coming? To talk about Damon, right? Why? To feed your morbid curiosity?"

The gloves were off. Mary didn't like Elizabeth. She would have to say she loathed Constance. She had never been a part of their confidences. She would be astonished to know that there *were* none. Elizabeth and Constance recognized the strengths in each other, and the vulnerabilities. Their lives were private.

"*You* found him, Elizabeth. I want to know about that. How, in the name of all that is holy, did you come to be in that hovel at that hour? I swear to God, I can't forget what Damon said about you. That you killed Ellen. I wanted to see your face. I wanted to see what a murderess looked like."

"Christ!" Constance said explosively, beneath her breath. She lit another cigarette from the first, and shook her head at Elizabeth.

"She's an idiot. I wish it *was* you or me, love, who was the killer. I'd make sure Mary was next."

"That's not funny, Constance! Not even close. How you can sit here and talk like that with Damon hardly cold . . ." Mary took a tissue from her purse, unfolded it, and blew her nose. Last night she had been on the brink of shattering like glass, but now she looked merely tired. She was never going to get to go home.

It was where Elizabeth would have been without Stephen. She said quietly, "Damon called me last night."

"Why?" Mary demanded stridently. "He was at your place with us last night. Couldn't you talk in front of us?"

"He wanted her to come over and inject him with pure heroin, Mary. What else?" Constance said contemptuously. She waved her empty wineglass at the waiter.

"I didn't kill him, Mary. The police say it was suicide."

"Suicide? Damon? He's been having too good a time killing himself by inches. He wouldn't want to miss a second of a lingering finale. He was murdered."

Constance nodded reluctantly.

"I won't go on record as agreeing with Mary about anything, but I can't see Damon going with a bang, either. I'd expect something more appealing to his bizarre sense of humor. Liver disease, kidney failure. But one thing you can make bank on: it wasn't an accident, as far as Damon goes. He knew his stuff. If it was pure, he knew it, and if it was stepped on, he'd know how many times. He was an expert."

"That's what I mean. He was murdered."

"And you think Elizabeth did it? That's your usual rubbish, Mary."

"Of course you would say that, Constance. She's your friend. But it can be stupid to be blindly loyal. Look at Damon."

"Great parallel," Constance mocked. "Damon wasn't loyal to anything but his own twisted needs."

Mary's eyes narrowed. She said sharply, "Oh, yes? Damon admitted he came to Phoenix because of Elizabeth. He said she was at the center of all this. He even said he saw her kill Ellen."

"He was trying to get a rise out of Elizabeth. You yelled him down yourself, Mary. Why don't you remember that, or is your memory selective?"

"It doesn't matter," Elizabeth intervened. "Damon was murdered. I saw the man who did it."

"God, Elizabeth!" Constance winced. "Have the police got him?"

"Not yet. They put together a composite drawing. They're looking for him."

"Who is it? It can't be a stranger."

"Why can't it be, Mary?" Constance demanded. "Because you know it isn't?"

"What's that supposed to mean? That I have intimate knowledge of the man? Get a grip. Nobody can accuse me of knowing anything about this."

"Too true," Constance agreed sardonically. "No one has ever accused you of knowing anything."

"Get over yourself, Constance! I'm saying it's not a stranger. Why would we all be tied in, unless it's one of us? Is it Stephen?"

"See a psychiatrist," Constance advised. She ground out her cigarette and looked at Elizabeth.

"Sorry, love. You can't say I didn't know better. I thought this way would be easier. Was I wrong, or what?"

Elizabeth smiled faintly.

"We'll get through this, Con," she promised. "We'll get together. Go bowling or something."

"We may get through it," Constance said dryly, "but we won't go bowling. Maybe the horse races. Or a little fine dining. I hope you'll call me."

"I will. I hope you'll call me. I imagine you know the number."

Constance grimaced.

"I do," she admitted. "Aren't you going to tell me to forget it?"

"No. I want to hear from you."

"You said you wouldn't expect me to be sorry if things had gone the other way. Would you have visited me?"

Elizabeth knew she wouldn't have. She couldn't have watched Stephen with Constance, with any woman. She shook her head.

"No," she admitted.

"Then you'll understand. Give me some time." Constance took another cigarette, but didn't light it. She said tautly, "You know, Elizabeth, I *did* behave badly. I can't justify it by saying you told me it was over between you and Stephen. I could see it wasn't. I heard it in your voice. I could see it every time he looked at you. I just wanted it to be different. I thought I could make it be different. I should have known better."

"Well, excuse me! Let's just say I'm not here, shall we? I'll run along to the restroom and check the mirror to see if I've become invisible!" Mary pushed back her chair and left the table. There was a small silence after her departure. And then Constance said pensively, "She really is gross. It's not my imagination."

Elizabeth chuckled.

"She's being sensitive. Giving us a chance to talk privately. We *were* rude, ignoring her."

"She brings out the rudeness in me. She's so whiny and sanctimonious. I wish she'd flown the hell out of here last night before this awful business with Damon. She's stuck here now."

"Is she? Can't she give her statement and catch the next flight out?"

"In your dreams! She has to stay until the inquest, at least. If they decide he was murdered, I doubt if they'll let her leave."

"You're probably right."

"I'd like to see the composite of the man you saw. Did you know him?"

"No. And if you've ever seen those police sketches, you know how unlikely it is you'd recognize a person from one of them. I'm working on some sketches."

"What does Sibben think? Does he believe you saw the killer?"

"Who knows what Sibben thinks? He called in an artist for the composite. But he's not too enthusiastic about the idea of keeping the case open."

"What *is* Sibben enthusiastic about? I can't imagine."

"Crime," Elizabeth said positively. "Mary's coming back. I guess we should order."

"God, let's not. I've lost my appetite. I can't sit opposite her and still eat a good meal."

Mary came and sat down.

"I've decided I won't stay. You two can exchange confidences to your heart's content, and I won't have to be insulted or eat where I'm not sure how well the silver has been washed."

"Right," Constance said dryly. "I was just planning my own exit."

"That leaves Elizabeth," Mary purred. "Maybe she would prefer to join her admirer."

"I've noticed," Constance smiled teasingly at Elizabeth. "The big man of Royce Chem himself. Too bad Elizabeth's already involved with someone."

Elizabeth followed their glances to a table across the room. There were a half-dozen men there, businessmen. One of them, a distinguished-looking man with steel-gray hair and cold blue eyes, was looking straight at her. She felt herself pale, her heart lurch.

It was the man who'd murdered Damon.

He didn't look away. His expression was coldly ironic. It was Elizabeth who flinched.

Her throat closed up. She couldn't breathe. A terrible, nightmarish possibility was pounding in her head.

"That's Randolph Royce? Is that what you're saying?"

Constance exhaled smoke toward the ceiling.

"Right the first time."

Mary nodded confirmation.

Chapter Thirty

Elizabeth could not remember how she'd gotten to the police station. She sat alone in a small cubicle with a table and two chairs. Sibben was supposed to be coming. He was on his way, the dispatcher said. She did what they told her, she waited where they said, and she wouldn't have noticed if it was the middle of Grand Avenue on a Friday afternoon at rush hour.

But it wasn't Friday. It was a late Saturday afternoon, and heaven knew where Sibben had gotten to. She *had* to speak to Sibben.

Elizabeth's head was pounding. Randolph Royce! By all that was holy, she had put the baby into the hands of a cold-blooded killer! And only a tissue-thin fabric of lies was keeping the boy alive.

How near was he to discovering the truth about the little boy? He had to be close! There was no guessing what he'd gotten out of Damon, but it could be everything. The boy could already be dead.

Elizabeth jumped to her feet and began to pace the small room. She hadn't smoked in two years, but if there had been a pack in front of her now, she'd have emptied it. There was a scream of urgency, of futility, closing her throat.

"Okay," Sibben said. He must have come straight to the interrogation room. He tossed beeper and keys, his ID badge, and a worn baseball cap on the table. He looked hot and irritable and ready to throw her out. "Here I am. What's the big shake-up? You've decided to confess?"

Elizabeth would never have believed she could be relieved to see the man. But he was here and he was going to help. He was going to prevent the death of a child. He had to.

Elizabeth said shakily, "I saw the murderer. I know his name."

"Is that a fact? What is it?"

"Randolph Royce. He's the head of the Royce Chemical Conglomerate."

Sibben whistled. He wasn't writing, he was leaning back in his chair, watching Elizabeth, and she couldn't begin to guess what he was thinking.

"Sure, I know who he is. A friend of the chief. The mayor's golfing partner."

"I'm sorry," Elizabeth said tautly. She *was* sorry, she was sick. "But it doesn't make him any less a killer."

Sibben didn't want to hear it. He pressed his fingers into his eye sockets.

"Where's Kenwood?"

"Stephen? He's at work. Why?"

"You'd better call him. You're going to want to talk this over with him before you start making accusations in that direction."

"I left a message. He'll come here when he gets it." Elizabeth drew a tremulous breath and sat down. She looked at Sibben. She held him with her intensity and her fear. "You're going to have to listen to me. A child will die if you don't."

"I'm listening. I just don't like it." He rubbed his chin with the back of his hand. "I want this on tape, unless you've got a good reason why it shouldn't be."

"It's all right. Unless it wastes time. We have to hurry."

Sibben took a small tape recorder from the desk drawer, rummaged for a blank tape, and clicked it on.

"Okay," he said. "Shoot."

Elizabeth startled him by reaching out quickly and switching it off. She left her hand there, over the microphone, as if it could still pick up her words.

"I'm sorry. Some of this has to be absolutely confidential."

"It can't be. It'll come out in court if the case gets that far."

Elizabeth leaned her head into her hands and thought frantically. Maybe even in this eleventh hour she had to keep the child out of it. If Royce went to trial for murder and was acquitted, he would walk away with all the information he needed to know. The boy wouldn't have a chance.

On the other hand, the case against Royce might rely on his motive for killing Ellen and Keith and Damon. Only the existence of the little boy could explain Royce's actions.

Elizabeth's head ached. She was desperate. She wished more fervently than Sibben did that Stephen were here.

Damon had said David Royce was the father of Ellen's baby and it must be true. Ellen's "they" who wanted the baby dead was the powerful Royce conglomerate. Ensuring no illegitimate heir to the Royce millions.

Oh, God, did that make sense? She couldn't think straight. If the baby was David's, was it such a natural conclusion Royce would want it killed that Ellen already knew it at the time of the child's birth? He hadn't killed anyone at that point. Or apparently hadn't. Unless the drug-tampering deaths laid at David's door were really his brother's work. Maybe he'd killed David.

Good Lord, she was reaching now! Constance had seen David commit suicide. Randolph Royce certainly had no hand in David's death. There was no reason to think he was behind the drug-tampering.

Elizabeth shivered. Perhaps it was some genetic weakness. Two brothers, both with blood on their hands. It was a nightmare. Like some absurd theme of madness in a gothic tale. She had always scoffed at such unlikely melodrama.

She pressed the button on the recorder.

"I'm ready," she said tensely.

"Good. Let's hear it."

"It was Randolph Royce I saw last night leaving the complex where Damon was killed. I can identify him."

"You said that. Tell me something new."

"He had to have killed Keith."

"Why? And where does the kid come in? You know, the one whose life depends on me."

Elizabeth bit her lip.

"What will it take to put Royce in prison?"

"A lot, lady. You can't even put him at the murder scene. Sure, he came from that direction, and it was

275

a dark, wet night in a neighborhood where nobody in their right mind would be. But you were there. Kenwood was. Give me some proof that this guy wasn't as innocent as you and Kenwood claim to be."

She had none. Without exposing the little boy, she couldn't even give them a reason for Royce to commit murder.

"What about the blackmail money?"

"Yeah, that's what I'd like to know. What about it? Somebody has been blackmailing *him,* not the other way around. And that's a supposition, if you'll recall. We haven't got diddly that Royce himself was behind the payments or that they were in any way criminal. Maybe he's making charitable donations."

"To *my* account," Elizabeth derided.

"Right. To your account. How do *you* explain it?"

"He's setting me up. It's a lot of money, but he's not going to miss it. He might consider it an investment. A way to discredit me as a witness against him."

Sibben opened a stick of chewing gum and rolled it up before putting it in his mouth.

"He didn't know you would need discrediting when he set up the account. He didn't know you were going to see him running away from Baille's."

Elizabeth hesitated. It was a fine line between the whole truth and half.

"He's been following me for years. Or having me followed. Keith must have worked for him."

"No kidding? Why would he follow you?"

"I have information he wants."

Sibben snorted.

"Yeah, that sounds about right. Maybe he's paying you for the information, and you're a little slow

276

on the uptake. Maybe maybe maybe. Maybe Van-fossen worked for him. What do we do for proof?"

"We'll ask him," Elizabeth said. She leaned forward, her eyes bright with fear. "I'll demand more money. I'll insist we meet."

"Right. You snap your fingers and Randolph Royce comes running."

"He knows that I know. He has to kill me."

"What about the information? That must be why you've never thought you were in danger, I take it? So now he just flushes that? He bumps you off?"

She stood up. She felt trapped in this little, airless room. But the resignation went as deeply as the terror. If this was ever going to end, she knew it had to be like this. There was no more hiding from a faceless killer. He had a face and he had a name and he was so close to the little boy that it terrified her.

"He'll get it some other way," she said flatly. "Maybe he killed Damon for it."

"So that's it! You think Baille talked?"

Did she? Would Royce have been sitting in a restaurant having a late lunch with business associates if he had just killed his son? God, he probably would! But she couldn't believe it. She couldn't let herself.

"No. He killed Damon because Damon knew who he was. It was just bad luck that I saw him leaving. But he'll have to weigh his priorities, and I'm dangerous alive. I'll expose him."

She remembered how he had looked at her across the busy room. Coldly ironic. Unsurprised. Waiting.

"So you demand more money," Sibben said thoughtfully. "It's risky. Say we wire you, cover the area. We've got to have a threat before we move in.

If you're right and it's him, he's going to move quickly. And damned effectively."

Elizabeth ran a finger across her lips. Her throat was tight, tight. She could almost feel the cold steel pressing against her flesh.

"He might talk about the killings. You'd have it on tape."

"Yeah, he might. But it's not likely. That's TV stuff. We're going to have to expect an attack. Anticipate it. That, together with placing him in the vicinity of Baille's death, is a start. We can get him behind bars while we tie him into the other killings."

Elizabeth took a deep breath and let it out.

"All right," she said faintly. "Let's do it.

Chapter Thirty-one

Elizabeth sat in the conference room. People came and went, uniformed officers. Someone brought her a cup of scalding coffee, but it didn't seem to warm her. She was locked inside herself. She was waiting.

She didn't want to die. She didn't want to come close to dying. There were so many things she wanted to do.

She wanted to lie in Stephen's arms until the dream quality was gone, until she began to believe that she could wake up any hour of the night and know he would be there. She wanted to throw the ball for Sam. She wanted to plant pansies in the yard.

Sibben said it was risky. That probably meant she didn't have a prayer. He probably couldn't help but get a kick out of the irony in this: the woman he'd been sure was a murderess or an accessory to murder being used as bait for the real killer.

She sat behind the long conference table with her back to the window. There was nothing to see through the glass but another wall, so close that if the window wasn't sealed, she could reach through and touch the cold brickwork. There were no winter flowers, no migratory birds singing, nothing. Elizabeth preferred facing the room, although it wasn't much itself.

She didn't know where she was, but it was far away. In Portland, perhaps, years ago. She didn't see Stephen until he was beside her.

He pulled out a chair and sat down, so close that Elizabeth could see the tiny fine lines that ran from the corners of his eyes. How colorless he was beneath the sun-brown warmth of his skin.

"You've seen Sibben," she said quietly, and it wasn't a question. She could see it in his face.

He leaned toward her and they could have been alone. Everything and everyone fell away. He took her cold hands between both of his.

"I won't let you do this, Elizabeth."

She was staggered. She searched his face and she didn't know what to say. Everything was set up but the phone call to Royce.

"Sibben thinks it will work."

"Of course he does!" Stephen ground out. "He's in no danger! No one he loves is! It's *Miami Vice* mentality. What he does best, I have no doubt."

Elizabeth's voice was low, but the words were quick and jerky.

"I have to get the little boy out of this, Stephen. It's my fault he's in the middle of it. I put him there."

"You didn't know. Christ, no one could have known! You aren't failing him just because you value your own life!"

"I *would* be failing him," she said quietly, "if I backed out now."

Stephen shook his head. His hands were holding her, but she was slipping away.

"What about us?" he asked bleakly. "What about me? Aren't you failing me?"

She knew she was. That was the worst of it.

"Yes," she admitted. There were tears in her voice. "But I don't know what else to do."

"Neither do I. But this isn't it. Meeting Royce. I pray to God you care enough about me not to put yourself into this danger."

"Don't you know?" she whispered.

Some of the tension went out of him.

"Tell me," he prompted.

Elizabeth chuckled softly.

"There are people listening," she reminded him.

"Good." He was ready to laugh, but it wasn't with amusement. It was going to be all right, better than all right. She was reaching out to him, not simply letting him reach out to her. His eyes crinkled at the corners. "I may need witnesses."

"Do you think so?"

"It couldn't hurt. I might need someone to remind me that you almost said you love me."

"Almost? I thought I said it."

"No," he smiled. "You didn't."

"Are you sure?"

"Positive."

"Hmmm," she said. She pushed back her chair and stood up. Half an hour ago her legs were too weak to hold her, but now she was laughing. She could have run the mile in her best time.

She took Stephen's hand and drew him down the length of the room to the door at the end. It was a small washroom. The basin was chipped and the floor was bare, cracked concrete.

"This is nice," he teased her.

"Good. I'm glad you like it."

Elizabeth put her arms around Stephen's neck. She leaned into him, pressed her mouth to his. The kiss was endless. She could feel the thick pounding of his heart, of hers.

"I love you," she said.

"Don't meet Royce."

Even in his arms she could feel the chill.

"If there's any other way, Stephen, I won't. I've racked my brain."

"There is. There *has* to be. If Sibben is forced to give up this idea, who knows what he might come up with? It's his job, for God's sake!"

"He wasn't pleased to hear it was Randolph Royce. He probably wishes we'd go home and forget it. I didn't tell him about the boy."

"No? That's best for the little boy, but I don't know how far Sibben will go without the whole story. How far he *can* go. He may decide to charge us with obstruction, or some such garbage."

"I'm sure he's hoping I'll change my mind about naming Royce."

"Then he's out of luck. Royce has to be this close to knowing who the boy is."

"I know. I've been scaring myself that Damon told him. They've got to arrest him right away, Stephen. It's the only chance that little boy has."

"We'll talk to Sibben." Stephen opened the door. Sibben and several other officers were sitting at the table.

"It's close in there," Sibben observed dryly. "That's why we usually go in one at a time." He tossed down the clipboard. "Don't tell me. We're moving to Plan B, right?"

"Right," Stephen said. "Unless you'd like to bring in *your* wife to use as decoy."

"Thanks. It's a good idea, but I don't think she'd go for it." He motioned to the other officers. "You met Nichols the night Vanfossen bought it. The other two are Watts and Fordyce. I guess I may as well send them back to their units."

"That's up to you. It's not going to be a fair fight, if that's what you mean."

Sibben grunted.

"I'll keep them. It's hard enough to requisition help without tossing them out with the bathwater." He drew the clipboard toward him. "This is what we're looking at: an old murder which may or may not be solved. Portland PD can worry about it. We're more concerned with the two fresh ones. Baille early this morning. Vanfossen little more than a week ago and just ID'd last night.

"Vanfossen was a PI. We know that much. We don't know who he was working for, but we know who he was tailing." He gave Elizabeth a sarcastic little nod. "There were no prints, nothing, at the murder scene. We wouldn't have known the identity of the victim until he floated up if Miss Purdin hadn't so generously helped us there.

"And the body's not doing us much good. Badly decomposed. Had his throat cut, which was obvious at the scene, with blood everywhere. It's pretty much a zero.

"Then there's Baille. Clear case of OD on heroin, pure stuff. A known user, one of Portland's favorite scrotes. To all intents and purposes, deciding to take a long walk off a short pier. Leaves a suicide note implicating himself in the other two murders.

Couldn't be tidier, right? Wrong. Miss Purdin, coincidentally in the neighborhood at 4:30 A.M., sees none other than our esteemed king of the pharmaceutical world, Randolph Royce, leaving Baille's apartment building. If that's not enough, he runs. Not a confession of guilt, of course, but a little uncharacteristic in a dignified pillar of the community.

"And then there's the small matter of a cut on Baille's neck. This wasn't a guy who shaved, you understand. He's got a superficial nick right over the artery to his brain. The same one as Vanfossen and the girl in Portland had severed as a cause of death, which, incidentally, was possible to determine after all this time because the slash was so deep it cut into the bone. Not a nice person, our killer.

"We've got no prints, of course. That would be asking too much. And that's about the size of what we're going on. It adds up, if you throw in a six-pack of beer, to exactly nothing. Zero. If anybody wants to argue that, I'm listening."

"I'll argue it," Stephen said sharply. "You've got $450,000 in blackmail money. In the name of a woman who doesn't know where it came from and didn't set up the account. You've got the word of a man who was an hour away from dying that he could name the killer and supply motive and means."

"Whoa, Kenwood. Let's hold up a minute. That business about motive intrigues me. What *is* the guy's motive, by the way? It's dirty business, murder. Not something an important, respected man takes on lightly. Not unless he's some kind of a psycho."

"He *is* some kind of a psycho, for God's sake! You must know about his brother. David was schizophrenic. He tampered with the prescription drugs he was

284

handling and several people died. He killed himself."

"Yeah, I've looked at that. But I don't like it. Schizophrenia is supposed to have some genetic tendencies, but nothing like this. You can't say a guy is a murderer because his brother was. If that was the case, we could lock up all the family members of any given felon and call it a job. Everything would be nice and they wouldn't need us anymore. No more crime."

"Royce has gone a long way to cover up what his brother did. He's paid blackmail to keep it quiet. He's killed."

"Uh-uh. That would mean he thought Vanfossen and then Baille were behind the blackmail. When all he has to do is look at the name on the account. If he wanted to kill the person blackmailing him, he would have taken out Miss Purdin.

"Anyway, there's no reason to let himself be blackmailed on his brother's behalf. Royce paid up at the time. He approached the families of the victims and settled with them privately. It's not like exposure now will net him time. It was all handled legally and above-board."

"It didn't reach the press."

"You're right on that. The great destroyer of credibility. Now, *that* I'll buy. He might pay plenty to keep it out of the public eye. But murder is stretching it. And as I said before, it's Miss Purdin who he'd be after. There's not even a tie-in between him and Baille. Or him and Vanfossen, for that matter. That's why it's going to take an open threat on Miss Purdin's life to hold him on any of this."

"There *is* a tie-in," Elizabeth said quietly. "Keith worked for Royce."

"You don't know that," Sibben demurred. "And you can't prove it. Besides, it's no crime to hire a man who later winds up dead."

"I *can* prove it. Royce killed Keith."

"Okay," Sibben leaned back and ran a hand across his eyes. "I'm game. Prove it."

"I have a phone tape of Keith's employer threatening to kill him. He doesn't give his name, but surely there are ways to identify his voice. Compare the recording to Royce's voice? It's got to be him."

"No kidding?" Sibben mocked. "Illegally obtained wiretaps don't go very far in court."

"It was my house. Maybe I should have asked his permission before I recorded him. I'll remember to do that the next time he threatens to kill someone on my phone."

"Okay, okay. We can give it a listen. But these things aren't usually admissible. What we'd need, assuming the tape's good and we could get a voice match on Royce, is his admission that Vanfossen worked for him. That sounds harmless enough. If we're talking to him, anyway, right, kids?" Sibben threw his hands wide for the silent officers. "See how easy it is, being a detective? Take a break. If they go together to pick up the tape, they may not be back for hours."

Chapter Thirty-two

"This isn't going to work," Elizabeth said bleakly. It had been her idea, but now she was frightened. Her lips were dry, and she still felt pinched and pale from hearing Keith's voice on the tape.

"Sure it is. Not going to chicken out now, are you, Miss Purdin?" Sibben couldn't resist. He added, "Not again?"

"Back off, Sibben," Stephen gritted.

The air crackled with tension. Sibben ran a hand over his jaw, across his forehead.

"Okay, maybe it's been a long day. There's a cure for it. Let's get this over with. Let's plug into Royce's number and see what we can get." He looked at Elizabeth. "Ready?"

"Not yet. Listen to me a minute. Are we heading in the right direction with this? Assume you get a match on the voice prints and even that he admits Keith worked for him. We're calling him from the police station, for heaven's sake. Isn't that entrapment or something?"

Sibben rolled his eyes.

"No," he said irritably. "It's not entrapment or something. Can we get this over with?"

"So if you get a voice match, what I'm really doing is getting him away from his home so you can arrest him, right?"

"That is *not* what you're doing. Just the opposite. We want the guy at home. He's less likely to come unglued around his family."

Elizabeth pressed her fingers to her eyes. Before God, it was the last thing she would let happen. Force Grace and the boy to witness Royce's arrest.

"In the meantime, we've got officers canvasing the neighborhoods where Vanfossen and Baille were wasted, showing everyone pictures of our man Royce. If he's the killer, somebody will recognize him. They'll place him at the murder scene."

"*I* placed him at the murder scene. It hasn't done much good."

"Now, don't get sensitive on us, Miss Purdin. It's nothing personal. We have to do better than his being in the vicinity when the victim himself is claiming suicide. And when," Sibben's voice thinned, "the suspect is God Himself."

"You don't like this much, do you, Sibben?" Stephen taunted.

"Like it? Christ, I hate it! We're not playing penny ante with some street scum here. This better be one righteous arrest, or my career is history. I'm selling cars for my brother-in-law. And I hate my brother-in-law."

"What if he won't admit Keith worked for him? You won't even question him, will you?"

"If the voice prints tally with the guy threatening to kill Vanfossen, we'll bring him in. If they don't, we

288

don't arrest him. That's simple enough. I'm not sticking my neck out, lady."

"All right," Elizabeth said quietly. "Let's call him."

"Right. You ready, Collings?" Sibben asked the electronics expert.

They were in a small, soundproof room. Royce's voice would be picked up on a receiver and transmitted into the room.

"Sure. Ready as I'll ever be. Lights, camera, action."

Sibben laughed. "What do you think this is? MTV? Next thing I know, you'll be doing music videos." He looked at Elizabeth. "Okay. You know the drill. Make it convincing. Nobody's going to deny we're dealing with one bright hombre here. Get him to admit his connection with Vanfossen if you can. Collings will be giving us the nod as he gets Royce's voice and compares it to the one on the tape. If it's thumbs up, we're in business.

"We want to know where we can find him when we come with the cuffs. That means we don't want him scared off. With his dough, he could be in Rio de Janeiro before we can blink an eye, so play it cool. Ready?"

"I'm ready. Try his office number first. He may not even be home."

Sibben shook his head in exasperation.

"You're a bleeding heart, Miss Purdin. It may not occur to you, but even murderers go home occasionally. It's two in the morning, you know."

She was too tired, too strung up, to have noticed the hour. These next few minutes could decide everything, end the hell they had all been living in. And she felt so brittle and spent that she might shatter.

Sibben nodded to Collings, giving him the go-ahead to ring Royce's office. The steady burr of the phone filled the room.

It was an answering service. Elizabeth was advised to call back in the morning, that the offices were empty. She waited grimly while Royce's home number was punched in.

A businesslike voice replied, "Royce residence. Mrs. Ardway speaking."

"I'd like to speak to Mr. Royce, please," Elizabeth said.

"I'm sorry. Mr. Royce has retired for the evening. If you would like to leave a message, you may be assured he will receive it first thing in the morning."

"I have to speak to him now, I'm afraid . . ." she hesitated. "Tell him it's Elizabeth Purdin calling."

"One moment, Miss Purdin." She was put on hold. The woman was probably consulting a list of persons whose calls Royce would take at any hour. Her name would be on it. A man had to be prepared to take calls from his blackmailer at a moment's notice, she thought bitterly.

"I'm ringing Mr. Royce, Miss Purdin."

She knew it. She could hear it. Royce saying a brusque, "Yes?" and Mrs. Ardway's voice telling him that an Elizabeth Purdin was on the line. The moment of hesitation from Royce, while Grace Royce's voice echoed Elizabeth's name faintly in the background. Elizabeth could feel her shock.

"I'll take the call in the study," Royce said curtly, and hung up the phone. Elizabeth wondered tautly if Grace would speak to her, if she would pick up the phone and listen to what Elizabeth and her husband might be saying. But she didn't. She was trusting Elizabeth to know what she was doing. Elizabeth wished her trust were justified. She was saving the boy, but she was destroying Grace's life just the same.

"Miss Purdin?" Royce said evenly. It was the voice from the recording with Keith. She knew now why there had been a whisper of familiarity in it. There was something, an enunciation, of his brother David. "You're changing your style. I hadn't thought an open confrontation would suit you."

"That's interesting, coming from you. A man who just happens to turn up where people are being killed."

"Yes. That was close, wasn't it? Another five minutes either way and no one would have been the wiser. You must have been appalled."

"I was," Elizabeth admitted. "I didn't expect to see you there."

"Then I had an advantage over you. Because I wasn't the least surprised to see you."

"Really? I wonder why you ran."

Royce laughed. There was no amusement in it.

"Do you? Do you indeed? It would seem obvious."

"You're right. One can't afford to be seen where one has just committed murder."

"A great truth, Miss Purdin. Which makes it all the more surprising that you should call me."

"I don't see why. I want more money."

"Of course you do. And I'm supposed to hand it over. You seem to be a little confused about who has what on whom."

"I'm not confused at all. David was the one who

291

was confused. Remember David? Your brother who killed people?"

There was a pause.

"How much do you want?" Royce asked.

"How much did you pay Keith Vanfossen?" Elizabeth taunted him.

"Not enough," Royce said bitterly. "Not nearly enough."

Elizabeth glanced at Sibben. He nodded, Collings was giving his own exaggerated nod that the voice prints appeared to be matching.

"Was he supposed to kill me?"

Royce snorted.

"Hardly. He was selling information and I was buying. But he was a bungler. In the long run, he was less than useless."

She didn't want to get into what the information was. She didn't want Sibben hearing about the boy. Royce wasn't going to admit on the telephone or anywhere else that he was stalking a child to kill him.

"I want $50,000." Elizabeth said.

"Is that all?" Royce mocked. "Aren't your deposits coming in on time? You should have gotten the last one a few days ago."

"The police are watching the account. I can't get a dime of it."

"Tut tut. You should have demanded it in cash. Or had it put into a Swiss account."

"The police wouldn't have found the account if they hadn't been watching me after Keith died. I can thank you for that."

"You can thank yourself. How soon do you want the money?"

Sibben was beginning to see where this was going.

292

He shook his head strongly at Elizabeth. He wrote on a pad and shoved it across the desk in front of her. *Home,* it read. She turned her chair so that he was behind her.

"In an hour," she said. "I'll meet you at your office."

"Where am I supposed to get $50,000 in cash in an hour?"

"I don't know. In your change pocket?"

"Why the office?"

That was what Sibben wanted to know. He underlined the word *Home* twice and walked around to stand in front of her. He held the pad close to her face.

She wasn't going to put Grace through that. Seeing him arrested. And the boy, whose life had never been any more secure than what his father read in the next day's mail.

"Why not? I've never been there. It's probably really something."

"No. *You're* really something." He spoke bitterly. He might have been angry, he had to be, but it was cold anger. It was calculated. It reminded Elizabeth of how glad she was that she *wasn't* meeting him in the darkened recesses of the Royce Chemical Conglomerate building. "One hour."

He dropped the phone back onto the hook.

Chapter Thirty-three

"Cute," Sibben rasped. "If one of my officers ends up injured because of that little stunt, I'll hold you personally responsible, Purdin. You knew the rules."

"I know the rules," she admitted tiredly. "But I wonder if you do. I wonder if you ever listen long enough to hear."

"Oh, I'm listening, all right. The guy admits he hired Vanfossen. That's what we wanted. But you blew the rest. I don't want Royce on the move. I don't want him out of his house. We could pick him up right now if you hadn't thrown in that monkey wrench. But no, you've given him an hour. You know what that hour's good for?"

"Yes," Elizabeth said tautly. "He's got an hour to kill me."

"Well, imagine that. She *is* playing with a full deck. Who would have thought?"

"Can it, Sibben," Stephen advised shortly. He stood up and drew Elizabeth to her feet. "Let's go home, Elizabeth."

Yes. That was what she wanted. She was exhausted. She couldn't remember how long it had been since she had last eaten. She and Constance and Mary had forgone a late lunch at the Olive Tree, and that had been ages ago.

"I need to pick up Sam. He's probably as hungry as I am."

Stephen's fingers closed around hers. She was too pale, but she was all right. In another hour they would have Royce and it would all be over. After all these years, another hour was child's play.

And she had always been in danger. Royce had wanted the information she had about the whereabouts of the child, but at any time he could have turned and struck out violently, as he had at Vanfossen and Damon. She couldn't delude herself any longer that she had been in no danger.

"We'll get Sam on our way. Sibben, we'll be waiting to hear from you. Call us as soon as you have Royce."

"It may be late," Sibben said sourly.

"We'll be up."

They drove to Elizabeth's rental. The lights were all off and the ghosts were back. They paced the darkened yard.

Stephen must have felt it, too, or felt her fear. They didn't go in. He took her keys and went to the gate at the side and let Sam out. Sam howled with delight and hunger, and he was more than pleased to leap into the car and be driven away.

"Poor Sam, poor puppy," Elizabeth commiserated. She scratched his ears. "Do you think Royce will be looking for me, Stephen? That he is now?"

"I don't know," he admitted. "But it doesn't matter. There's nothing he can do. We'll be home before he can drive that far. And once you're inside, he can't harm you. If he tried to get in, the police would have him in minutes. The security is very tight."

He reached out and brushed her white face with his fingers. He was driving fast. There was very little traffic.

"You did beautifully tonight, Libby. You gave Grace Royce and her son the distance they'll need. I was proud of you."

"So was Sibben."

Stephen grinned.

"To hell with Sibben."

The house was quiet. They went in through the garage and there was no one there. There were no shadows or menace or death. Elizabeth let out her breath on a long sigh and leaned against Stephen.

"May I have my nervous breakdown now?" she asked. "Or should I feed Sam first?"

"I think Sam would like to eat first. We'll eat, too. Then maybe it will be too late to bother."

"You're right. I am a little too tired for hysterics. Do you have a bowl for Sam? I'll have to get his things tomorrow."

"I'll feed him. Why don't you put a match to the fire and get warm. They're on the mantel."

Elizabeth wandered along to the living room. She wanted to see a clock, and she *was* cold. The hour she had given Royce wasn't half over and it was threatening to crawl.

She lit the fire and sank down on her knees before it.

The seven years since she had taken Ellen's baby and walked out into the snow hadn't seemed to pass as slowly as this hour was passing. Waiting for it to all be over, waiting to hear that a murderer was neutralized.

Neutralized. That was an odd choice of words. But he would still exist, he wasn't dead, like Ellen and Damon and Keith. His crimes were still there, fresh and bleeding. They weren't exorcised, they were only pending.

If they got him. If he hadn't suspected a trap and fled with his usual timing and skill. Elizabeth shivered.

They ate sitting close together in front of the fire. Sam lay with his head on his paws and watched them. He wasn't allowed to beg, and he was full besides, but it did no harm hoping that something would fall. He'd know where to look when he was given permission to get up.

Elizabeth grew quieter. She watched the slow hands of the clock. If she had fallen asleep she would probably have slept for twenty-four hours, but she wasn't sleeping, she was waiting. She was as tense as a coiled spring.

"He's not going to call," she said bleakly at last.

"He'll call." Stephen set their plates aside and put his arms around her. She leaned into him and closed her eyes.

"It made me sick, hearing that tape again," she said. "Keith's voice, Royce's. He sounds a little like David, enough to make me think I'd heard him before.

"I moved in with Constance the same day as I listened to that tape. I was having terrible dreams and I thought maybe they would go away. But I took them with me."

"I know," Stephen said grimly. "I know about bad nights.

"After you left, I went to Denver. I guess I told you. I hated it. It was the loneliest place on earth. And it was me.

"Sometimes I would almost believe I was going to make it. And then one night I would slam awake, as if I'd hit a brick wall, and your voice would be in my head. Calling me. Needing me.

"The last time it happened I just gave it up. I called Sara. She's always kept track of where you were, and when she said you were in Phoenix, I came here. And then Constance transferred, and it looked like I could come back into your life naturally." He shook his head, his words were quick and intense. "But if it hadn't worked out like that, I'd have found some other way. Even if it meant seeing again in your eyes that you thought I'd killed Ellen."

"Sometimes I thought you had," Elizabeth admitted starkly. "I had nightmares about it. But you were still all I ever wanted."

The telephone shrilled.

Elizabeth jumped violently. She looked at Stephen and the color that had come back into her face leached away.

"This is it," Stephen said. He got to his feet and pulled her up. "It's all over, Elizabeth."

She knew it. It must be over. But she couldn't move, she couldn't pick up the phone in case it wasn't, in case it was only to learn that Royce had gotten away.

Stephen lifted the receiver.

"Kenwood here."

"It's Sibben. We got him."

She was standing in the curve of Stephen's arm and she could hear Sibben's voice. He sounded like he was on an adrenaline high.

"That's wonderful. Tell Elizabeth." Stephen put the phone into her hand and smiled at her, and it was all right, his eyes and his voice said it was and he had never lied to her.

"Hello?" she said.

"Yeah. I told Kenwood. We got Royce."

"Was he . . . was he armed?"

"You bet. Snub-nosed .38. Makes a nasty hole."

She didn't doubt it. She asked faintly, "Was anyone hurt?"

"Nope. Royce is furious, but he still thinks his lawyers can pull him out."

"Can they?"

Sibben gave a hard laugh.

"Guess again," he said. "We got an eyewitness. Came out from under a rock to tell us he and Baille scored some grass a few times. Lets himself into the vacant apartment next to Baille's whenever he doesn't feel like crashing at the park. He ID'd Royce as the man he saw going into Baille's place the night and the time that Baille died. We got Royce cold."

Elizabeth let out her breath on a long, shaken sigh. She put down the phone and turned to put her arms around Stephen. She began to cry.

Chapter Thirty-four

Elizabeth sat in the square of sunshine that streamed in through the window. She had a thousand things to do, boxes to pack and sort and label, but she did none of them. She watched Sam play with his tennis ball in the back yard.

It was a beautiful November morning. A few hardy flowers bloomed along the back fence, a memory of previous renters. Every bird that had migrated from the north must have come to Phoenix for the winter. Doves and mockingbirds called from the trees, and small sparrows rustled in the palm fronds. Pigeons made fast, darting shadows overhead. Even an occasional hawk circled lazily over the city.

Elizabeth sat cross-legged, her elbows upon her knees. It was over. There *was* an end to hell, it wasn't interminable. There was a day when one opened one's eyes and the shadows were gone, and the fear, and the dread. It was happening for Elizabeth.

She had handed her last three designs over to Bill this morning and it was wonderful. It was a load off her shoulders, but it was nothing compared to seeing a murderer behind bars. It was insignificant beside knowing that a child she had momentarily nurtured was out of danger. She had longed for the day.

Sam came to stare at her through the glass. He dropped the ball hopefully and it rolled across the cement. She was supposed to be tantalized into coming out to throw it for him.

Elizabeth laughed. She had never felt like this. Free and alive and filled with confidence in the future. She got up and went outside.

"Okay, Sam. I'm wasting time anyway. I might as well be constructive about it." She threw the ball and watched him kick up dry grass and bits of sod in his enthusiastic pursuit of the missile. The sun was warm on her head.

She was stooping to take the ball from Sam when she heard the telephone ringing.

"One more," she told Sam, and threw the ball again before going back into the house.

"Hello?"

"Elizabeth?"

Something in that one word sent a chill down Elizabeth's spine.

"Grace?"

"Yes. It's Grace. I've got to see you."

Elizabeth drew a chair toward her and sat down. She ran a hand across her forehead.

There was still a hell for Grace Royce. Her boy was safe but she was losing her husband, her friend, in the most horrible way. Stripped of respect, of decency. Dragged through the legal system, the press, publicly and privately destroyed, while his wife could do nothing but watch.

"Grace, I can't tell you how sorry I am at how this turned out."

301

There was a long pause. And then Grace said in a flat, strained voice, "I don't blame you. You've got to know that."

"I helped the police, Grace, but there was no way I could have warned you. I'm sorry."

"It doesn't matter," Grace said, and she sounded as if she meant it, as if her will and strength were gone. She sounded broken.

"Is your little boy all right?" Elizabeth asked sharply. She didn't know what it was, but she sensed something. Something badly wrong.

Either that, or she had thought in such channels for too long.

Grace took an audible breath. It shivered on the phone as if she had been crying.

"He's fine. I'm sorry, Elizabeth. I should be thanking you for everything you've done. Protecting my son. But it's hard. I'm . . . I'm still shattered."

"I know," Elizabeth sighed. She had been imagining things where none existed. "Grace, is there someone I could call for you? You shouldn't be alone."

"I'm all right. I will be. But I need to see you. You're the only one who can understand the nightmare this has been."

Yes, Elizabeth understood the nightmare. That was the reason she dreaded seeing Grace Royce. She wanted it to be over.

It *was* over for her. She was selfish, but she didn't want to relive it, she didn't want to hear a murderer spoken of with love, with grief. She wanted to hate him. She *needed* to hate him.

"I'm sorry, Grace. I'm not sure I'm ready. You must have friends, family . . ."

"Please, Elizabeth . . ."

If Elizabeth had picked up the phone now, she would never have recognized the broken voice as Grace Royce's. The warning chill ran along Elizabeth's flesh again. Something wasn't right. Elizabeth had lived with fear, with caution, too long. Her senses shivered.

"Grace, I have to ask. Have the police released your husband?"

"No," she sobbed. "They never will. They'll execute him."

It was possible. It was probable.

"Where's your son?"

"He's with friends. I haven't been able to tell him yet. Oh, God, Elizabeth, please. I'm begging you. I need to see you."

Elizabeth shook her head. She ran her hand across her hair.

"Where are you?"

"I'm home." Grace made an effort to steady her voice. She asked, "Are you coming?"

"I'm sorry, Grace. I think it's a bad idea. The last thing either of us needs emotionally is to relive what we've been through. Give yourself some time. We can talk later, when it isn't so new and devastating."

"Oh, Elizabeth, don't you see? It will always be devastating. The only relief is to talk. To gain some kind of perspective.

"Elizabeth, you cared enough for a tiny baby to risk everything to save him. Please help me now." Her voice broke raggedly. "Please, Elizabeth. For Christopher's sake."

Christopher. That was an irony. It was the first time Elizabeth had heard the boy's name.

Christopher Royce. The young adopted son of a murderer. Through her own misguided judgment.

"All right, Grace," she said with resignation. "But I don't know where you live. Can we meet somewhere?"

"No, please. Come here. I'm in no condition to drive and I'm blessedly alone for the moment. No one will interrupt. Let me give you the address."

She gave it to Elizabeth. Her voice caught on little sobs, but it was stronger. She sounded more like herself.

It was an address of exclusive private homes along Camelback Mountain.

"I can find it. Give me half an hour, Grace."

"Thank you. Thank you, Elizabeth."

Elizabeth would have said all her tears had been cried last night in Stephen's arms. But now she was trembling, she didn't know what to think, to do. Grace's pain was as real as her own. It was unfinished business and she wanted it finished, she had promised herself that it already was.

She shook her head.

"Half an hour," she repeated, and put down the phone.

Elizabeth leaned her head into her hands. The sun wasn't warm anymore. She couldn't feel it. Sam waited with the ball in his mouth, but she didn't notice.

Grace Royce had no Stephen. Her strength had been illusion, worse than illusion. Hers had been a ruthless killer.

Elizabeth didn't want to think about it. She didn't want to walk back into the shadows. She was selfish, but she wanted the sunshine.

And it was more than that. A feeling, a cold breath of caution. A whisper that Grace Royce was desperate beyond the horror of the circumstances.

Uncharacteristic. The word came to Elizabeth. A conversation with Detective Sibben, an argument, probably. They had spoken of "uncharacteristic behavior." It was what Elizabeth was sensing in Grace Royce.

Or Elizabeth was paranoid. God knew, she had been. It was what had kept her alive.

But it wasn't as if they had all the answers yet. She still didn't know how Royce had gotten a copy of her key and killed Keith in her house. What about the blackmail money? She would have to know everything before she could drop her guard.

Elizabeth picked up the phone. She dialed Stephen's number at work. It was busy.

She dialed the police station next and asked for Sibben. She doubted that he was in, and he wasn't. He was probably celebrating having one of the most important men in the country in his jail. Or ruing it. It was difficult to know with Sibben. But he made a big deal about working weekends and nights and he had done both lately, and it was Sunday. He could have taken his phone off the hook or left town, but he wasn't coming in, and Elizabeth could understand that. She wished she had followed his example.

She didn't have to speak to Sibben. She knew half the detectives by now and more of the field officers.

She asked about Randolph Royce. She was being suspicious, but she didn't want to find out too late that Royce had been released. That she was walking into a trap that Royce had forced Grace to set for her.

Royce was in custody. They were certain about that. He was going nowhere. His arraignment wouldn't be until early in the week.

Elizabeth let out her breath. She *was* paranoid. She tried Stephen's number again and this time she got the receptionist, who assured her Stephen would get her message as soon as he came back to the lab. Elizabeth left Grace Royce's phone number with her.

It was all right. No more than a grieving woman's pain and her dependence on the only person who had, in a sense, shared the same burden of fear. Elizabeth gave Sam a pat, told him to wait, and went out to her car.

But still she was careful. She drove slowly past the huge two-story brick house. It was set well back from the road and surrounded by a high stone wall that almost obscured it from view. A long drive ran between the gate pillars. The gate was open.

It was beautiful, almost pastoral. In the heart of a desert city, and yet it was remote, with vast clipped grounds that were as flawless as a golf course.

There was nothing to make Elizabeth hesitate, but she sat in her car another handful of seconds and watched the house. Nothing stirred. She started the engine and drove slowly up the concrete drive.

There was no evidence that a little boy lived here. There might be a swing set, something, in the back, but here there was only cool elegance, mature taste that did not include a noisy young child and his friends.

Perhaps Grace had never dared let him be a normal boy. Perhaps her fear had kept him indoors. It was sad, if true. His father could have found him anywhere.

Everything was quiet. A small tractor-mower sat beside a utility shed, as if the operator was on the verge of putting it away, but she didn't see him. She stopped the car and got out.

Elizabeth went up the semicircle of stone steps to the front door. She pressed the doorbell.

She couldn't hear the chimes ringing inside the house. The silence was complete. After a moment she pushed the bell again.

Her spine tingled. She had lived with fear too long. There was something wrong.

She didn't move at once. Perhaps she could get back to her car, drive away. She slid her fingers along the door. It moved inward on oiled hinges.

After the bright light of the outdoors, it took a moment for Elizabeth to focus her eyes on the shadows within. She stood taut, poised for retreat, as the room slowly took shape.

"I'm sorry, Elizabeth."

Grace Royce was a small, broken figure bound to a chair in the shadows ahead of Elizabeth. Her voice was cracked, hoarse, almost unrecognizable.

In the window embrasure just over Elizabeth's head there came the sudden, unmistakable crash of a shotgun thrusting a shell into the chamber.

Chapter Thirty-five

Elizabeth couldn't move. She knew the gun was pointed at her. She could feel it. But her limbs were frozen. She couldn't even raise her head to that deadly sound above her. And then Grace Royce said raggedly, "I'm sorry, Elizabeth. You can't run. You're trapped." And she began to cry in deep, broken sobs.

Elizabeth stepped down into the cool shadows of the house.

Grace sat hunched in a dining room chair. Her hands were bound behind her and her ankles were tied to the chair legs. Her face was wet with tears and blood and dirt. There were scratches on her cheeks and arms, and a long, razorlike gash ran the length of her jaw. Blood darkened her white silk blouse.

Elizabeth stumbled over debris as she hurried to her. The electricity had been cut. The shadows were filled with the ugly shapes of destruction. The furniture had been viciously slashed and broken, the carpet ripped and torn loose from the floor. Even the wallpaper had been scored, and in places hung limply from the walls.

The thin cord around Grace's wrists bit so deeply the flesh had swollen around it. Her hands were bluish white, useless. Elizabeth fumbled with the knots, but there was no way. She would have to have a knife, something sharp, and there was none.

"I can't get you loose," she agonized. "I'll go out the back. I'll get help. I'll hurry."

Grace shook her head.

"The doors are jammed."

"A window . . ."

"Iron grilling. And the phone's been cut." Grace sounded resigned. She said it. "We're dead, Elizabeth. You and I. Christopher . . ." tears ran weakly down her face.

"Where *is* Christopher?" Elizabeth demanded sharply.

Grace's face contorted.

"On his way home. He should have been here already."

"How is he getting here?"

"A friend's mother. She'll drop him at the gate. Elizabeth . . ."

"We'll yell to her. She'll call Christopher back and go for help."

"No," Grace said bleakly. "She'll be killed, too. Like Leon, our gardener. He's dead. We're all going to be dead."

Elizabeth's heart was pounding in her throat. She went to the open door and stared out into the brilliant white sunlight.

"There's got to be someone close enough to hear if we scream for help," Elizabeth argued. "A neighbor."

"No. Just Leon."

Elizabeth turned and scrambled through the debris to the kitchen. She had to find a knife to cut Grace's wrists loose. To fight for their lives.

There were none. The drawers had been emptied in the middle of the floor, and the knives were gone.

Perhaps she'd always known it would end like this. Elizabeth let her hands fall to her sides. She went through the half-darkness to the stairs. She began to climb.

There was no sound overhead. Elizabeth's feet crunched on broken glass and mirror, crushed plaster, as she climbed.

And then she heard the car turning up the drive.

Elizabeth froze. And then she came down fast, her feet flying. She had to wave them away, turn them back. But it was too late. The dark blue sedan drew to a halt beneath the window where the killer sat.

"No!" Grace implored Elizabeth, halting her forward rush. "Please! They'll all be killed! Two more little boys, their mother. Please!"

Elizabeth paused. The voices of young boys rang cheerfully. A car door slammed, the motor revved slightly. The car pulled away.

Elizabeth could feel the pounding of her heart in her head. She could scarcely hear for the roar.

Three small boys came into the house.

It stunned them both, Grace and Elizabeth. But it fired something in Grace, some lost hope. She cried out sharply, "Stay with the other boys, Christopher!"

They were frozen in amazement and horror.

"Mother, what . . . ?"

"I mean it, Christopher! Don't come to me! And don't tell who you are. None of you. Don't tell."

310

The boys didn't move. They stared in round-eyed shock at Grace, at the destruction.

Elizabeth shattered the deadly tableau. She rushed forward, grasping small, stiff arms in hands that shook.

"Come with me," she demanded urgently. The only thing she could think of, their only hope, was what small overhang the eaves afforded. If she could move them along the wall outside, out of the killer's vision for a few seconds, a minute, they could run. They could flee like frightened young quail. She pushed them toward the door.

There was a sound on the stairs behind them.

One might run from a knife, but not from a shotgun. Not at this range. Elizabeth stopped, the small boys trembling against her. She turned to watch the figure come down the stairs.

"Hello, Elizabeth," Constance said.

Perhaps Elizabeth was too numb to grasp it. Perhaps she never would. She could feel the terrified stiffness of the little shoulders beneath her fingers, but nothing else, nothing. She couldn't drag her eyes away.

Constance carried the shotgun across her bent left arm. Her right hand held the grip as if it were a pistol, a finger upon the trigger. She smiled languidly, beautifully, in the half-light. She wore tailored trousers and a silk blouse, and her gold-blond hair gleamed in a sleek, flawless chignon.

"Here we are, Elizabeth. At the beginning and at the end. Just like we've always been."

She crossed to where Elizabeth had dropped her handbag. She dumped the contents onto the mutilated sofa.

"Damn," she said mildly. "I hoped you'd bring my knife. The one I'm using now isn't half as good."

Somehow Elizabeth found her voice. She said shakily, "Don't hurt the boys, Constance."

Constance laughed. She had never seemed more alive, more herself.

"No can do, love. Christ, the trouble I've gone to. You wouldn't believe. Or maybe you would. You've been the cause of most of it. You've led me one hell of a merry chase, Elizabeth."

She didn't seem angry, distraught. She crossed to the front door and pushed it shut hard. She took a table knife from under the torn corner of the rug and jammed it into the hinge, and then slammed the bolt that lay above the boys' reach.

"Okay," she said. "Let's play 'find the boy.'"

She walked across to where Grace slumped in the chair. Taking a handful of her dark, matted hair, Constance jerked her head back viciously. Grace cried out.

Elizabeth felt the small shoulder twist protestingly beneath her hand. She said sharply, warningly, "No!" as much to the child as to Constance. She came around the boys and stood between them and Constance and Grace.

"No, Constance. Let the boys go. Let Grace go. This is between you and me."

"Sure it is," Constance agreed. "You and me and a certain little brat. He's not leaving here alive any more than you are, Elizabeth."

"The police have Randolph Royce, Constance. They're charging him with the murders. If you don't hurt anyone now, you can walk away free. No one will be the wiser."

Constance laughed.

"Yeah. That's a good one. Randolph Royce, and you ID'd him. It's too rich." She dropped Grace's hair, and backed up to sit casually on the arm of a chair. The shotgun nestled in the curve of her arm. "But what good is it going to do me? Without money, I'm no better off than when I started."

"No one's touched the money you got from Royce. It's still in the bank."

"Half a million dollars? Don't be naive, Elizabeth. I'm talking millions. Maybe billions. I want it all."

"Royce will pay to have his family safe."

"Oh, sure. While he's rotting in a jail cell with my name on it. No way. I want it all. Legitimately. I've worked damned hard for it. Damned hard."

Elizabeth couldn't follow her. Constance was cool and sober, she wasn't a raving lunatic, a maniac. She knew what she was saying and she knew what she was doing. She knew what she had to do.

"Legitimately?" Elizabeth echoed. "Through Ellen's son?"

"Through David Royce's son."

"It had nothing to do with Ellen?"

"Christ! It had everything to do with Ellen! The little bitch was sleeping with my ticket to the big time. When David got rattled and told me about the baby, I knew I had to get rid of her before it was born. Another example of my rotten luck, you'll have to appreciate.

"Ellen laughed. She said it was a real kick how popular her baby was. How everybody wanted it. But *you* had it, Elizabeth. And you were gone."

"You followed me."

"Sure. Halfway across the damned country. And you didn't even have the brat. I was furious."

"So you killed Ellen."

"Oh, I'd already done that. She had to be disposed of before I could start after you. That's what slowed me down. Otherwise, I would have had you before you hit the Dalles."

The boys stirred behind Elizabeth. They could scatter, they could fragment the fragile web of control that was keeping them alive.

"I don't understand. I don't see what the baby had to do with anything."

Constance sighed in exasperation.

"You probably don't. How you could be so damned obstructive without even knowing the bigger picture is beyond me. But obstructive you have been, Elizabeth. I won't be sorry to see the last of you." She stroked the wooden stock of the shotgun. "David and I took a little trip to Las Vegas one weekend, you see. Tied the old knot. He wasn't *real* enthusiastic, but anyone with half a mind could make him do what they wanted.

"So there I was, my hand virtually on the Royce millions, and David ready to do himself in any time. I'd be a very, very rich widow.

"We came back from Vegas to find that David's little venture into drug-tampering had broken. I wasn't going to say anything then, when he was in line for hard time or the loony bin. I must have been a little naive about what big money could do with nasty publicity. It went under the rug so fast poor David's head was still spinning. Spinning so fast, in fact, he blabbed to me about him and Ellen. About their little bundle of joy that was on the way.

314

"Even an illegitimate kid had a stronger claim to the Royce money than I did. I saw the kind of high-powered clout Randolph Royce could wield when he covered up what was virtually murder for David. And people weren't exactly going to stand in line to testify that David was of sound mind when he married me, were they? All I needed was an illegitimate brat on hand to prove that David had . . . shall we say, 'other interests' at the time he married me. The kid would get it all.

"So the first thing was to get rid of the kid. Then, when David did himself, there I would be, the grieving widow, afraid to come forward sooner because of my sensitivity to the family's troubles and my devotion to poor, sick David. I would rake it in."

Elizabeth shook her head bemusedly. Her mind was reeling.

"But . . ."

It didn't matter. She could live with the unanswered questions, the missing points, if someone would just come. If the police would question the security breach at the Royce home, the dead phone.

But she had to keep Constance talking. When she was through talking, everybody would die.

Chapter Thirty-six

"I'm sorry," Elizabeth said. "I don't understand."

But she did. Damon had said it. Damon had said it a dozen times, and no one had listened.

"Poor, naive Elizabeth. Okay. When David drowned, his body wasn't recovered. Even with eye-witnesses, Royce refused to petition the court to have David declared legally dead. He could have done that. But no. He's kept everything in limbo while the seven requisite years pass before he'll settle the estate. That's in April. The boy has to be dead by then."

She shook her head. Her golden hair shone in the half-darkness. "It's my bad luck he's made it this far. You've been a formidable opponent, Elizabeth. Every step of the way. A dozen times I thought of killing you, but I always hesitated. You knew where the brat was. I didn't dare cut off that corridor of information, even though I knew I couldn't torture it out of you. You could slip, you could misstep. Only you didn't, did you, Elizabeth? Until now."

"I can help you get away. You can take my car."

Constance made an exasperated sound.

"I don't want to get away. I've got work to do."

She lifted the gun until the bore pointed straight at Elizabeth's chest. She came close. The barrel brushed Elizabeth, froze her. "Come here, boys. Now."

They came from behind Elizabeth, single file. Their faces were deathly pale. One of them had been crying quietly. They looked at Constance in inarticulate terror.

"Which of you is young Mr. Royce? Tell me the truth, and I'll let the other two go."

They were very small, only six or seven years old. They trembled. And then one of them, the blond, said on a rough voice of tears, "No, you won't. You'll kill us."

Constance was amused.

"Will I? What makes you think so?"

"Because you gotta. We'll tell."

Constance straightened. She made a wry face at Elizabeth.

"Sharp," she said. "But not David's. The Royces would insist on perfect grammar. Even in a crisis." She looked at Grace Royce. "Right, Mother?"

Grace didn't answer. Her chin had sunk forward onto her chest. She could have been unconscious, by the lifeless look of her.

Constance made an irritated clucking sound in her throat. She came close to Grace's chair.

"*Right,* Mother?" she repeated with an edge.

Grace stirred.

"Don't talk," she muttered. "Don't tell her anything."

"God, that's moving," Constance mocked. She looked at Elizabeth. "You must congratulate yourself every day that you picked such a devoted mother

317

for your little foundling. Not that it's going to do him much good."

"You don't want to hurt the boys, Constance," Elizabeth said quietly.

"Don't I? What *do* I want to do?"

"You want to hurt *me*. Because of Stephen."

Constance laughed.

"You've got *that* right. Because of Stephen, and because of everything. Christ, nearly dead with pneumonia you defeated me! You were babbling your head off about Ellen and the baby until I tried to find out where the kid was. And you clammed up. I told you what I'd done to Ellen. Do you remember? I didn't think you were going to make it. I wasn't sure I was going to let you make it. But just like a Timex, you kept on ticking. Or should I say, like a time bomb? There was a while there when I expected at any minute you'd tell someone that I'd killed Ellen. But you didn't. And guess who comes through to save you from the wrath of the college board? Me. Your best friend and ally. It amused the hell out of me. I needed you where I could see you, watch you."

"I know. And then Keith got in your way."

"You *know?*" Constance sneered. "You know nothing!"

She waved the shotgun in the faces of the boys. "Come closer, children. I want you to see this. You can stay where you are, Elizabeth. And I'd advise you not to move."

Elizabeth tensed. The boys inched forward, their eyes big with horror in their white faces.

"Don't harm them, Constance."

"Oh, shut up, Elizabeth. I know what you're trying to do. You want to keep me talking until you think

318

of some way to get out of this. Forget it . . . and forget anyone coming. I had our good friend the gardener call the police and phone company to confirm that power and security systems were off. He was a great help. And then I thanked him very nicely and killed him."

One of the boys gasped. Constance whipped her glance to them.

"Yeah. Leon. That was his name, wasn't it? Any of you know Leon?"

There was silence.

Elizabeth could feel the violence building in Constance. She was on the verge of shattering them all with a blast from the shotgun. Elizabeth moved an inch nearer.

"I don't understand about Keith. How you got into my house. If no one is coming, it doesn't matter if you take a minute to tell me."

Constance snorted.

"I'll tell you what doesn't matter: you knowing all the details. Dead people don't much care, Elizabeth. You'll find that out soon enough."

"I thought not," Elizabeth taunted. "You didn't get into the house at all. Keith found a way in. You always were an opportunist, Constance."

Constance stroked the trigger thoughtfully. It was pointed at the boys, but Elizabeth was behind them. It would probably cut a pattern that would catch all four of them.

"Don't be cute, Elizabeth. I had the key. It was while you were staying with me, remember? I unlocked the bathroom door when you were in the shower and took your copy and went down to Walmart. I was back before you had finished rinsing the shampoo from your hair. It was child's play."

"And was Keith? He must have weighed 180 pounds. You couldn't have moved him without help."

"You're transparent, Elizabeth. I expected better of you. God knows, you gave me fits enough. Slashing your own tires so you would have an alibi for Keith's death. Christ! What was the point if it wasn't to hang it on you?"

"I don't know. What *was* the point? I thought it was to scare me into running to the boy."

"Hardly. I'd given up on that years ago. You were supposed to look at some hard time. And when you were ready to snap, I'd come forward with an alibi. You'd be vulnerable. You'd talk.

"But no. That sixth sense of yours that Sibben makes fun of is no joke. You knew something was happening and you protected yourself. Too bad it went bust on you today."

"It wasn't like that," Elizabeth demurred. "Keith called me. He warned me."

"No kidding? Maybe he was smarter than I thought. But he wasn't being altruistic. He must have found out that it was your house we were meeting at. He didn't want you to catch us there together." She laughed suddenly, as if she were genuinely amused. "God, that would have been rich! If you had slashed your tires when there was nothing more going on then him and me in bed together at your place! It's an expensive way to conduct an affair."

Elizabeth willed the boys not to move, not to draw Constance's attention back to them. She was talking, she was letting herself be stalled, if only momentarily.

Please God, the children wouldn't force a confrontation by their terror.

"You always could draw any man you wanted."

"Yeah. Except one," Constance rasped. "Guess who that was."

"He was already married to me."

"Like hell. He was mine first. I don't suppose you even bother to remember. I introduced you. He was *my* date."

Maybe it had been like that. Stephen was with someone, she didn't remember who. She had been with someone, too, but it hadn't mattered. Nothing had.

"Am I supposed to say I'm sorry?"

"Don't bother. Insincere apologies bore me." Constance leaned close to the trembling boys. She drew them away from Elizabeth, positioning them in a ragged quarter circle around Grace's nearly inert form. "Now, stand still. I want to see your faces. Elizabeth, stay where you are. If you don't quit trying to get nearer, I'll finish you now. It doesn't make a lot of difference, except that I'd like for you to see this."

She sounded in control, calm. She took a knife from her pocket and opened it. The blade was long and sharp and silver in the half-light.

"Good," she said. "Don't anybody move." She ran the smooth edge of the blade down Grace Royce's face. "Wake up, Gracie. I want you to call your boy."

Grace pulled her head away from the knife, not quickly, but as if the last of her strength were gone. As if she could no longer recognize the threat, or no longer felt it.

321

"No," she said.

Constance needed an extra hand. She ejected the shells from the chamber of the shotgun and leaned it against the wall. She tossed the shells away into the darkness.

"Now," Constance said. "Let's get serious." With catlike quickness she shoved the chair Grace was tied to. It went over forward. Grace's unprotected forehead struck the bare tile of the hearth with a blood-chilling crack. She didn't move.

"Mother!" Christopher Royce cried. He flung himself at Constance.

"Good," Constance said coolly. She caught him by the arm and twisted it until he quit struggling. Then she drew back his head and pressed the cold steel to his throat.

Chapter Thirty-seven

Elizabeth had no time to think. She shoved the two boys and they scattered, they ran. The house was dark and there were a thousand darker corners to hold a small, hiding body. She flung herself into Constance.

They both went down, the boy beneath them, but he was up first. Elizabeth didn't know if he had been cut. Someone had. She could feel the warmth of blood upon her arm.

She found something, the shotgun. Still on her knees, she swung it with all her strength. It caught Constance hard in the shoulder and knocked her back, but she didn't drop the knife. She held it before her, the tendons in her hand and forearm standing out from the fury with which she grasped it. The ache to plunge it into warm flesh.

Elizabeth scrambled to her feet and swung the gun again. Constance ducked it, but it threw her off balance. She tried to claw it from Elizabeth's grip.

Elizabeth jerked backwards. She almost fell as the gun came loose from Constance's grasp.

"Christopher!" Elizabeth cried. She didn't know if

he was hiding, if his leap away from them had been a death throe. There was blood all down her arm. Constance could have plunged the knife into his exposed throat before Elizabeth had hit her.

He materialized out of the darkness and he wasn't bleeding, he didn't seem to be. There was dirt and plaster on his face, and his eyes were big enough to drown in. Elizabeth pushed him past Constance, up the stairs.

Constance was on her knees now. She was dirty and tousled, there was blood on her blouse, but she wasn't really shaken. She held the knife in the steadiest hand Elizabeth had ever seen.

"Stay back," Elizabeth panted. She held the barrel of the shotgun like a club, but the blood was making her grasp slip. She didn't dare lose her grip on the gun.

Constance got to her feet. She looked from Elizabeth to the boy who had paused halfway up the stairs and was watching them. She began to ease her way toward him.

Elizabeth wiped her palm on her trouser leg. She gauged the distance. She was cold now. She was as hard as she had to be.

"Get off the stairs," she commanded.

Constance hurled herself from the wall. She came at Elizabeth like a tiger, a mad thing, lost to reason with the scent of blood.

She was almost too quick for Elizabeth. The knife sliced the air beside her face. Elizabeth winced. She went to one knee and with the force of her strength, brought the gun butt up in a short, thrusting blow into Constance's ribs. She scrambled up and took the stairs two at a time. When she reached the boy, she stopped and looked down.

Constance was getting her breath. She stood at the bottom. Her head was back and her face was a white, expressionless oval in the gloom. She put a hand on the banister, the hand that didn't hold the knife. She began to climb.

The boy dragged at Elizabeth's arm. She looked down and saw the blood, *her* blood, running down into her hand. The arm was going numb. She was already losing the strength to hold the shotgun.

Constance knew it. She paused a moment on the third stair. She smiled thinly and changed hands with the knife. She flexed her fingers.

She had taken a hard blow to the ribcage. One rib might be cracked, but her stamina was untried, her wind sound. She could sit here and wait Elizabeth out, watch her blood drip away and her will to fight with it. There was no hurry now.

It unnerved Elizabeth, her silence. There was something worse than horror in her voiceless watching. A predator and its prey.

The boy tugged harder. He could have run, he should have. He was taking Elizabeth with him.

Elizabeth looked down at Constance from the wide landing at the top of the stair. Constance hadn't moved. She leaned against the wall as if she had all the time in the world, and she did. Her face was upturned, watching.

Elizabeth looked for something to block the staircase, anything. There was nothing. She couldn't search the rooms without leaving the stairs unattended, and it would be no more than a temporary barrier, at any rate.

She let the boy pull her along. She hoped he knew where he was going, that he wasn't acting out of blind panic.

He knew, all right. But they were too late. Constance had been there before them. She had shattered the lock on the heavy study door with a blast from the shotgun.

They heard the sudden crunch of glass on the stairway and knew Constance was following them. Elizabeth's fingers closed tightly on the boy's hand and she ran down the hall, away from that sound of pursuit. In one of these dark, ravaged rooms, Constance had waited, watching Elizabeth drive up. The window would be open.

She found it. The master bedroom. The pale blue drapes, shredded, stirred in a lazy breeze. The cast-iron grilling meant to keep trespassers out kept them in. Even a small boy couldn't squeeze between the bars.

Elizabeth was going to have to let go of the boy's hand or the shotgun, one or the other. She had only one hand now. The other was lost to sensation and strength. And she needed a respite, a moment to bind the arm, stop the flow of blood before she was too weak to do it. She was going to have to drop the shotgun.

But she tucked it under her arm for a few more steps. It was probably useless to her now, but it was something, it had thrust back the slashing fury of death for a little while.

And finally they were trapped. There were no more rooms, there was no more chance of finding a door whose lock was not destroyed. They went into the last room.

It was a guest room, apparently. It had been. Now it was a place to die.

Even here the violence was complete. The waterbed had been slashed, and the carpet squished wetly underfoot. The silk coverlet, pillows, the sheets, had been mutilated. The bureau mirror had been shattered, the old oak wood gashed. The draperies had been pulled from the windows and rent, and something, a chair, perhaps, smashed repeatedly against the pale beige plaster of the walls.

There was a clothes hamper sitting drunkenly at the foot of the bed. Elizabeth hesitated. Constance might think like that. She might have laid it as a trap. On the verge of hiding the boy in the hamper, she drew back. They could hear footsteps just outside. Elizabeth pressed the boy silently back into the closet.

She still had the gun, but it was useless now. In the close quarters she couldn't swing it. She could get no force behind a blow with only one arm. She put an unnecessary hand over the child's mouth and they sank deeper into the shadows of the closet.

Elizabeth could see a four-foot square of floor through the crack in the closet door. She could see their footprints in the sodden carpet.

Constance could see them, too. She laughed.

Not a real laugh. A hoarse grate of mockery, of angry satisfaction. But she was wary. Elizabeth was bleeding, but she wasn't finished.

"Well, Elizabeth?" Constance said calmly, so close that Elizabeth and the boy jumped. Or perhaps it was her voice, as natural as if there weren't a knife in her hand. After all her silent, mad struggles down below. "You were the one who wanted to talk. Come out

327

and we'll talk. I'll tell you everything. About Keith
About Damon. The letters I wrote, the clippings
sent you. You deserve to hear. You've put a lot o
energy into this."

Elizabeth could hardly believe it was really Con
stance beyond the door. Her oldest friend, her best
Wanting to talk together, to laugh. To share un
spoken trials and pain.

"Elizabeth?" Constance's shadow moved past the
closet door, over their faces. She approached the
clothes hamper where Elizabeth had almost hidder
the boy. She plunged the knife through the wicke
webbing.

She laughed.

"Come on, Elizabeth. Play fair. Show me your
predictable side. Do what I would do."

As if anyone knew. As if anyone could read Con
stance. Beyond the certainty that she would kill.

Constance turned. She looked at the closet, but she
was more concerned with the bathroom. Elizabeth
had the room to swing the shotgun in there, she had
used it with unexpected strength.

But that was before the blood loss had begun to
tell on her. She might be powerless now. She might be
hiding, too weak to raise a hand.

Constance wasn't going to take the chance. She
hesitated. She stared thoughtfully at the bathroom
door, hanging off its bottom hinge. She ran her
tongue over her lips.

She was close enough to touch. Elizabeth could see
the fine pores in her face, the lines of concentration
that made tiny webs at the corners of her beautifu
blue eyes. The iron resolve in the set of her head.

The boy scarcely breathed. If he had been hysteri

328

cal, weeping, they would have been lost already. But he wasn't. He was a small, wild creature as bent on survival as any that had been born into danger. He waited.

Chapter Thirty-eight

Constance was uncertain. It wasn't like her, but the circumstances were unfamiliar. She had killed three people—no, four—and it had been easy. They hadn't lifted a finger. Even Damon, who knew what was going to happen when he looked up and saw her in the doorway of his sleazy apartment. He had gone like a lamb to the slaughter. She had grown to expect such docility, such resignation.

Not that Keith Vanfossen had been resigned, of course. He had suspected nothing. She couldn't have overpowered so large a man. She had had a devil of a time just wrapping his body in a sheet and dragging him into the garage and into her car. He had been heavier than she expected.

But it had still been comparatively easy. The deaths had been. These should be even simpler. A small boy, and a woman who weighed not much over a hundred pounds. It wasn't worthy of her caution.

But still she was wary. She backed up until she was out of Elizabeth's line of vision and paused indecisively in the doorway.

She had to remind herself that there was no hurry.

There had been before. She'd had to plan every detail, every second, to the tiniest degree.

Elizabeth had still almost run into her at Damon's apartment. If Randolph Royce's unexpected appearance at Damon's door hadn't unnerved her into taking instant flight, she would have been there when Elizabeth came. It couldn't have been closer.

But there was time now.

"The kid seems to trust you, Elizabeth," Constance said suddenly, shattering the eerie silence. "Can you figure it? Maybe he would like to hear how everyone thinks you wrote in a dead man's blood. That's a story a boy would like. Tell him about it, Elizabeth."

Perhaps Constance thought to frighten Christopher into running. He pressed more closely against Elizabeth. She was afraid she could hear him breathing, but maybe it was herself. Maybe it was Constance. Elizabeth forced herself not to shiver.

"Come out, Elizabeth. Your arm must be hurting. We'll sit down and talk. We'll get you to a doctor.

"I didn't mean to cut you. I wanted the boy, and you got in the way." Constance's voice hardened, she was finding it difficult to wait, to reason. She wanted to finish it. Finish Elizabeth and the boy. She ached to see their blood, feel it gushing over her hands.

"You always get in the way, don't you, Elizabeth? Always. With Stephen. With Ellen and the baby. With Damon. Christ, Damon almost told you everything, didn't he? He could have, on the phone. If he hadn't been so paranoid, you would have had me."

Constance came close to the closet door. It creaked from her weight as she pressed her eye to the crack.

Elizabeth's heart stood still. They were trapped.

331

There was nowhere to run. She should have picked up something, anything, to wield with her undamaged hand. A broken shard of mirror or glass. Anything.

But she hadn't. She had been too intent on hiding. And then she knew her heart hadn't stopped. It filled the dark interior of the closet with its deafening roar. It pounded in her ears.

"Elizabeth?"

Constance's lips were against the crack in the closet door. Elizabeth pressed her hand over the boy's mouth. If the door had opened out, she could have slammed against it, flung Constance off balance. But it folded, and she could get no force. Constance would have only to step back and let them tumble out onto the floor.

"Are you in there, Elizabeth?" Her voice was distorted by the proximity of the door. "Wouldn't you like to come out and play?"

The boy stirred. Elizabeth tightened her fingers over his mouth warningly. She had to convey to him that they mustn't move, that fleeing would be fatal.

He didn't make a sound. He put his small, sweaty hand against the back of hers and there was something hard in it. He was trying to press something into her hand.

Elizabeth was afraid Constance would see the slightest movement, hear it. Her fingers stirred. She almost couldn't get them to move, she was so taut. And when she did, what if the boy gave way to his terror and made a sound?

"Elizabeth? Come out, Elizabeth. I know you're in there."

As soon as Elizabeth's hand loosened on his

mouth, Christopher pressed the object into her palm. Her fingers closed around a shotgun shell.

She could have wept. It explained his absence while she and Constance had struggled downstairs. He had plunged into the darkness after the shells that Constance had flung away. He had found one of them. And it would do no good.

If she had five uninterrupted minutes and two good arms, it was possible that Elizabeth could figure out the loading and firing mechanism of a pump shotgun. It was possible.

But there was no time. The shotgun leaned beside her, jammed in by the press of their bodies. As good as useless.

God, he was a fighter. Something stirred in Elizabeth, some outrage at the persecution this child had suffered. She wasn't going to let him die like this.

She opened the closet door and stepped out.

Constance retreated abruptly, but then she laughed at her wariness. Elizabeth had left the shotgun somewhere. She was defenseless.

"Good girl," Constance approved. "Now, where is the little snot?"

"I want to talk about that," Elizabeth said. "But you'll have to let me wrap up my arm first."

Constance shook her head.

"You know, Elizabeth, you never quit. You always seem to think you make the decisions, that everything is going to work out your way. I don't get it. You're a loser and you don't even know it."

"You're afraid of me," Elizabeth taunted. "You don't know what I might do."

"I know, all right. You'll die. You'll do your damnedest to save some kid who couldn't mean a

333

thing to you. And then you'll die and so will he, and I hope you wonder as you're going how anyone could be so stupid. Because you are, Elizabeth. Always helping the lame duck.

"You must have thought of me as one of your projects when you pulled me out of the fire and designed that 'Cloud Creation' to get me on with Marston's. Christ! I hated you for that! And you, with your artistic talent, designing Christmas cards! It makes me sick!

"But don't worry about it. There will probably be one hell of a rush on your cards when you die so young and violently. The public eats up that kind of thing. You'll be remembered for some flickering, useless moment. I'll drink a toast to you."

There was a small sound from the closet. Elizabeth hoped Constance hadn't heard, but of course she had. She shook her head at Elizabeth.

"No great big complicated plan. Just a couple of children hiding in the first dark corner they can find. I'm disappointed, Elizabeth." She moved along the wall toward the closet, keeping her eyes on Elizabeth.

Elizabeth moved in front of her, blocking the closet with her body.

"I don't know why you think I'll let you hurt him," she said, and it was cold, it was as hard as steel. It was as if she held a deadly weapon in her hand instead of cradling an injured arm.

Constance hesitated. She could still feel the staggering blow she had taken to the shoulder, to the ribs. She wasn't hurt, but she could be. She wasn't as invulnerable to pain as she'd considered herself to be. As immune to failure.

She settled the knife more comfortably in her grip.

"How are you going to stop me?" she mocked.

Elizabeth said, every word ice, "I'll kill you."

Constance laughed.

"You and who else?" she taunted, and she sprang at Elizabeth. She aimed a powerful, slashing stroke at Elizabeth's unprotected throat.

Elizabeth felt the swish of the blade as she fell back. She caught hold of Constance's wrist as the swing expended its force and hung on.

She wasn't as strong as Constance, but her desperation was immeasurable. When she felt Constance twisting away, Elizabeth drew up her knees and drove them into the other woman's chest.

It had the force to rock Constance. She staggered back and struck the wall. She leaned there a moment catching her breath while Elizabeth scrambled to her feet.

"This is getting old, Elizabeth. You're ruining my manicure." And she came forward again, this time at a more measured pace, closing in, wary, stalking. She wanted blood.

Elizabeth's arm was bleeding again. It dripped off her fingers and dotted the wet carpet. Constance came nearer, the blade gleaming as brightly as her eyes.

But she didn't use the knife this time. Elizabeth was expecting it. She was ready for such a move. Constance feinted with the knife and then lunged in from the left. She caught a handful of Elizabeth's hair and jerked her off balance. Pinning her with a knee in her chest, she put the knife to the hollow in Elizabeth's throat.

"Now," she said with satisfaction. "This is more like it." Her breath came short. She wasn't used to fighting to gain her ends. "You can come out, kid. I've got Elizabeth. You can see her die." She reached up a hand and pounded loudly on the closet door.

Elizabeth wasn't ready to die. In the second that Constance diverted her attention, Elizabeth struck her in the face with a doubled fist. She felt the knife nick her flesh, a scratch, and she struck again. She grasped Constance's wrist with her good hand and threw her weight sideways, trying to pin the arm beneath her.

Constance swore. She was flung off balance and she struggled, twisting the knife in an effort to cut flesh, resisting Elizabeth's efforts to render the knife ineffectual. She was on top and her own weight helped Elizabeth pin the arm beneath her.

The closet door opened and the muzzle of the shotgun protruded. The boy pumped the shell into the chamber.

Chapter Thirty-nine

They both froze. And then Constance laughed. She was so close her breath stirred Elizabeth's hair.

"Christ!" she said. "He had me for a second. I thought it was loaded."

Elizabeth said tautly, expressionlessly,

"It is."

"Sure," Constance mocked. "I believe it. Why not?" But then she paused. There was something in Elizabeth's face, a controlled wince, perhaps. She looked like a woman might who had a loaded shotgun pointed at her. Constance looked back at the boy.

The shotgun was too heavy for him and too long. It wavered in his small hands, but it wouldn't have to be dead accurate at this range. The pattern of the shot would be large enough that he couldn't miss.

"It doesn't matter," Constance decided at last. "One way or the other. He can't pull the trigger without killing you as well as me. And he's not going to do that."

Constance must have gambled a thousand times since the day she'd coerced David Royce into marrying her. The chances she had taken every time she stalked another victim and then brushed away the evidence of her guilt. And it wasn't simply luck. She had put everything that was in her into the planning and the execution.

And now she was gambling again.

But it had never been like this. An untried child's mind. She had never understood children, had never liked them. And he was only six, and terrified. He had seen her kill his mother.

Almost kill her. Grace could still be alive.

Constance could feel a prickling in her spine. She looked at Elizabeth's white face so close to hers. Elizabeth's blood was warm where her injured arm was trapped between them. She could see the pain etched in her eyes. And something else.

"Do it, Christopher," Elizabeth said, and it was quiet, steady, but she might have shouted it. It filled the room like an echo.

He didn't come near. He knew how strong Constance was, and how quick. He walked around behind the bed and rested the muzzle of the gun on it so all the weight wasn't on his trembling arms.

"I might hurt you," he quavered to Elizabeth.

God yes, he might, he would. She would be killed. But her strength was fading and she couldn't hold Constance's arm much longer. And then they would both die, she and the boy. And Grace, if she still lived, and the two little boys hiding downstairs in the darkness. Everyone.

It was survival. As simple and as ugly and as violent as that. He could die, or he could live with an image in his mind more terrible than a person's worst nightmare.

It was a horrendous burden to place on a child.

"He won't do it," Constance mocked. "I told you he wouldn't." And she gave a sudden, wrenching jerk that freed her hand and the knife. She settled the blade at Elizabeth's throat.

"Okay," she said. "We've got an impasse. If I kill you, the kid will kill me. But he won't shoot as long as he risks hitting you. It's your basic standoff, wouldn't you say?"

"No," Elizabeth said. "It's not. Because someone's coming."

Constance's head came up like a startled deer. She forgot the boy, discounted him. She listened.

"I don't hear anything," she clipped.

Elizabeth was silent. Her breath went out on a little sigh that froze something in Constance. It meant Elizabeth wasn't bluffing. There was relief in it, deliverance.

"Nobody can get in here," Constance reminded her, reminded herself.

The boy looked out the window. He could see nothing. They could read it in his face. But his hearing was better, younger. He could hear what Elizabeth had detected only because she was lying on the floor. He took a shaken step backwards and sat down on the windowsill, the shotgun across his lap.

"Christ!" Constance swore. She believed it now, she had to. She had to end this swiftly, coolly. She had to be free to stalk the interloper, finish him. "Come on, Elizabeth. Get to your feet." She rolled free, but dragged Elizabeth with her. She didn't dare be more than a few inches from Elizabeth.

Elizabeth got up slowly, coming awkwardly to her knees and then to her feet. Her head swam.

The boy stood up, too. The muzzle lifted to follow them.

"Save it," Constance grated, and fell away, through the door into the hall, dragging Elizabeth with her. They crashed to the floor amid glass and plaster, but Constance rolled. She sprang to her feet, and as the boy flung himself through the doorway behind them, she grasped the shotgun muzzle and ripped it from his grasp.

Elizabeth was on her knees. She plunged forward as Constance moved, grasping her ankle and letting the momentum carry Constance sprawling to the floor.

But Constance was quick. She let the shotgun go and came up with the knife, forcing Elizabeth back. She laughed harshly.

"Now," she said. "This is better." Without taking her eyes off Elizabeth or the boy, she picked up the shotgun and ejected the shell. "Let's try this again," she mocked, and retrieved the shell and tossed it over the balcony to the room below.

Stephen came down the hall.

There was no reading in his face the hell he had been through. His eyes went past Constance to Elizabeth, and God, thank God, she was alive, she was lovely. Cut and battered, but she was breathing, she was on her feet. She was probably, if he knew Elizabeth, a long way from beaten.

"Don't come any closer," Constance warned. She was momentarily unnerved, but she wouldn't let it be anything more than that. Nothing had changed. It was only one man. It wasn't the police.

She edged along the wall. She didn't want to be

between them. She had already made the mistake of thinking that Elizabeth was too weak to fight.

The boy said into the silence: "Is my mother dead?"

There was something blood-curdling in the simple question.

"No," Stephen said. "But she's badly hurt. We'll have to get her to a hospital."

Constance laughed. She had moved along the wall past Elizabeth and the boy. She held the knife in front of her body, and it was sharp, it was swift. Stephen came nearer.

"It's a great theory," Constance taunted. She wished she had kept the shotgun. "It's too bad it won't work. Brain hemorrhages, that sort of thing, they need quick attention. It's already too late. It will be, by the time they find her. Find all of you." And she lunged. She got her fingers into the boy's hair and jerked him to her.

He should have screamed, cried out. He didn't make a sound. Constance raised the knife and slashed it across his throat.

It met the resistance of his fingers.

And her luck ran out. It slipped between her fingers like the boy's blood. They were upon her and Stephen was strong. He ripped the knife from her grasp. Elizabeth fell with her, struggling for the boy who was wriggling to get free of Constance.

And then they all broke apart. Constance was left sitting in the rubble she had created and Elizabeth was cradling the boy. She was holding back the flow of blood from his fingers with pressure from her hand.

Stephen closed the knife with a snap and it was

useless, meaningless, and Constance no more than a paper tiger. She began to laugh.

Stephen lifted Elizabeth and the boy to their feet and put his arms around them, both of them.

"Thank God," he breathed, and he could feel their trembling, but it was all right, he was trembling, too. They were warm and their hearts were beating. He had feared when he had pried open the door from the garage that it wouldn't be that way. When he had found Grace.

"The police are coming," Stephen said. "I flagged down a motorist. We'll get you both to a doctor right away." The pain must be terrible, Elizabeth's pain. The boy's hand might still be numb, and please God it would stay that way until he reached the hospital. "All right?"

Elizabeth nodded, but she looked at Constance. She couldn't drag her eyes away.

"Lord, if you could see yourself, Elizabeth," Constance mocked. "You're a mess. You look dead on your feet." That was good, that was amusing. She wished Elizabeth *were* dead. She wished Stephen had seen her die.

Her luck had been bad. Damn, it had always been bad where Elizabeth was concerned. It seemed as if every time it came back to that.

"I hope you hate me, Elizabeth, as much as I hate you," she grated. "I hope you never stop being afraid that I'll get out. Because I will. It's the old story. Cop an insanity plea. I should know. I've been there before.

"Lakeside Sanitarium. Doesn't that have a nice ring? I did two years there. Two God-damned years. You must have missed me every day, right, Eliza-

342

beth? While you were free and happy, marrying the man I wanted.

"They don't use the electric chair on the 'insane,' you know. That's me. Your basic model inmate. I'll get a few years, and then you'll have to start worrying about who's behind you. *Knowing* who's behind you. It'll be me." She laughed harshly. She inched toward the shotgun.

Stephen moved it out of her reach. He was waiting for the sound of sirens. He had to have Constance secured before he could take Elizabeth and the boy downstairs.

"It's empty," Constance jeered. "Be a sport. Help me set up my insanity plea. There's nothing like a suicide attempt to convince the jury."

"It *is* empty," Elizabeth agreed. She was beginning to feel ill. Her legs didn't want to support her. "I need to sit down, Stephen."

They heard the sirens. They could hear them slow at the gate and then rise to a shuddering crescendo. They stopped outside the house.

Constance stood up. She was only a few feet from the window, and she went to it and looked down.

"Christ! They seem to think they need an army." She turned around and came back, moving jerkily, tautly, as if she were about to snap. She picked up the shotgun.

"Don't be stupid," Stephen warned. "They aren't going to shoot you if we tell them it's not loaded."

Constance laughed.

"Guess who's stupid," she mocked. "I don't want them to kill me. Why should I? I'm going to do my time as nice as you please so I can get out and kill Elizabeth. I want you to think of that every day and

343

every night. I want you to wait for me, and know tha
I'll be coming." She cocked the shotgun and the
placed the butt at the juncture of the floor and wall.
She found the trigger and leaned into the barrel. She
pulled the trigger.

In the last second, millisecond, Elizabeth knew. I
was in the almost catatonic rigidity of the boy sittin
within the circle of her arms. She clasped a hand over
his eyes, she screamed, "No!" even as the roar of the
shotgun shook the walls, reverberated the windows.

The shotgun and the body crashed heavily to the
floor.

Chapter Forty

Elizabeth stirred restlessly in the hospital bed. Her arm beneath the heavy bandage ached, throbbed. She needed something for the pain, but she waited. She put the nurses off. It might be too strong. She had to stay awake, oriented, to hear about Grace.

Stephen held her uninjured hand between both of his. There should be word soon. It had been hours already.

Randolph Royce came along the corridor. He was looking at the numbers on the doors, but blindly, without focus. He moved like a drunken man.

Elizabeth's heart lurched. She would have called to him, stopped him, but the lines in his face took the words away. Her fingers tightened convulsively on Stephen's.

Stephen knew what hell was. He knew what it was like when it was over. He said, "It's all right, Libby," and she knew he meant it. He could read something in Randolph Royce that her fear could not. He went to the door.

Royce paused, looking at Stephen and then

beyond, to Elizabeth. He ran a hand over his face as if he were just awakening from a bad dream.

"Sorry," he managed. "I guess I'm wandering aimlessly. I was looking for your room . . . the doctors said you were waiting to hear. Am I intruding?"

"No," Stephen said gently. "We've been waiting for you." He pulled up a chair and drew Royce to it.

There was no resistance. Royce sat down as obediently as a child.

Elizabeth looked from the lines of shock in the man's face to Stephen with deep anxiety. Stephen said it was all right, he said Grace was okay, but she couldn't reconcile his confidence with what she saw in Royce's shattered demeanor.

"Grace?" she said, a whisper. "Is Grace out of surgery?"

"Yes, God yes. Finally." Royce drew a shuddering breath. He had come straight here from recovery and he hadn't found his composure. He couldn't think. He was still in shock.

"Tell me," Elizabeth said sharply.

"She's going to be all right. The doctors expect a full recovery." Royce swallowed and said again, as if he had to hear it, "She's going to be all right."

Elizabeth let out her breath on a shaken sigh.

"Thank God," she breathed. She leaned her face against Stephen's sleeve in thankfulness and apology.

"Yes," Royce said. "Thank God."

"Are *you* all right?" she asked Royce.

"Yes, thank you. I can't think straight yet, but I've never been better. I'm . . . it could have gone the other way so easily. I can't imagine life . . ." he cleared his throat of huskiness. "Sorry. I shouldn't have come

346

straight here, but I wanted to tell you myself. I owe you that, both of you. You saved my son's life."

Stephen touched Elizabeth's hair.

"Elizabeth did," he said.

"Yes. Elizabeth did. And not just today. That other day, that dark day when his life might have ended before it started. Grace and I might never have known Christopher if it hadn't been for Elizabeth."

"He's a wonderful boy," Elizabeth said. "You must be proud of him."

"I am. Foolishly so, I don't doubt. He's been tormenting the nurses to let him come visit you. I hope you don't mind."

"I'd love it. I didn't know . . . I thought you might object to my seeing him."

Royce shook his head.

"On the contrary. I'd like nothing better. And when Grace is well enough, she'll insist upon it. I . . ." Royce hesitated. He was rapidly regaining his equilibrium, but now he paused and ran a hand over his eyes. ". . . I really don't know what to say, Elizabeth. 'Thank you' is as inadequate as 'I'm sorry,' but they both come from the bottom of my heart. I drew every possible wrong conclusion about you and your motives. And I *am* sorry.

"The only thing I can say in my defense is that I was sure you were a murderess. Every mistake that followed came back to that." Royce looked helplessly at Stephen. "In retrospect, I must have been out of my mind. I don't believe there was a move I made that wasn't grossly in error."

"There was one," Stephen demurred. "You adopted a great son."

"Yes. Despite myself." Royce laughed bemusedly.

"Through the sound good sense and long-sighted-ness of my wife and Elizabeth. My God, this is all new to me! I can't absorb it."

"I'm surprised you know," Stephen said.

"Grace was conscious before they took her to surgery. She wanted to be sure that I understood, in case . . . in the event that something went wrong. She told me that Chris is David's son." He shook his head. "I've spent the better part of seven years trying to find a needle in a haystack. Trying to find a tiny baby that disappeared off the face of the earth in the arms of Elizabeth Purdin."

"How did you know there *was* a baby? Did David tell you?"

"No," Royce said, and there was a touch of weariness in it, of old pain. "Not as I believe you mean, in any case. Not in the months before his death. Several days after he . . . died, I received a letter in the mail from David. It was a suicide letter. He mentioned the baby then, and said Ellen Glover was the mother.

"Ellen had been missing for nearly four months at that time. He believed she was dead. He chose . . . he chose the same for himself.

"I began an immediate search for the infant, but the trail had grown cold, of course. At times I really doubted that the child had survived, but I couldn't give up. Not if there was the slimmest chance that David's little boy was alive and was needing his family." Royce cleared his throat. "You were the only one who knew, Elizabeth. I didn't dare let you slip away. When you came to Phoenix, I packed up my family and moved here. I had to keep track of you."

"I knew I was being followed."

"Lord, yes. I can't count the man-hours put into

having you watched. To no end. The only constant was that my investigators always found traces that someone had been ahead of them. Every step you took you were followed by a killer. My men came after."

Elizabeth shivered. Stephen could feel her tension through the fingers that he held.

"I know," she said. "I know now. It was Constance."

"My attorneys have found the record of her marriage to David. It wouldn't have stood up. David's illness was too far advanced." Royce sighed heavily. "I have his guilt in the drug-tampering deaths to live with. I should have foreseen it. I should have insisted that he surrender his license when his illness became apparent.

"I'd like to say that I knew what I was doing where David was concerned. I thought I did. I believed that once he began to deteriorate we had safeguards to prevent him causing harm. I was wrong.

"My devotion to David blinded me. He was much younger than me, he was my responsibility. I couldn't seem to find the moment to take away the one crutch that he clung to, his work. And then it was too late."

"You couldn't have foreseen it," Stephen said. "We all worked with him. We saw him every day. And we couldn't have guessed where his illness was leading him."

"I appreciate that," Royce said. "It's difficult having any perspective from where I stand. I did what I could to rectify an impossible situation. We settled generously with the families, if there is such a thing as putting a price on a life. I did what I could to bury it on David's behalf.

"And then David found his own way out, but not without leaving us the reality of his son. And the blackmail began and I had to protect his name for his child. It all seemed so futile when we couldn't even find the boy."

"The blackmail was paid in David's name," Stephen said.

"Yes. My own twisted efforts to get under the skin of the recipient. Elizabeth, as I thought. I had my accountant copy it from old documents of David's. And I used the Royce Pharmaceutical drafts from David's business, covering the checks even though the company had folded."

"You did the same with David's car, didn't you? Kept the license and registration in his name?"

"Yes. I deliberately let the security guard get the number of the plates. I wanted to scare you." Royce shook his head. "It was rapidly coming home to me that you didn't scare very easily.

"Of course, that only strengthened my conviction that you were a murderess. Vanfossen had been killed in your home. You were at Baille's in the middle of the night and his body still warm. The night you called me and wanted to meet, I thought you as good as admitted you killed Baille. It was only later I realized how ambiguous our conversation had been.

"But at the time I believed you were going to make an attempt on my life. I took a gun." He made a wry face and said dryly, "I can't tell you how pleased the police were to find it on me."

"I had a phone recording of a conversation you had with Keith."

"I figured that out sitting in custody. I threatened to kill him as I recall. A very ill-timed loss of temper."

"In my own defense, I can only say I was desperate. Desperate and frustrated. David's baby was growing up somewhere without his family, under God knew what conditions, because of you. It was all I could think of. It was an obsession."

"I didn't know the baby was David's," Elizabeth said. She looked at Stephen and her eyes were soft.

He touched the dark gleam of her hair. She was pale and tired, and her arm must be hurting scarcely to be borne, but the ghosts were leaving her, the hell. In her own way, she was as resilient as Christopher.

"Grace told me. She worked side by side with me looking for David's child. She was as eager as I was to take him in, rear him with Chris. It was only when ... when she learned that David was the father of Ellen Glover's baby that she knew it *was* Christopher."

"Ellen told me the baby was Stephen's," Elizabeth said. "Once I knew she was lying, I was no closer to the truth. Until I saw you at Damon's apartment and found out who you were. In some mad, impossible way, it all made sense. I did everything in my power to help the police get you."

"I realize that. I suppose Hell has a corner for people who think what I did about you. What I *said* about you." Royce grinned crookedly. "Maybe Kenwood would like to settle with me."

Elizabeth chuckled.

"Stephen will be busy," she said. She looked up at Stephen and she forgot the pain in her arm. "We're going to Portland. I'm going to see my sister."